# The QUEEN of WAR

# ALEX LINWOOD

# The QUEEN of WAR

## VOLUME I OF THE GODDESS OF DESTINY

GREENLEES
PUBLISHING

Published by Greenlees Publishing,

contact@greenleespublishing.com

eBook ISBN-13: 978-1-951098-22-3

Hardcover ISBN-13: 978-1-951098-21-6

Paperback ISBN-13: 978-1-951098-19-3

Large Print Paperback ISBN-13: 978-1-951098-20-9

Artwork by Iurii Marin, Mikhail Hoika, Sachith Palipane, Stephanie Wittenburg & Anzhelika Pavlova

Cover Design by Alex Linwood

*To all those who also wish
they had a time machine.*

# I

Wind whisked through the open stone window, sending snowflakes swirling along the floor and blowing the long hairs of the fur coverlet that had been thrown carelessly down on the flagstones. It lay in a heap next to Valentina's best dress, having only slightly fewer patches than the dress she wore at the moment, and the tattered remains of her thrice mended stockings and shawl.

Valentina stared at the heap of clothing from her place on the floor, sitting with her back to the cold stone wall, as far from the heavy locked door and nearby open window as she could manage. Repeatedly, she had thought she should stand and clean up the mess. Repeatedly, her mind whirled and she found herself staring into space, unwilling or unable to move.

The tapestry that should have covered the gaping window and protected the room was now torn to shreds, some stringy remains hanging from the nails embedded in the walls above and writhing in the wind, while other bits had long exited out the window, thrown in a fit of rage.

Large airy snowflakes collected in the curl of spilled porridge and in the broken fragments of brown stone pottery strewn on the floor, the only kind of dishes allowed up in the tower. The royal blue boneware never made it up the curved steps on the trays carried by the servants. Now Valentina wondered if any dishes at all would find their way up again. No servants had returned since early morning. Yesterday's fire in the hearth had long since burned out, and she'd never been allowed more wood than what would last for a day or two. Manservants were not allowed to enter the tower, not even so far as the bottom steps, nor in the grounds outside, and the thin women servants complained enough about bringing up the trays and the daily bits of wood. They would never bring more than absolutely commanded by those below.

And those below would never command more than the absolute minimum to keep Valentina alive. Only fear of the gods held them back from locking the door and never opening it again. Valentina shivered, rubbing her arms and pulling her woolen dress close.

The increasingly cold air pouring in from the darkening exterior finally pushed her enough to move and grab the fur coverlet. Pulling it close, she wrapped it around her shoulders and tucked it beneath her legs, curling herself into a ball and trying to even pull it over her head. When she'd first entered the tower as a young girl of twelve, she would have fit neatly within the fur, but now at fifteen her limbs were too long and she had to choose what to not fit within its the warm folds. She settled on leaving her head out, but tucking her hair closely around her neck and laying her cheek on the soft hairs of the fur covering her knees.

White scars on the stone wall around the window glimmered in the dimming light, showing the path the sword had taken when cutting the tapestry down. Flesh would have held no resistance to it.

The wind howled its agreement.

.   .   .

Sleep came uneasy in the cold night. No one came.

The morning sun shone weakly through hazy clouds, a weak sunbeam coming through the open window and hitting Valentina's face. She woke slowly, eyes bleary as she stirred under the fur. Her nose was cold, and her lungs felt tight in the brisk air. She stirred, stiff from the night spent crouched in one position.

The chaos of the room remained as the night before. Only a few hands-height of snow in the middle of the room spoke of any passage of time. The weak sunbeam melted the edge of the pile of fluffy white flakes, sending a small rivulet of water creeping toward her on the uneven floor.

Valentina stood, stretching her arms, feeling the anxiety in her stomach loosening from the tight ball it had been yesterday that had kept her crouched and low. Hunger and time had dulled the sheer wall of panic to only a constant background noise in her heart.

*You should not be alive. You should not be alive.*

She shook her head. It was not her voice. She would not believe it. No matter how many seasons it continued.

Brushing the snow off her shoulders and out of her hair, she gathered the fur to herself once again, and this time was able to bend down and pick up her old dress and stockings. She tried to fold them into some semblance of order, but her fingers were too stiff with the cold to do more than roll them into a rough ball. At least they found their way back on the unfinished shelf that stood next to the shredded remains of what had been her straw pallet. The ticking, slashed and torn, lay on the floor amidst the crushed old straw it had once contained. Valentina picked up a long piece of it. The material was strong, and there was lots of it.

She walked to the window and looked down.

The window was high enough that it took her breath away. She had never been brave when it came to heights, and this was the highest building she'd ever been in. It took at least three circles of the stairs to reach the height of the tower and she imagined it was five or six of her standing foot to shoulder in total. Leaping was not a possibility, not if she wanted to live. She glanced back into the room. There was no place to tie the material, at least no place firmly anchored into the wall.

Maybe if she broke the shelving and tied one end of the ticking to it and set the wood across the stone window, it would hold long enough for her to crawl her way down the makeshift ladder to the ground below. Her head felt dizzy, and her feet tingled at the very thought of it. It terrified her.

Her stomach growled, reminding her that her only choice might be which way she died. Would falling to one's death be worse than starving to death? She didn't know.

Returning to the shelving, she crouched down to examine the detritus below it, the few precious belongings she had. A broken urn. A few crushed leaves she had snatched from the blowing wind the fall before, and cherished for their touch of something from the outside. A broken piece of plate armor she'd found long ago as a child and used as a mirror.

A glimmer of red caught her eye and hope leapt, but a brush of her hand on the covering snow only revealed a few snatches of thread carefully wound around a sliver of wood pried from the shelf. Her own homemade spool of thread for repairing her dresses. Her heart sank as she looked.

Then she spied it, tucked half-hidden below a stone at the base of the wall that was not laid even with its neighbors, jutting into the room itself to hide a small space underneath its granite surface. The yellow metal showing beneath it gleamed at her, almost a wink. A small bladed knife with dull red jewels embedded in the hilt and a blade only as long as her fingers. She gave a cry, then quickly silenced herself as she leapt to grab it. Taking a smaller piece of the torn ticking, she wrapped the blade within it and tucked it into her bodice. They must not have seen it. Or thought the dull thing beyond concern.

It was bright as diamond treasure to her.

A scratching at the door caught Valentina's ear and she whirled, crouching defensively. The roughhewn shelving was the only furniture in the room, and its open structure and spindly sides hardly made a weapon that could hold up against a sword. But there was nothing else, so she grabbed it roughly, ready to shove it ahead between whoever was at the door and herself. Her heart thudded so loudly in her chest she was afraid it would stop or burst forth from her mouth.

The soft click echoed in the room as the lock was thrown from the other side. Then the scrape of the key exiting the keyhole roared in her ears, though Valentina knew it could be no louder than a mouse's squeak.

The door slowly pushed open.

The soft face of her elderly nurse, a face Valentina barely remembered from years ago, peered slowly around the dark stained door. Concerned black eyes flicked around the room under thick gray brows that furrowed into lines disappearing into the linen cap above. The woman was so stooped with age she was barely taller than Valentina's own height while crouching.

Their eyes met and the nurse gasped, then quickly covered her mouth with one hand. Her eyes watered.

Valentina inhaled to speak and her nurse shook her head violently, holding out a finger for Valentina's silence while pushing into the room and quietly shutting the door behind her.

Her nurse's small stature shocked Valentina. Her memory was of a sturdy woman with warm, strong arms. The woman before her looked like a soft doll sewn together out of a bundle of sheep's wool, and topped off with a white doll's cap. She looked like a doll in all ways, except for the bright intelligence of her eyes.

"How—" Valentina started, unsure of what even she was going to ask.

But by then the nurse had reached her, having shuffled through the snow in the middle of the room, and reached up to place a hand on her mouth. The warmth of the woman's fingers burned on Valentina's lips.

"No time, child," the nurse said, her voice hoarse with age and something else Valentina couldn't place. "They fight amongst themselves, forgetting you for the moment, but that won't last."

"Fight?" Valentina asked, pulling back from the woman's fingers over her lips.

"The blood... How it could get worse, I do not even know." The woman looked down, then shoved something toward Valentina, whose eyes focused for the first time on the burden the nurse carried.

It was a heavy package wrapped in dark green cloth and tied with leather thongs, along with a thick carrying strap meant to go over one's shoulder. It looked too fine and out of place. Valentina raised her eyebrows as she glanced back up to her nurse.

"It's owner will never miss it." A dark look passed over the nurse's face and she turned to mutter, "He'll never miss anything again."

Valentina sucked in her breath, feeling dizzy.

Being forgotten in the tower had not been the worst fate for someone yesterday.

The nurse pulled herself together. "No matter. Nothing to be done now." Her black eyes searched Valentina's face. "Except for you. That can be done. You must leave here, child, before they remember they left you here."

"Leave?" Valentina repeated.

"Yes, child," her nurse said, looking up at her and reaching a hand for her cheek.

Valentina's heart danced in her chest.

Leaving.

Something she dreamed of for years. But now, in the depth of winter, and with the rage of those around her, it terrified her.

This was nothing like her fantasy of leaving on a warm summer's day to the welcome of those below.

They would never welcome her.

Her nurse shoved her, bringing her out of her thoughts.

"Now, child," her nurse said, the voice from her small body suddenly like iron. It brooked no argument. "Run. Far as you can, then change. Burn those clothes if you can." Her nurse grabbed the sleeve of Valentina's bodice. "Or at least bury them. Everything you need is in the bag."

Everything she needed? The bag was heavy in Valentina's arms, but not heavy enough to hide a father or a guide or a home.

But now it was everything she had.

She stared down at the bag.

"Come with me," Valentina said, her voice cracking.

"I cannot," the nurse said.

"Please," Valentina said, not caring how pathetic her begging sounded.

"I will only slow you down, and you must *run*."

A horn sounded in the distance, followed by the baying of dogs.

"No no no. So soon." Her nurse grabbed her by the arms and twisted Valentina's body around to shove her toward the door.

The horn sounded again, breaking Valentina from her paralysis. She slung the fine bag over her shoulder and securely across her body, then grabbed the fur from the floor as they ran across the room to the door opening ahead. An ominous maw. A threshold she had not crossed in three years.

A moment later, it was gone behind her.

. . .

She went down the stairs, sliding along the outer stone wall as her legs struggled with the unfamiliar action.

Her nurse followed, but could not keep up the pace, and Valentina reached the bottom alone.

The outer door stood ajar. Blinding white light came in, bouncing off the crisp snow outside.

How could she get away? Her tracks in the snow would lead directly to her.

Valentina looked back up at her nurse still on the stairs. Fear washed over her, strong as it had been yesterday.

"Go! Pick one and send the rest flying," the nurse said as she nearly missed a step and fell to her knees on the steep wood stair. The structure rang and echoed like a death bell.

Pick one? Pick what?

Valentina took one last look at her nurse and recognized the formidable look that bid her to go. She exited the tower for the first time in three years.

Outside, stamping in the snow and blowing clouds of white vapors under the hazy light stood a dozen black horses.

It must be half the royal stables.

How had that tiny woman corralled all these horses here?

Valentina turned back to the tower, but as if to remind her of her peril, the dogs in the distance bayed again.

No.

She had to go on.

Turning back, she faced the dozen beautiful animals, their hides slick and shiny even under the dull light. Their necks curved in pride. Not one wore a harness or saddle.

And they were huge.

These were warhorses, not ponies young princesses rode.

Good.

She needed a strong horse. Lifting her chin she walked toward them. One of the horses strode forward, as if to greet her. Valentina nodded and reached out a hand, carefully keeping her palm flat. The horse sniffed, then whinnied and presented its side to Valentina.

Valentina grabbed its mane and leapt up the best she could, trying to not pull too hard on the horse's hair.

It gave no sign of irritation, only waiting till she was settled before it turned away from the direction of the coming dogs and horses and ran over the snow covered and pristine sloping meadow, the snow cover not even marred by a single rabbit track.

They raced toward the tree line ahead, a mixture of skeletal, leafless trees sown in with towering snow-laden pines that could hide near anything within their dense branches.

The Forbidden Woods.

The woods that stretched from horizon to horizon and marked the edge of the kingdom. Woods rumored to hold all the ills of the outside world. Woods she'd stared at for hours when she had dared to pull aside the tapestry and reach her head out the window, and even so, she could just barely see them.

Not once in the hours she'd gazed at them had she seen a living creature enter or exit.

As if on cue, when Valentina's horse ran, all the other horses also ran, fanning out in all directions. Many of them also angled toward the woods, but others circled back over the rolling hills, up the gentle slope leading to the main complex. Others still took the last of the compass directions. The horses crossed each other's paths and left winding trails in the snow. Some even rolling in the snow as if playing.

As Valentina and her ride raced to the deep shadows of the woods ahead, the horses called out to them as if in farewell. Her horse replied in a bellowing call as it carried them both into the cold depth of the woods, the weak sun suddenly gone in the shadows. The smell of dead wood and pine sap filled Valentina's nose. Cold air—colder than night—washed over her and wrapped around her body.

Valentina shivered and wrapped the fur she'd clutched in her hands around her shoulders and over her head. She pulled it tight against the frigid air as she tucked tight to the horse to avoid the branches flying by.

Her thoughts raced back to her nurse's face. Valentina hoped she was all right. She feared what would become of her if the riders and their dogs found her old nurse at the forbidden tower and its former inhabitant gone.

Twisting on the horse's back to face the way they'd come, Valentina strained to hear more trumpets, or even a dog's cry, but only the sounds of the horse's hooves breaking the sticks and pine needles on the forest floor below reached her ears. The horse swished his tail in her face, as if nudging her to face forward again.

Valentina obliged, turning back to face the dark woods. Suddenly, the smell of sap cloying in her nose made her stomach clench and spasm. Her hands dug into the horse's mane and she leaned over to slide off. She was going to be sick.

But the horse skidded to a stop and sidled up to a thin black tree, trapping Valentina's leg between the animal's side and the sharp, flaking bark of the tree. The bark looked fragile, but its edges were strong enough to feel like a knife's edge even through the wool of her dress.

"I need to get down," she said, gasping, as if the horse could understand her.

It snorted.

She twisted on the horse's back, trying to pull her leg free from the pinch between the animal and the tree trunk, but the horse only leaned harder against the tree. Not hard enough to injure her, but hard enough to keep her secure.

Valentina stopped struggling.

The horse turned its head back to face her, blowing a bit of mist at her and lowering its lashes.

Its breath smelled of summer grass. Normally a pleasant smell, it was too much in addition to the sap and rot filling the air.

Her stomach clenched violently and powerfully. She bent over and gagged. Another powerful cramp came and Valentina twisted to the side, throwing up a thin stream of liquid over the side of the horse, just managing to miss its flank. Her teeth ached.

When her stomach stopped convulsing, she slowly sat up and wiped her mouth with her hand.

"I guess I don't need to get down," Valentina finally said gingerly.

The horse blinked at her.

"I won't get down," Valentina said more firmly, reassuring it.

The horse huffed and bobbed its head, its black mane bouncing and shining even in the low light. It turned its head away from her again and slowly walked forward, gracefully avoiding the steaming remains of what had been in her stomach and keeping close to the trees, as if waiting for her to attempt to dismount again. Valentina ducked to keep from getting struck by a low branch reaching out across their path, only to fail to see the next branch and get walloped across the chest and face by the quill-sized fingers of the winter slumbering tree.

Valentina blinked in surprise, then a laugh bubbled up in her chest, surprising even herself.

"I guess I understand not trusting someone." She patted the horse's curved neck. Warmth flowed up through the short hairs there. Valentina pressed both hands down onto its withers, leaning into the warmth.

The horse walked closer to the middle of the path through the trees.

The horse seemed to know where it was going. It had taken her directly away from the danger at the tower, so Valentina thought there could be much worse things than trusting it now. She held onto its mane and watched wide-eyed as they walked through the deep shadows of the feared Woods she'd only dreamed about from her tall tower.

# 2

The acrid smell of woodsmoke roused Valentina from her half slumber on the horse's back. The rocking motion of the ride from each step of its powerful legs had lulled her eyes shut. Now, opening them, the deep shadows of the woods appeared unchanged. As before, some snow lay powdered between the trees and on the limbs of the thick blue-green pines, and rested on the black twisting limbs of the other leafless trees. As before, no birds called, no small animals scurried.

Only the sounds of breaking underbrush and discarded needles underneath the horse's hooves and small branches breaking in their progress carried through the seemingly endless wood around her.

Twisting on the horse's back, Valentina checked behind and all around to see if she could spot the red glow of fire in the distance, or even smoke overhead. White lights dotted the deep blue above, the color of not night, and not day, but somewhere between. Had they walked all night?

As if sensing her thoughts, the horse increased his pace. Valentina grabbed its mane and adjusted her position. It broke into a trot, and then a gallop. She pressed her knees into the sides of the horse to steady herself and not slide off. She wished for nothing more in that moment but for a saddle with a pair of stirrups and a pommel to hold on to. But there was nothing like that here, so instead she twisted her fingers into the coarse black hairs of the horse's mane and leaned forward and kept low.

They rode on and on. Valentina's breath grew ragged with the effort it took to hang on so tightly. The muscles in her forearms ached and cramped, her fingers grew numb, the blood cut off from the tightness of the hairs wrapped around them, and her thighs cramped with the effort to squeeze her mount tightly, but she didn't dare relax, for every time she did, she started to slide off to one side or the other of the slicked back of the horse. Even in the coolness of the woods, the animal was sweaty with exertion.

Finally, the horse slowed back to a trot and then a walk, huffing and steaming in the cool air. Cautiously, Valentina sat up again and looked around. Perhaps she was imagining it, but the woods ahead appeared to be thinning, the trees less tightly packed.

The horse stopped and whinnied softly. Valentina looked around, unsure what it was reacting to. It whinnied again. She froze in place, trapped by an ominous feeling.

It turned its head to her, and shook it, as if saying 'no', the hairs along its neck and head flying out wildly in a beautiful cloud of black.

She stared into its huge brown-black eyes, then suddenly gripped its mane as she felt herself sliding forward. The horse had leapt with his rear two legs, sending her off-balance, then shook its head again after its rear feet landed again.

"Okay, I get it, I get it," Valentina said, her heart racing. She leaned forward then stiffly lifted one leg and brought it over the back of the horse and awkwardly slid off. Her legs, shaking and weak with exhaustion, gave way so instead of standing, she landed in a pile on the ground by the horse's hooves. Flakes of snow flew up around her, and the wetness of the ground immediately soaked into her gown where it touched the ground.

She scrambled away from her position on all fours, sacrificing the dignity of standing first for the safety of getting away from the feet of the enormous animal.

It made a sound that in any other creature she would have thought was a laugh.

"Fun for you," she said as she turned away, put one foot on the ground, and pushed herself upright. It felt good to stand, although the ground seemed to be still moving under her. She reached out a hand for the horse and steadied herself. Her breath slowly returned to normal.

Now that they were no longer walking and crashing through the undergrowth, a faint, musical tinkling reached her. Water. Valentina licked her lips.

A creek flowed through a nearby dense section of pine trees. It was narrow but looked deep and fast running. That must be how the waters were not frozen. Anything slower would have succumbed to ice in the coldness of the wood.

Valentina found a stub on a tree at eye level where a thick branch had broken off and hung her green bag on it, having taken it from her shoulders. It hung safely over the wet ground.

She gingerly walked toward the water, her thin leather shoes quickly soaked and blackened. They offered no purchase and she slid several times, narrowly missing ending up in the creek itself. Scanning the length of the banks, she finally found what she was looking for.

A branch the size of her forearm reached toward the waters, low enough to be within easy grasp. Testing it first with several sharp yanks, she then grasped it and used it as an anchor as she leaned down to the waters and took in several long droughts. No feast was ever so splendid.

The horse, more sure of itself in the water, drank downstream from her. It finished before she did and waded through the waters to her, corralling her back to solid land.

"Fine, fine. You are a bossy one," Valentina said.

It nudged her toward her bag.

Valentina remembered her nurse's instructions. She walked to her bag, waving the horse away, and set to opening it. Her cold and stiff fingers worked at the leather thongs. Finally freeing the bag of its ties, she opened it to be overwhelmed by the smell of cheese. Inside lay a pile of fabric, the glint of a buckle, and the tops of two sturdy boots. Nestled alongside the boots, sat a small linen bag with a slight grease stain. It probably held the cheese, and hopefully more foods besides.

Her stomach growled.

The horse side-eyed her.

"What? I bet you ate while we were going," Valentina said. Her face turned red as she realized she was probably wrong. It had walked without stopping, indeed without sleeping as she had, and all while carrying her. Suddenly she felt shame.

"Sorry, sorry," she said to the horse and reached out to touch its forelock. To her relief, it let her. She exhaled.

Holding up the clothing, she found they were a boy's set of breeches and tunic. Thick and well made, but in a dull wood brown and mossy green, the stitching plain. Only touching it would reveal how well made the set was.

"Wait here," Valentina said to the horse. Taking the clothing, she went into a nearby circle of pine trees. She felt silly being modest in front of the horse, but others could come through the woods, as unlikely as that was, and she wanted some shelter around her if she was to change.

Emerging from the circle of pines a few moments later, she felt like a different person. The clothing fit well. How had Nurse managed that? Even the boots fit, cradling her feet. Valentina stuck one foot out, admiring the design. Something thick had been applied to the bottom of the leathers that prevented water from soaking into the boot itself. The coating reached to the ankle, and was camouflaged to look as part of a decorative design. That was the only decoration on the entire outfit. Valentina wriggled her toes. It felt so good to have dry feet she could have cried.

Walking back to the bag still hanging on the tree stub, Valentina looked around for some place to put the bundle of her old clothes she held in her arms. Spying a nearby crotch in the branches of a tree next to the one she was standing, she shoved the clothes there. They were wet and dirty, but she couldn't bring herself to set them down in the snow and mud.

Inside the green bag, Valentina found a small cap. She remembered young grooms wearing caps of that style years ago. Putting a hand up, she felt the thick length of her hair. It would never fit within the double-thick linen cap. Nurse must have included it for a reason though.

Valentina held the cap, turning it inside and out, and then looked around the woods. She made a decision. Going back to the bundle of clothes she had set in the tree, she dug around until she found the ticking-wrapped knife she carried in her bodice the entire ride. Pulling the knife out, the metal itself felt warm, not the cold she expected in the winter air. It fit in her hand comfortably.

Reaching up, she gathered a section of hair and used the knife to cut it off at the level of her shoulder. Looking around uncertainly with the length of hair in her hand, her gaze stopped at the water. Walking over to the bank of the creek, she threw the lock of hair in the center of the flowing waters the best she could. The curl of chestnut hair floated at first, then slowly separated into individual sections and was sucked under the flowing waters.

It was quick work to cut the rest of her hair to match. Her head felt light on her neck as her waist-length hair was reduced to a shoulder-length bob, a style young pages and servants alike favored.

With any luck, between the clothing and her hair, she would be taken for a boy.

The horse came to stand beside her just as she was finishing her hair. It stared down at her, then reached out and nuzzled at her neck with its nose. Valentina froze in place at the unexpected attention, feeling its hot breath on her neck and the gentle touch of the animal's chin hairs gliding along her cheek.

"Well, hello to you too," Valentina said. She wished she had a pocket of sugar cubes, or really anything, to give this gracious creature.

The horse backed up then bobbed its head and snorted. While Valentina was trying to figure out what it was doing, it then quickly trotted to where her old woolen dress and leather slippers nestled in the crotch of the nearby tree. The horse reached out its long neck, and with its big square teeth it grabbed a hold of the whole mass and pulled it from the tree, the gown hanging down while the shoes stuck out of its mouth in a ridiculous fashion.

"Hey!" Valentina cried, holding out a hand and running toward the horse. It eyed her with one white-rimmed eye, then whirled and took off between the trees, running in great strides the way they had come.

Valentina ran after the receding horse, her boots sliding in the mud. She had no chance to catch it, but couldn't stop herself from trying anyhow. Her breath grew ragged and her lungs burned.

Ahead, the horse turned a corner around a snow-laden pine and was gone. Soon the sounds of its hooves were gone too, quickly muffled by the snowfall and the thick trees around them.

Valentina ran after for a few more lengths but then gave up the chase, bending over and holding her side as her ribs ached. Surprise and shock ran through her. She'd only been with the horse for less than a day, but already its disappearance felt like a betrayal.

Staggering, she walked back to where her bag still hung from the tree. Crouching down, she felt around in the dead leaves and snow and mud until she found her knife half buried in filth where she had dropped it. She wiped it off the best she could with some dead leaves she found under the snowpack and rewrapped it in the ticking that she had luckily placed in her pocket instead of with the rest of her old clothing. Tucking the secured blade into the bag, she looked around for any other items. Only the leather ties lay on the ground. Grabbing those too, she shoved them in the bag and then shouldered it.

She looked around the woods.

She had no idea where she was, what time it was, or how she would eat when the food in her bag was gone.

More than she ever had felt in the tower, now she felt truly alone.

She rubbed her arms against the cold.


Valentina trudged through the snow, occasionally looking up to check the sky. Its blue had lightened to a cerulean blue with only the faintest wisps of white spread across it, at least as far as she could see. She hoped to see a trace of smoke and know where to go to find others, but there had been nothing after the smell of wood burning had disappeared yesterday.

Trees crowded her with snow covered needles on the enormous pines and the black twisted branches of their companion trees, making it hard to see far in any direction. Some of the pines were so large a house could have hidden within the branches. Valentina had pushed inside a few of those monstrous trees to see if anything or anyone was hiding within, feeling the snow fall on her head and down her back as she disturbed the branches. There was never anything inside the massive branches except the heavy sweet smell of sap and dried needles underfoot. Even being careful, she had gotten sap on her clothing and fingers. And now sap covered her fur and bag from using them as a bed under last night's tree.

At least it had been warmer within the embrace of the tree. Emerging into the cold morning air had been a shock.

Once she'd come out that morning, she'd checked her mark on a nearby tree from the night before and set her direction. As much as she missed the horse, she knew it would be folly to go back the way they had come to look for it. Nothing good waited for her there.

At her feet the snow lifted in powdery flakes with each step. The mud was long gone under yesterday's new snowfall, and the newly crisp temperatures kept it hard beneath the snow. Valentina's fingers numbed with the chill. She blew on them and pulled the fur around her shoulders closer.

Her stomach growled its complaint. She'd eaten the last of Nurse's cheese and dried fruit this morning.

Valentina looked through the woods as she walked for any animal tracks or plants she might recognize as food. Even with these efforts, she'd not seen one set of animal tracks. Confounding things, snow covered all the foliage. No mind; anything below the white pack was probably long dead for winter anyhow. Still, she couldn't stop herself from walking to every higher pile of snow that promised bushes beneath and brushing off the covering snow, looking and hoping for some overlooked berries beneath. It made for slow going.

Ahead, one long row of snow-covered bushes ran between two large black and twisted trees. Despite her cold and exhaustion, Valentina's pace quickened as she pushed through the calf-deep snow. Wrapping the fur around her hand, she used it to brush off the snow. It lay so thick and heavy on the bushes that the snow ran up her arm as she pushed it away. She ignored the chill as the gleam of tiny purple-blue shriveled berries on the thorned branches caught her eye. Success! Berries of the Wild Women.

Nurse had loved feeding her the juicy, bittersweet berries in the summer while telling her tales of the warrior women who had supposedly planted them all over the lands. The berries were to feed all those in need.

Once Valentina had complained of getting a bitter berry and Nurse had shushed her so abruptly by covering Valentina's mouth with her thick calloused hand that Valentina burst into tears. "Never, ever complain of the warrior berries, child," Nurse had said in a low tone, a warning in her voice Valentina had never heard from her before. Valentina had nodded, her eyes wide over Nurse's hand. They had never spoken of it again.

Now she just gave thoughts of thanks as she pulled on the tiny berries. Each fruit gave the lightest of resistance before releasing from the bush with a gentle pop. She put three into her mouth. At first, she couldn't taste anything except the cold of ice on the frozen fruit, but then they warmed and filled her mouth with an earthy flavor of summer and tart juice. Valentina closed her eyes, savoring the flavor as the berries melted. Her mouth watered.

"Taking your fill, eh?" a rough voice asked.

Valentina turned. Behind her stood a young man, dressed in a dark gray tunic over matching pants. He had tall boots, taller than hers, with the same design as her own. Long raven hair showed at his shoulders beneath a hat pulled down low that shaded his eyes. His face, only slightly gaunt and with high cheekbones, held no hint of a smile.

She did not look at his face long though, for she was distracted by the glint of silver in his hands.

A knife as long as her forearm wavered just slightly in his grip. Just enough to get her attention.

# 3

The young man stepped forward, his broad shoulders framed perfectly between two large pines behind him. Valentina wondered what he looked like beneath his hat, wondering if perhaps she was a little hysterical at his sudden appearance. She forced herself to breathe and not move as he approached.

As if his appearance had brought it, the smell of smoke tickled her nose, bringing with it the burning sensation in the back of her throat that woodsmoke always brought. How had she not noticed? There must be people around. At least one. Hopefully more. Even more hopefully, strangers and not the ones she was running from.

The young man drew close enough that Valentina could see the wear on his clothing. Threads on the elbows of the fine gray tunic shone with much washing and usage. A patch, as finely stitched it was, showed at his right shoulder and betrayed the age of the garment. Long scratches and darkened spots on his boots spoke of their age.

But his skin, clean-shaven, was that of a young person.

He pushed back his cap. His eyes, a light gray, drew her to them.

Valentina focused on her breathing. Her only weapon, the tiny knife, was wrapped in its ticking deep in her bag. She cursed herself for such trusting foolishness. A weapon should be out and reachable.

He stopped about ten paces from her and appraised her. "I've not seen you these ways before," he said.

Valentina shook her head.

"Do you have a voice? Or are you one of the mute ones?" he asked.

Mute ones?

"No... I mean, yes I have a voice," Valentina said, her voice cracking from the last few days of disuse.

"And a name?" he asked in the same neutral tone.

"Va—, I mean, Wiley," Valentina said, scrambling for a false name. Her face reddened. She couldn't take her eyes away from him. Is this what the rabbit felt like under the gaze of the wolf?

He raised one eyebrow.

"Val, Vee... Those are nicknames. The other kids teased that I was not smart enough to be Wiley and so called me other things," Valentina said. That much had been true, but he did not need to know the other kids had also been royals as she was.

"I see you also know children raised by the same heathens I once knew." Nodding at her as if satisfied, he sheathed the knife into a leather holder hanging from his belt.

Valentina exhaled a breath she had not realized she was holding. Her eyes flickered over the woods behind him.

"There is no one else. Just me," he said, the hint of a smile showing for the first time.

"And you are?" Valentina said, with more bravado than she felt. She had tried to make her voice lower, like that of a boy, but it had only resulted in another crack.

"Mercato. I have allowed no nicknames." He looked entirely too smug about that. Valentina turned from him and back to the bushes, marveling at her own bravery. He could probably kill her now even with his bare hands, so she decided not to worry about it.

Besides, she was hungry.

Shoving more snow off the bushes, she busied herself with pulling as many berries off as she could. They stained her palm as they melted in the heat of her hand, so she shoved them into her mouth and then quickly wiped her hand on the snow.

"You aren't worried about those?" Mercato asked.

"No," Valentina said. "They aren't poisonous."

"That's not what I meant," Mercato said.

"They're for the needy. Right now I'm needy," Valentina answered around a mouthful of berries. She gripped her hands into fists as the cold of the fruit filled her head. She had to slow down, no matter how hungry she was.

"Ahhh..." Mercato said, watching her with amusement.

Valentina turned to him. He ate none of the fruit, not even the ones directly in front of him where she had cleared away the snow.

"And you are not?" she asked.

"Apparently not," he answered.

She stood and glanced between him and the fruit, hesitant to continue eating in front of him. It made her uneasy.

"They are for everybody," she said.

"So the stories say," he said. "I'm just surprised you know them."

"Doesn't every child?" she asked. Really, he was too much.

"No," he said.

She huffed.

"Come. I have something much better than fruit dried by the winter days." He turned without another word and walked back toward the trees, retracing his tracks visible in the snow. Valentina watched him, then took one last longing look at the berries before running after him.

·  ·  ·

They walked through the woods for what seemed half the morning, though Valentina was sure it was less than that. Only her growling stomach made it seem so long. Mercato laughed at its noisiness, but didn't break his long stride. Valentina questioned her decision to follow him with each passing moment. Behind her was certain food. Who knew what lay ahead?

The snow on the ground thinned, leaving some spots barren. With the lack of snow and the hard frozen ground, it would be difficult for someone to follow them here. At least that was in her favor.

A thick grove of pines lay ahead, growing so close together that their branches intertwined like fingers. Mercato walked directly toward the mess and then pushed through. One moment he had just been a few paces ahead of her, and the next he was going into what looked like an impenetrable thicket of branches. Valentina stopped and stared. She was in no mood to be scratched by the trees and wear yet more sap on her body and clothing.

Behind her, a crack echoed throughout the wood, as if a large branch had broken. Whirling, she saw nothing, only the dim shadows between the trees and the browns and greens of the winter woods.

Repressing a shiver, she turned back to the thicket of trees. She gritted her teeth, lowered her head, and held out her arms as she pushed through the tree branches. They gave way with surprising ease, and she stepped into a clearing. An unbroken ring of tall pines with interlocking branches encircled an open courtyard in front of a tiny stone cottage. A curl of gray smoke rose straight to the sky from the neat stone chimney.

The stones of the building were of all sizes and shapes and seemed to magically fit together like a gigantic puzzle with the barest of mortar between them.

Mercato stood in the doorway, holding the door open and revealing a yellow warm light behind him from the interior of the cottage. "I thought you changed your mind for a moment," he said, a smirk revealing his teasing.

The rich odor of a stew reached Valentina for the first time. She stared over Mercato's shoulder, trying to peer into the cottage. Her stomach growled yet again.

"What are you waiting for?" he asked.

"Insufferable," Valentina muttered under her breath. She walked to the cottage and pushed past Mercato into its warm interior.

"Travelers' greetings to you," a thin voice said, startling Valentina. Sitting by the fire in a spindly rocking chair sat a tiny woman tightly bundled so thickly in blankets and shawls that Valentina at first thought it was just a pile of cloth. The woman's ancient face crinkled as she smiled, reminding Valentina of the tiny spring apples she'd find in the ground after a long winter, back in the days when she roamed the grounds freely.

"I'm... I'm sorry... I didn't know you were here," Valentina stuttered, as she stopped and bowed awkwardly. She couldn't remember how the young men had done it in court. It had been so long since she'd been there. "Greetings to you."

"Yes, good to mind your manners around her," Mercato said as he came into the room and motioned to the figure in the chair. "She is much more fearsome than I am any day."

Valentina looked to him and then to the tiny woman and back again. He seemed perfectly serious.

The woman smiled at Valentina. "He kids."

"I do not," he said. He pulled three cups from an open shelf and put them on the nearby table, then poured water from a pitcher. He gave one glass to Valentina with a nod. "Even I must mind my manners." He gave another glass to the old lady, who cradled it gently.

Turning back to Valentina, he motioned to the woman in the chair. "This is my most esteemed grandmother, Jessop."

"I'm Wiley, but you can call me Val," Valentina said. A warmth flushed her face at the lie, but she already said as much to Mercato.

The old lady grinned conspiratorially at Valentina and gave her a wink, as if she knew her secret.

Flustered, Valentina looked down and drank the water. It was empty in no time. She was thirstier than she thought.

Mercato filled the glass again, and gratefully Valentina drank it.

"Welcome, Wiley," Jessop said. "Have your supper with us. We rarely get visitors this far out, although I think that is about to change."

Mercato scowled at Jessop's words. He turned and fussed with the stewpot over the fire while Valentina found a chair.


Valentina and Jessop sat at the table as the candlelight flickered in the small house.

Supper had been good, but modest. Thankfully, neither Jessop nor Mercato asked Valentina how she came to be in the woods and she didn't volunteer it. Instead, the two of them had chatted about the weather and the coming spring while Valentina looked down at her plate and studiously studied the light blue flower pattern in the stoneware as she ate. She hadn't met new people in years and felt awkward.

Soon after, Mercato excused himself to go tend to the chores outside, while Jessop and Valentina quickly cleaned the kitchen, which mostly meant Valentina washed the dishes in a shallow basin of warm water while Jessop supervised from her chair.

Afterwards, they sat at the table with cups of tea.

"He must have a lot of chores outside," Valentina said at Mercato's extended absence.

Jessop waved Valentina's comment away. "Sometimes he goes hunting in the twilight."

The tiny woman stared at Valentina, her dark eyes searching

Valentina's face. "I'm sorry, youn'un, but you know you cannot stay here, much as I would love you to."

"I would never ask such a thing," Valentina said. She sat back. Where had that come from?

Jessop leaned in to Valentina. "I know who you are." She hooked a thumb and motioned outside. "He does not."

A rushing filled Valentina's ears. Her face must have shown some of her panic, because Jessop patted her hand with her own.

"No worries, child. I have not lived here all these years, waiting for you, only to murder you when you come by. But you cannot stay. For your own sake. There is one place you can go to be safe, for now. You must hurry there."

Valentina looked down. She concentrated on trying to calm her stomach that had jumped within her at the woman's words. A bitter disappointment tugged at her. She'd only been in this cottage for a few hours, enjoying its warmth and companionship, and already she was forced to go. Perhaps she should be grateful she was not being held prisoner yet again, but it felt like small comfort.

What had she ever done to deserve such treatment?

Jessop inhaled sharply. "What are you thinking, youn'un?"

Reluctantly, Valentina looked up and met the old lady's eyes. Whether it was from the disappointment, or exhaustion of the last few days, she ignored what she knew to be good manners and spoke bluntly. "Why?"

The old lady leaned back. She appraised Valentina from head to toe. "I see. I think I know who you are better than you know yourself. And it's not forever, child. For good or for ill, nothing is forever."

Jessop slowly rose from her seat at the table, her shawl falling from her shoulders as she stood from the wood seat. She hobbled over to a low wooden cupboard, her fine white hairs waving gently with her steps, and pulled out a small brown linen bag, drawn tightly shut with two woven linen strings. It bulged with its contents. Retreating to the table, she slid the bag across the table to Valentina.

"This is my gift to you. To any others that check, it will look like a bag of dried herbs—cheap ones at that. Only you can see its true contents."

Valentina picked up the bag. It was surprisingly light, despite its fullness. A familiar scent reached her, but she couldn't quite place it. "What is it?"

"That is for you to find out, my dear. That is part of the gift. Do not lose it though. Even if others cannot recognize it, it doesn't mean it cannot be dangerous in others' hands." Jessop gave Valentina a smile so broad that her eyes nearly disappeared within the folds of skin around them.

Despite the aching around her heart, Valentina could not deny the sincerity of the old lady. She returned the smile the best she could and held onto the bag.

"Try to not open that bag around others," Jessop cautioned. "If you must, you can dissemble by treating it as cooking herbs, but do try to not make others eat too much of them." Jessop cackled at some unknown joke.

# 4

Valentina and Mercato rode two older piebald horses next to the rutted and slushy road. Warmth had overcome the land, melting the frozen mud crossed with wagon ruts. Valentina doubted any more wagons could make further passage on the road until the weather improved and the road dried. As it was, the horses struggled in the damp ground next to the road, even with the thick patches of vegetation they trod on to steady their steps.

They'd been traveling for two days, having left early the next morning after Valentina's dinner with Jessop and Mercato. Jessop had nudged her awake before dawn and pressed two heavy saddlebags into her hands. "Your breakfast is inside. Mercato has the water skins."

Before Valentina could blink herself completely awake, she was standing outside of the cottage in the chilled predawn air, holding her bag and the two saddlebags. Her fur was tucked under her arm, where Jessop had put it. Before she could even turn to say her goodbyes, the cottage door shut and locked.

"Well, goodbye to you then, and thank you, Jessop," Valentina said under her breath.

Mercato came round from the back of the cottage at that moment. "Excellent. You're here. Ready?" He motioned for Valentina to follow him. He moved with a quickness Valentina didn't feel.

"You're in a good mood," she said, trying to keep the sullenness out of her voice.

"I am," he said. He turned back to check her progress and waved impatiently as she slowly trod after him. "I've been waiting to make this trip for ages. Jessop promised it would happen, and after more years than I want to count, it finally is."

Valentina squinted at him. "Where exactly are we going?"

"The capital of capitals. The center of all the Empire."

Empire?

"What's an Empire?" Valentina asked. "Is that like a kingdom?"

Mercato stopped in his tracks and turned on his heel to stare at her. "You jest?"

Valentina stopped walking. She shook her head.

Mercato swooped down and picked up a pinecone. He held it up for Valentina to see, then motioned with it to a tree towering above them. "An Empire is what this mighty pine tree is to this pinecone." He held the pinecone aloft higher. "This is a kingdom." He pointed to the tree. "That magnificent thing is the Empire. We are going to the center of our universe."

He twirled around as if doing a dance and then whipped the pinecone off into the woods, letting loose his excitement with a hard throw.

"Why is that so exciting? Isn't it just more people?" Valentina asked. She'd not had the best of luck with people lately. The thought of going into crowds of them didn't thrill her heart.

Mercato just gave her comment an exasperated look and motioned her to hurry.

He tried over the next several days to explain it to her, but at some point in their trip he had finally given up. Valentina had gathered he had great ambitions that vaguely had to do with commerce and being a businessperson that could not be satisfied in the depths of the woods. To her, it wasn't enough to take the risk of so many people.

That reluctance of hers to enter the city was why Valentina so regretted not pressing Jessop for more information. Jessop had not told her why this trip was so important for Valentina, but the last thing she had said to her that night was that Valentina must make it to the destination with Mercato. No matter what.

Now, after two days of riding, she was achy all over and ready to be off her horse.

The pine trees had thinned after their first day, and once they had joined up with the road, landscaping quickly changed to the bare branches of slumbering leafy trees and open fields. The occasional farmer labored in the distance, but none showed any interest in them.

Mercato and Valentina encouraged the lack of interest by keeping their distance and sleeping huddled under one of the few pine trees still in the changing landscape the previous night. The good-natured horses had not complained of the night outside and of only having a thin wool blanket apiece.

At Mercato's urgings, Valentina had hidden her fur and used a spare cape of his to huddle under for warmth. It let more of the chill in, but the unremarkable and unnoticeable gray linen was worth the exchange for the flashy fur that would only invite questions Valentina did not want to answer.

"Okay, so you want to go to Valderhorn to be a merchant? What about me?" Valentina asked as she shifted in her saddle, trying to find a comfortable position. The weak sun overhead lit the land, but did not give much warmth.

Mercato looked at her sharply. "Jessop said you're going to the stables."

"I am?" Valentina asked, confused. "As if I'm a horse?"

"No. Not stables like those. The Stables. It's the nickname for the school of all kingdoms. Stanasbrisson, but everyone just calls it The Stables," he said. He glanced at her quickly, then looked away, as if considering asking a question or not. They rode on in silence.

"Why am I going there?" Valentina asked.

"All who attend there are safe under the headmaster for the duration of their training. It is an oasis and a sanctuary. Many nobles send their children there."

Valentina huffed. "I am neither a noble nor a child." She turned away so he would not see the blush on her face at the first lie. As far as he knew, she was a nobody.

As far as she knew, it was now true.

"Everyone who qualifies can attend. Jessop said to make sure you got there and got in," Mercato said, looking a little uncertain for the first time on their trip.

"How does one qualify?" Valentina asked.

"No one knows for sure. The master comes out and looks at each applicant."

Valentina groaned. This sounded like a fool's errand. Worse, she would be in the middle of a crowded city, a difficult place to run quickly from. Maybe she could hide in the masses, but she doubted her meager disguise of a short haircut and boy's clothes would fool many for long. She rode on, ignoring Mercato for the rest of the afternoon.

The sun was dipping toward the horizon when the bellowing of a trumpet call rang out from behind them. The road had widened over the afternoon as several other roads joined up with it. They'd spotted a wagon or two in the distance, but had crossed paths with none.

Valentina turned at the noise and pulled up her horse. In the distance, six horses galloped, riding dangerously fast on the still wet ground. In the front, two dark horses took the lead, both with pendants flying. The gleam of a trumpet shone in the hands of one of the front riders.

Behind the front two, four white horses rode, all blanketed with brilliant red beneath their saddles. Their riders wore outfits of jewel colors: amethyst, citrine, ruby, and sapphire. One, in flowing robes of shades of amethyst purple, was a woman, but the other three were men. One of them, the one in citrine, seemed to be staring at Valentina. Even at their distance, Valentina felt a rush at his stare.

Tagging behind, in much less brilliant colors of muted browns and burgundies, was a cluster of more servants on horseback, surrounding a supply wagon pulled by the most massive horses Valentina had ever seen. Their labored chuffing reached Mercato and Valentina where they stood several furlongs away.

"Who are they?" Valentina asked quietly, though the riders were not close enough to hear.

Mercato only shook his head. He backed up his horse away from the road to make way for the riders. Valentina followed suit.

The front two riders, dressed in trim black uniforms, galloped past, sparing only a glace to Valentina and Mercato sitting on their mounts several lengths from the road. Valentina noted the polished sword on the first rider's back. The second had a bow and arrows lashed to the saddle of his horse. Valentina had no doubt they could pull their weapons quickly, and would, if either rider had thought them a threat.

The cluster of four behind the vanguard rode fast upon them. Valentina thought they too would pass in a rush, but one, the one dressed in ruby velvet, peeled off his horse from the rest and circled back to Mercato and Valentina. The remaining three slowed and turned to watch the ruby rider.

His horse was enormous. Its muscles bunched and shone in stark relief in the low dusky light. It arched its neck as if showing off its beauty. Valentina couldn't help but be entranced, until its rider cleared his throat, demanding her attention.

If the horse was beautiful, its rider was even more so. Sharp lines dominated his cheek bones and jaw, despite the youthful glow of his skin. Beautiful green eyes fringed with brown lashes stared at her. His hair, a rich brown in color, was combed back, forcing the curls to behave somewhat, though a single curl had pulled loose and hung on his forehead.

Only his scowl was ugly.

And it was focused on Valentina.

"You dare stare at your betters?" he asked as he pulled his horse back to a walk.

Beside her, Mercato pulled his horse back and looked down. Valentina knew she should do the same, but something about the rider's attitude told her that would be only the beginning of the torment, not the end.

"Are you my betters? What makes you so?" Valentina asked.

Mercato sucked in his breath sharply.

A flash of surprise flitted across the ruby rider's face, quickly replaced with a look of fury. He glanced back at the three other riders. They were steadily approaching, their horses huffing despite the easy walk, recovering from their earlier gallop.

"You dare..." he ground out.

Valentina too late realized her mistake. Bowing down could invite bullying, but humiliating one such as this in front of his peers would be a worse offense. Whoever the ruby rider was, he had to make her pay for losing face.

"Genedron," called out the woman in the amethyst dress.

"What, Nereen?" the ruby rider answered testily. Genedron.

"We are almost there. Master Silas does not want—"

Genedron whirled to glare at Nereen. Her words stopped abruptly.

"I am not your charge," he said in a low voice.

A tense silence filled the air. Valentina glanced at Mercato, but he was transfixed by the drama going on by the four ahead of them.

"No, of course not," Nereen answered. She tried to put a light tone in it, but faltered, her voice cracking.

Genedron turned back to Valentina. "Who are you?"

*No one*, Valentina wanted to say. Instead, she lifted her chin and said, "Wiley."

To Valentina's surprise, the rider in sapphire burst out laughing, his black eyes near hidden with cheeks curved with glee. He shook back his black hair and stopped laughing, giving the two others standing by him a shrug as they stared at him.

The one in citrine with blond wavy hair turned from his friend and stared at Valentina, as if to ask, *what do you think of this?* Unnerved by his half smile, Valentina had to look away and back to Genedron.

Genedron had not moved his eyes from Valentina's. "Apparently, Alcorn thinks that a funny joke. I would too, but I'm in no mood for fun. What is your name?" he said.

"Wiley," Valentina repeated. She could feel her pulse beating in her neck and in her palms. She wanted to get away from this group, but it was too late for that now.

"You insist on that?" Genedron asked.

"I would not insult my mother by doing otherwise," Valentina said.

Genedron snorted at that. "Your mother did not teach you to bow down to the royal houses when you saw them?"

"We saw no such people as you," Valentina said. It was true in some sense. In the years before the tower, she'd never seen these people, if they were indeed royals.

"Just as well. But you're seeing them now, you mongrel mutt. Bow your head," Genedron said.

Valentina stared back at Genedron.

His green eyes narrowed. "Now!" he yelled.

Valentina felt a nudge at her side. Mercato. She flicked a glance at him. He looked down, and had poked her with a booted toe to her leg. Screaming rebellion inside, Valentina slowly looked down.

Genedron gave another snort, this one of satisfaction. "A start. A poor start, but look what we are working with."

"Genedron," Nereen called out again. Her voice floated musically over the ground. She too, like the rest, was stunningly beautiful, her red hair falling in waves and layers that echoed the complex layered construction of her amethyst dress. Valentina watched her through her lashes as Genedron turned to go. He joined the rest, and the four of them turned their horses and trotted after the vanguard, the blond the last to look away.

Valentina lifted her head to watch them leave. When they were a furlong away, the blond one in citrine orange velvet turned back to look at them, then quickly turned away again.

"Well, that was fun," Mercato muttered as they waited for the final group of servants to pass them by.

"Who were they?" Valentina asked.

"I don't know," Mercato admitted. "We are going to the meeting place of many kingdoms. They could be from anywhere."

Valentina turned her horse back to the road and set off. Mercato followed.

"Why did you just bow to them?" Valentina finally asked after several moments of quiet riding.

"Why wouldn't I?" Mercato asked. "Do you think ones such as they would respect us because we asked them to? No. As things stand now, that just gives an excuse for their cruelty. It is another reason for me to want to become a rich merchant. It is the only way for a common folk such as I to have a chance at society, and even then, it's a thin chance at best."

"Why would you want their society if they are so unkind?" Valentina asked.

"Because that is how the world works. You have money or

power, or you die in poverty and discomfort," Mercato said before he nudged his horse ahead of Valentina's, and marking the end of his willingness to talk about the subject.

Valentina studied the movements of his horse as she thought about his words and the meaning of respect and royalty.

They camped next to a merchant convoy that night. Mercato had flipped a coin to the merchants' captain of arms, and that had earned them the right to sleep next to the circled wagons of the main caravan. It also meant they were safe enough to have a fire. The drivers of the merchants' convoy crowded around their own roaring fire in good spirits because they would reach their home of Valderhorn on the morrow, but Mercato and Valentina had demurred their invitation, instead settling for their own quiet fire with their horses nearby. Old habits die hard, Mercato had said.

Valentina was glad to avoid the company as much as possible. The chances of any of the drivers knowing who Valentina was, or of her kingdom, were slight, but it still worried her. Hopefully, she was keeping ahead of any possible pursuers, if there were any.

Jessop had seemed to think there would be people coming after her, at least as far as the cottage. Valentina pushed further thoughts of it out of her mind. It was too frightening to think of such things in the darkness.

The laughter of the drivers and the guards rang out in the night air, competing with hooting of the night owls, and calming her with its banal ordinariness. It was not yet warm enough for insects to be calling, but the lightness of spring filled the air. Everything was starting to move.

Valentina chewed the last of the cheese and bread that was their supper. Across the fire, Mercato whittled at a stick with a long knife. Valentina realized with a start this might be their last night of companionship. She'd gotten used to having a friend.

"So, are you going to The Stables too?" she asked Mercato.

"That I am not. I want to be out in the real world," he said.

"I do too," Valentina answered. Did she? She wasn't sure, but committing herself to this unknown place in the name of safety worried her.

"Ha," Mercato said.

"What do you mean by that?"

"There are protections at The Stables. And training. I don't know why," he paused in his whittling and stared at her, "but Jessop said it was important that you go there."

"You don't question her?" Valentina asked, surprised at his lack of curiosity.

"No. One of my first lessons was the danger of asking for more than I needed to know." He grimaced, then went back to his wood-working. "Jessop is different. She has... *thoughts*, that are more than just thoughts. It is hard to explain. But she knows more than you and I ever will, even if we grew to be ancient with snow-white hair all over."

"If we should be so lucky," Valentina muttered to herself.

Mercato glanced at her, but did not ask for her to repeat herself.

Valentina watched Mercato work for a bit more. He concentrated on his whittling as if she were not there.

She pulled out her own knife from its hiding spot within her tunic, slipped inside a sash she kept wrapped around her middle. Unwrapping the ticking that now was one of her few reminders of the Tower, she held the yellow handle and stared at the three ruby stones in it. They looked dull during the day, but now the stones caught the firelight and glinted and gleamed, as if wakened by the flames. As always, the handle felt warm. It had never not been warm to her touch.

She could not remember a time she'd ever been without the blade. It was important for some reason, but try as she might to remember, the reason evaded her.

# 5

Valderhorn nestled in a valley that abutted a large southern sea. It was a coastal city that also stood at the meeting place of four great kingdoms, so it had a massive harbor, as well as wide, well-traveled roads that came from north, east, and west.

Valentina and Mercato paused on the crest of the hill, taking in the sight of the metropolis below. The whites of the sails of the enormous ships in the harbor competed with the red tile roofs and fancy walled pavilions of the residents for Valentina's attention. A massive circular forum rested on the highest hilltop near the city center. Several large buildings flanked it, all with wide porticos with imposing columns and front plazas. More plazas and public buildings rose scattered amongst the vast stretches of residential compounds.

Nowhere could Valentina see smaller homes, or cottages, or shacks. All was massive and richly constructed.

Most of the buildings were a brilliant white, trimmed in bright colors. Statues, also painted bright colors, rose several stories tall in each plaza, easily visible from the crest of the hill where Valentina and Mercato stood atop their mounts, taking in the spectacle.

The merchant caravan they had slept by had left early in the predawn hours. Valentina had started to find them gone when she awoke. It amazed her that so many wagons, horses, and men had snuck off silently as ghosts without waking her or Mercato. She'd given a silent thanks for the honesty of the people of the caravan, for her and Mercato's horses and all their possessions were just as they'd left them when they'd fallen asleep the previous night.

So she and Mercato completed the journey to the capital on their own. Not that they were truly alone, for the closer they got to the city, the fuller the roads became. The silence of the horses riding on vegetation was replaced by the sounds of wagon wheels and iron horseshoes on the paving stones, the first such stones Valentina had ever seen. Her horse, unphased, had walked right up upon them. Mercato had a good laugh at the look on Valentina's face.

"I'm sorry. I've been here before," he explained. "I probably had the same expression as you do now."

"Thanks," Valentina muttered, but she was glad for his words. She didn't like being surprised, and lately surprises seemed to be all she was getting.

They rode down the long sloping hill to the city. It took until late afternoon before they reached the nearest gate.

The first sight of the city from the top of the hill had been deceptive. Based on the sizes of the building, she'd thought they had been closer, but she'd severely misjudged their scale. The stone structures were far larger than she thought possible. The wall itself around the city was several stories tall, not the single one she'd first estimated. Even the foundation pieces of one of the nearest buildings towered over her head while she sat mounted on her ride. She marveled at how such large pieces of stone had been moved.

"Halt," called one of the guards at the metal and wood gate. He moved stiffly, the red bristles on his helmet bouncing with each step. The greaves of his armor clinked as he walked, and his red cape flowed behind him, his dress finer than any Valentina had remembered of the nobles from the years she had been allowed within the court sessions back home. The years before things had gone wrong.

"What business have you?" the guard asked Mercato and Valentina.

Mercato leaned in. "We are going to The Stables."

The guard scowled at Mercato.

"I mean, we are going to Stanasbrisson, to see the master," Mercato said, quickly correcting himself.

The guard corrected his pronunciation of the school but then waived them in. "I expect if either of you are not admitted, that you will come back and pay the head tax required of all visitors staying beyond a day. I am assuming neither of you are city citizens." His smile revealed a broken tooth on one side.

Valentina shook her head.

"Note the display in the square of those who do not pay their taxes." He motioned to the square just inside the city gates and gave them two chits that allowed passage in the city for the day only. Valentina could not see what he meant due to the crush of wagons and people and guards, but as soon as they got inside the city and free of the masses squeezing through the gate, she saw quite clearly.

A family of four—a man, a woman, and two small children—stood in stocks. Two city boys pelted the man with rotten tomatoes, but blessedly left the children alone. It probably had something to do with the formidable guards holding spears standing nearby.

"So, you're going to pay that tax," Valentina said quickly to Mercato.

"Oh yes I am. I hope that you are not," he answered.

For the first time, Valentina hoped he was right.

．　．　．

42

The day was half over, so they didn't dally with visiting the marketplaces or touring the city. "You'll have time for that later," Mercato said. Instead, they had made their way directly to the gates of the school, which rested on the far edge of the city near a flat open area.

While they slowly made their way through the crowded city streets, Valentina kept her face down, paranoid that some stranger would recognize her and call her out. What they would do to her, she could not imagine, but she feared being dragged back to the tower. Or worse.

Valentina sweated under the sun and heavy salt air of the city, it being much warmer than the lands they had left behind. The white of the buildings around them reflected and increased the sun's power, so some stretches of the boulevards felt like the inside of an oven.

The city residents, most clothed in white linen and sandals, made way for them and their horses. They didn't greet them, but didn't seem unfriendly either. Just busy.

Only once did they have to make way themselves. A chair resting on two poles and carried by six burly men came racing up one of the smaller streets they had taken. The men ran in the late afternoon sun, their corded muscles shining with the effort. They were so fast that Valentina and Mercato had just enough time to convince their horses to move back and out of the way. Valentina stared, but the chair was covered with billowing fabrics hung from poles and hid whoever was riding within.

After the encounter with the sedan chair, they emerged from the narrow boulevard and set upon another main street, which was also closer to the many-stories high, thin wall-like structure towering over the buildings below it. Instead of being of solid construction like a brick wall, the thing was instead row upon row of arced stones layered upon each other. It looked like a fancy layered midwinter festival cake, but with arches instead of angel food. Valentina had seen the wall-like structure on their approach to the city, but now that they were near enough to touch it, she wanted to know what it was.

"Water," Mercato explained when she'd asked of its significance. This clarified nothing for Valentina. She stopped her horse and made as if to change course to get closer to the strange structure.

"That won't help you," Mercato said. "There is nothing to see at the base. The water is at the top." He pointed to the top layer of the arcs. "They bring it in from the mountains."

Mountains?

Valentina turned in her saddle. The nearest mountains were just faint blue and white peaks many days' journey away, far outside the city. That could not be.

"Yes, those mountains," Mercato said, not waiting for Valentina to ask. "They have enormous baths here and fountains and marvels you could not even begin to guess at."

Valentina could think of nothing to say to that. She let Mercato pull her horse's lead to follow him without complaint. Her massive tower and compound that had been her entire world until just a few days ago now seemed tiny and insignificant.

The city was so large that even making a direct path, it took many candlemarks to reach the school compound.

The main building of the school rested on a gigantic plinth, as if it had been carved in one piece from the hillside behind it. Eight columns spanned the front and reached up at least three stories, but Valentina thought possibly four. Dancing figures clothed in robes twisted and covered the pediment far above, along with a band of writing carved into the stone that she could not read, for the letters were foreign to her. A wall ran from each side of the building and encircled a vast area behind it, tall enough that Valentina could not see what lay inside except for the red clay roof tiles of several smaller structures.

The columns on the main building didn't stop at the front. Over the wall, she could see at least one other face of the building, this one longer and having seventeen columns, but only the upper portions were visible. To see more, one had to be within the walls of the school proper.

"This is a school for children?" Valentina asked Mercato, disbelief coloring her voice.

"Well..." He gave her a guilty look. "It is a vast place of learning. People come from all over the lands to study here. Or try to."

A chill overcame Valentina. Suddenly, the walls of the school reminded her of the walls of her tower, equally adept at keeping someone in as keeping others out. She walked her horse out of the shadow of the wall and into the sun in an effort to stop her shivers, and turned away from Mercato until she could control her expression.

Two guards stood at the base of the stairs that led to the front face of the school building. They wore the same greaves and metal plate as the guards at the city gate, but these had capes of a deep midnight blue, as well as blue-dyed horsehair on their helmets.

Mercato dismounted from his horse and gave the reins to Valentina. He approached one of the guards. "We're here to see the master."

The guard did not move.

Valentina dismounted her own horse and led both animals to a nearby post where she tied the reins. She went to join Mercato.

Mercato tried again. "This one," he motioned to Valentina, "would like to apply."

Again, the guard did not move.

Valentina and Mercato exchanged glances. Was there some trick to this?

Mercato opened his mouth to speak again, but Valentina held up a hand to stop him. "Please," she said to the guard. "If there is some custom we are missing, please let us know."

As if she had said some magic password, the guard nodded at her words and without explanation backed up and then climbed the stairs of the building. Valentina hoped that was a good sign and not a bad one. Surely, if they had done something wrong the other guard would have changed his stance. Instead, the second guard stared ahead as if Valentina and Mercato did not even exist.

Valentina looked around the streets while they waited. This section of the city was strangely empty, the pedestrians in their sandals and robes long since thinned to nothing. Even the birds were quiet here. It was as if the city was holding its breath for some reason. They had passed through several residential areas, the houses and compounds only slightly smaller than the main buildings in the center of the city that culminated in the massive palace on the hill that overlooked the forum.

Finally, the slap of leather on stone alerted Valentina that someone was coming down from the portico of the building. A tall thin man with iron-gray hair and a thick iron-gray beard, dressed in a linen robe trimmed with the dark midnight blue of the guards' capes, came quickly down the stairs, followed by the guard that struggled to keep up.

Next to her, Mercato whispered to her, "That must be Master Silas. Jessop tried to describe him to me, though it's been many years since she was here."

There was no time for more before the tall imposing man stood in front of Valentina. "So, you wish to join Stanasbrisson?" He spoke the words strangely, with the rhythm as if it was the beginning of a song. Was this a riddle?

"I do," Valentina said.

"Why?" the man asked.

Flustered, Valentina glanced at Mercato, but he only reddened. Valentina could understand he would not volunteer that she was joining because his grandmother said she should. She would have to figure this one out on her own.

"To learn," Valentina said.

The man pulled himself up and looked down at Valentina. "Your name?"

Valentina hesitated, then finally spoke. "Wiley."

A flash of anger flared from his eyes, but was quickly extinguished. His face became expressionless; it looked as if it were carved from stone.

"Are you?" he asked.

Feeling trapped but unable to change her answer, Valentina pushed forward. She lifted her chin. "Yes." She felt as if her lie were so obvious any passerby on the street could see it, if there had been anyone out. She glanced at the guards, but neither one was looking at her, instead maintaining their pose and staring off into the distance. They might as well have been statues.

"Why are you wearing that?" the man asked. He motioned to Valentina's pants and tunic and cap.

The strangeness of the question confused Valentina so much she stepped back. "They are clothes." She knew he meant something else, but wasn't sure what. "They protect me," she stuttered out.

The man's face relaxed. "Ah. Is that what you seek here then, protection?"

"Yes," Valentina boldly answered.

"Is that it?" he pressed.

"No, I want to learn too. There is so much I want to know." The last words flew out of Valentina's mouth, surprising even herself, but she realized the moment she said it that it was true. Coming to the city had shown her how narrow her thinking had become after three years of being isolated in the tower and in what she thought was the largest kingdom in the lands. She wanted to know what this place was.

She wanted to know why she had been put in the tower.

# 6

Valentina and Mercato watched the master climb back up the stairs of the school's main building, his blue trimmed robes flowing. He said he'd wait for her at the top. The face of a young man, his curls falling over his eyes, peered down the stairs but quickly disappeared when it saw the master climbing the stairs.

The two guards nearby stood impassively.

Valentina turned to Mercato. The anxiety of going into a new situation mixed with her sadness at saying goodbye. He shifted awkwardly from foot to foot, then pulled her away from the front guards so they could speak more privately.

"Here, I made this for you. Find some linseed oil to stain it and protect the wood. Sorry I could not get that done. It's more precious than it looks. Someday you'll know why," he said as he pressed a carved medallion of wood into her hand. It was about the thickness and size of a morning biscuit. Intricate carved deer decorated the front and back, the delicate arch of their neck and bank antlers preserved in the fine grain of the wood, while a crisscross texture decorated the thin edge of the medallion.

Valentina held the medallion, amazed at the intricacy of the work. "Did you make this last night?"

"Some of the work I did last night," he said, looking both pleased and embarrassed at her reaction. "Don't lose it. It's from both Jessop and I."

"I won't," Valentina said. She hesitated, then stepped forward and looked up into his gray eyes and gave him a hug. He was surprisingly solid. After a moment's hesitation, he returned her hug, awkwardly patting her back before finally pulling away.

"Find some oil for it. I'm sorry I didn't have time to finish it." His expression turned serious again. "I'll be back to check on you," he promised. "Right now, though, I better get back to the gate and pay the tax. I'll be in town for a while. I'll try to stop by once on my way out to make sure you're alright."

"Will the guards let me know that you're here?" Valentina asked. She turned to look at the guards standing behind them to see if they would answer, but they looked ahead as always, and either were pretending to not have heard her question, or really hadn't.

"Don't worry. I'll find a way to talk to you," Mercato said.

They stood awkwardly for a second, staring at each other before Valentina put the medallion into the safety of her bag, then turned and ran up the stairs, unable to face actually saying the word goodbye. Someday she would say the words and not have her final goodbyes be her running away from someone.

She reached the top of the stairs and glanced down behind her, just quick enough to get a glance of Mercato riding away and leading her horse. She'd forgotten about the animal but it was too late now. Hopefully she would not need one in the school. Besides, it wasn't hers. Jessop and Mercato's help of getting her into the school, and its promised safety, was more than enough of a gift from anyone.

She turned back to the darkened entrance, cool under the shadow of the enormous roof above them.

. . .

Valentina hurried to keep up behind Master Silas as he walked quickly through the maze of single-story buildings, all with red tile roofs. Much to her disappointment, they had merely walked through the outer set of columns of the enormous main school building to a stairway set on the other side where they descended into the main grounds of the school. The interior of the large building was closed behind windowless walls and Valentina had itched to open the wide double doors decorated with blue and yellow artwork to its mysterious interior.

The rest of the campus looked much like the city, but on a smaller scale, complete with statues and plazas. All the buildings had the same open construction and wide windows, their only acknowledgment of the weather being metal shutters that could be swung over the windows and fastened against the wind. Exotic plants grew in small clumps along the gravel pathways between buildings.

It was beautiful, clean, and well-tended. Gardeners, marked by their tanned skin and brown linen uniforms of shirts and pants, walked everywhere, pulling off small dead leaves and sweeping the wide expanses.

With a grimace, Valentina realized she looked more like a gardener than a student, if indeed all the students wore robes in the same style that Master Silas did.

He walked ahead of her, seeming to pick up the pace even further as they went past a large field where both men and women were practicing with swords, spears, and another weapon she couldn't identify that swung around on chains and made strange noises, like the wind whistling through the woods.

Finally, he turned the corner and then stopped abruptly. She nearly ran into him, not expecting him to be standing still when she turned the corner herself. He stood facing a small building next to a

51

much larger one. A horse called from inside the larger building. Beyond the larger building, a large courtyard held several chariots, and past that a roaring fire and the ringing hammer of a smith.

Master Silas stood with his hands behind his back and rocked on his feet while staring at Valentina. "This will be your new home for now. An attendant will come and explain the smaller details that you will need to know on the morrow. One of your new house-mates will show you where to get dinner. Do you have any questions?"

Did she have any questions? She struggled with which one was the most important, but before she could get it out of her mouth, Master Silas had already turned on his heel and walked away. "Very good," he called back to her.

Valentina watched him turn the corner and disappear.

A feminine laugh rang out above her head. Self-consciously, Valentina shut her mouth that she realized was hanging open, then looked up to find the voice.

A young girl sat on the ledge of a second-story window in the smaller building. Blond shoulder-length hair partially hid her face with its brilliant blue eyes.

She smiled down at Valentina. "He's always like that. You wouldn't know he left heads of state in the forum cooling their heels while he came to meet you by his ways, would you?"

"He what?" Valentina asked.

"It's the day before the High Spring Rites. All the fancy rulers and their fancy advisors come to pay their respects to the school and he rewards them with a lecture, which he must have inter-rupted to bring you here."

"Why would he do such a thing? Couldn't he send an assistant—"

"The student is the most important thing, he always says," the girl said, interrupting Valentina. "I think he rather likes it, actually. Making all those important hoity-toity pooh-bahs sit around and wait for him, because if you think about it, today they are his students too."

Good point.

The girl jumped down from her perch on the windowsill and then leaned out the window. "Wait there. I'll be right down."

Valentina wouldn't have known where to go anyway, so she was happy to stand and wait for the girl to come out from the small building. Much to Valentina's surprise, the girl emerged wearing a short blue woven dress that hung to her knees but with a soldier's plated metal chest and back pieces, and a metal skirt of plates hung from her waist over the short dress like the petals of a large and strange flower. While her outfit looked like the uniform of a common soldier, all the hammered metal pieces must have been custom made to fit her tiny frame.

The girl noticed Valentina's surprise and smiled again in response. "There are all sorts of things to study at The Stables. I prefer the annals of the army and all the ways of war."

"You get to choose?" Valentina asked, too surprised to be tactful.

"You do. To a point. Master Silas would say your studies choose you." The girl twirled for Valentina, showing her the uniform front and back. "I don't normally get to wear the dress uniform, but we're preparing the ceremonies tomorrow. I'm Clelia," the girl said.

"Wiley," Valentina said, indicating herself.

"So how did you get in?" Clelia asked.

"I... don't know," Valentina answered. "Should I?"

"Not necessarily. I keep hoping I'll ask someone one day and they'll know how they got in. I can guess for half of the students here." She waved off to some distant buildings. "The half that are royalty or those that spent all their lives studying and talk in philosophy riddles. But you, you're one of the odd ones, like me. The non-royals.

"How do you know I'm not royal?" Valentina asked, unable to stop herself.

"Because you're here. For this building. I've been here long enough to know how Master Silas sorts his students."

Valentina hoped she was right. Powerful master or no, she was safer if no one knew who she was.

Valentina's stomach growled loudly as she lifted the shovel of dirty hay and dumped it in the wheelbarrow. Sun filtered through the dusty and hay borne air of the long barn. Despite being near the horizon, the sun had found near the only window in the barn and managed to get into her eyes as she tried to work. Despite most of the stalls being empty, there were still nearly twenty horses shifting in their stalls and whinnying, as if greeting her while she passed by with the loaded wheelbarrow.

Something didn't seem right here. She'd not had her dinner. Nor did she have a horse anymore. Yet here she was feeding these horses and caretaking for them before she had anything to eat herself.

The promised attendant who was to instruct her on what to do had only come and dragged her to the barn and quickly told her the chores expected of her. When Valentina had tried to ask about dinner, the woman only said, "Later, later." Valentina pressed her lips tightly and forced herself not to press further. Even she could see the woman was harried and stressed, her hair coming loose with wisps flying out on either side of the tight bun in the back. Apparently, this was not a good day to become a new student at the Stanasbrisson.

Clelia had melted away when the attendant showed up. Valentina didn't blame her. She wouldn't want to do chores either. Besides, Clelia had her dress uniform on. Valentina was still filthy from the road.

Valentina glanced back at her bag hanging from one nail at the end of the barn. She didn't dare let it out of her sight. She'd not been given rooms yet, and didn't know how safe anything was here. She owned few things in this world, and she'd hate to lose the very last of them. Without thinking, she patted her chest just above her belly to verify the knife was still tucked in its hiding spot, now shared with the wooden medallion that Mercato had given her.

She stepped back and looked at her handiwork in the barn. She had completed cleaning the stalls all the way down one side of the huge structure and now worked at the last stall on that side. Its owner was gone, like many of the other stalls, but this stall had been particularly well used and needed cleaning. Her work wasn't perfect, but she was too tired to dig for the last pieces of the hay along the wall. She stood the shovel up against the wall and turned to grab the loaded wheelbarrow and take it outside to the compost pile she'd been shown to use by the attendant on her hurried way out the door.

The barn was two stories tall, and Valentina had discovered that the fresh hay was on the second floor. She'd been dragging the bundles of clean hay down the loft stairs, an exhausting task, but since the horse was gone for this particular stall, she decided she could just toss it over the barrier on the second-floor loft and let it fall to the stall floor below. Valentina climbed the stairs to the loft, then grabbed the remains of half a bundle, took a quick glance over the half wall of the loft, and let the hay fly down. A yelp from below ran through the barn, startling the horses and Valentina. Her heart pounded.

"Ye gods! Who did that?" a male voice said.

A very angry male voice.

Slowly, Valentina leaned toward the half wall of the loft and peered over. A red-faced blond boy not much older than her stared up at her through a cloud of hay and whirling dust. The bundle of hay must have hit him and burst apart. His horse nearby gleamed with good grooming and had not a speck of hay on its freshly washed white hairs, unstained with any yellow. The horse looked up at her. She could have sworn it gave her a smile.

"Sorry," Valentina said quietly to the boy. "You weren't there before."

He put his hands on his hips and glared at her. "When did you check? Certainly not right before you drop that pile—"

"I said I'm sorry," she said.

"How could you be so careless? You could have hurt my sweet girl. Her—"

"Hey! I said I was sorry." Valentina wiped at the stinging sweat that ran in her eye. Now she was getting mad. "Shouldn't you be doing this for your horse, if that is your horse?" She motioned to the hay and the stall she had just cleaned out.

"How dare you..." he said, then ran out of things to curse her for.

"Clean out your horse's stall and take care of it," she supplied unhelpfully.

He indicated his hay covered clothing. "How is this taking care of my horse?" he asked.

"It's called making a new bed. It's not my fault you got in the way," Valentina said, then she pulled her head back. She sat for a moment up on the wooden floor of the loft and waited for the boy to leave, but he did not. She could hear him fussing with his horse. She closed her eyes in a grimace and decided there was no use for it. She had to go down. She still had half the barn to take care of, and she had a bad feeling that she wasn't going to get her own dinner until she completed the task.

# 7

Valentina slowly descended the rough stairs of the loft, her footsteps echoing in the high ceiling of the massive barn. She hoped against hope that the boy would leave by the time she reached the bottom. No such luck. Her foot touched the packed dirt of the barn floor, and she slowly turned the corner to gaze down the long aisle to the end of the barn where the boy and his horse stood high-lighted in the red rays of the setting sun coming through the open barn door. He'd left the door open to his horse's stall and was busily brushing the animal, debris flying up and highlighted as small moats in the last of the day's rays. His back was to her, but Valentina guessed he knew she was there.

Her wheelbarrow was nearby, but she'd left the shovel in the stall where the boy and his horse stood. Besides, she had to even out the hay in the stall and finish the job there. Valentina clenched her hands in frustration and squeezed her eyes shut before taking a deep breath and opening them again. She'd been here not even half the day and already did something to anger someone. Even if it wasn't her fault.

Maybe she should not even have come to the city at all.

Her chances might have been better out in the woods.

"Are you going to finish the job, or just stand there staring?" he said without even turning to look at her while continuing to brush his horse.

Valentina huffed. Unbelievable. She stomped down the long corridor to the end stall, several horses turning to look at her curiously as she went by. As she approached, she realized she'd made a mistake. This was no young boy. He was young, yes, but nearer to a man. He stood near a hand's breadth taller than her, and at least twice as wide in the shoulders. His blond hair hung in curls and just touched the collar of his finely tailored yellow linen jacket and riding pants. If she wasn't so mad, she would have felt some remorse at the stalks of hay stuck in his hair and covering the back of his jacket. As she turned sideways to squeeze by him—for he made no effort to get out of her way—she noted his high cheekbones revealed under the hair pushed back behind his ears.

He was so unexpectedly good-looking it made it hard to breathe for a moment.

Walking into the double-sized stall, she grabbed the handle of the shovel tightly, feeling the wood grain under her fingers ground her. Without turning to face him, she motioned to the stall he was blocking. "If you please," she said. She needed him and the horse to move if she was to complete her work.

Without saying a word, he led his horse back out into the aisle and continued brushing it there.

Valentina shoveled the hay into an even layer on the stall floor, taking more time than needed. Whether to stay close to the man, or avoiding having to pass by him again, she did not know. Finally, she could put it off no longer. She turned to him. "All done."

She expected him to at least look at her, if not thank her. He did neither. It was as if she didn't exist.

"Fine," she muttered under her breath. She squeezed by him once again and made her way back to the wheelbarrow at the far end of the barn. She'd start her work on the far end of the barn from him and, goddess willing, by the time she reached this end again he'd be gone.

But she'd only walked half the distance back to the wheelbarrow when she heard him speak. "Hopefully you learn your job better here."

Job? Did he think her a gardener or hired hand? Valentina's shoulders tensed, but she forced herself to ignore him. It was just as well, and she'd probably never see his face again.

With any luck.

What seemed like an eternity later, Valentina completed her work in the dusty barn. She'd been so focused she hadn't even noticed when the boy had left. Just as well. She was too irritated to have said a polite goodbye.

Almost the moment Valentina leaned the wheelbarrow up against the back wall with a sigh, Clelia appeared holding a burning torch. Valentina realized with a start that it was dark outside. She narrowed her eyes at the girl. Had Clelia been spying and waiting for the moment Valentina completed her task before appearing?

Clelia ignored Valentina's look. "Ready for dinner?" she asked sunnily.

Valentina glared at her.

"Oh, come on. It's not that bad," Clelia said. "Everyone in our house has had to do it."

Valentina relented with a groan. "Fine. Do I at least get to clean up?"

"Only if you're fast. Tonight it's just scraps in the kitchen. The dining hall is closed in preparation for tomorrow. The cooks will have no problem throwing us out if we miss our appointed time, unlike the royals who get their dinner sent to their rooms."

Her entire body aching, Valentina went back into the barn one last time to grab her bag that was hanging from a hook halfway down the long aisle. She said a soft goodbye to the horses she left there, then forced herself to jog back to Clelia. She didn't know what she was looking forward to more, getting a chance to wash up, or getting some food.

Bathing turned out to be five minutes by the pump in the back of the kitchen gardens. Clelia worked the handle while Valentina splashed the water on her face and her neck, using her hands to wipe the grime from behind her ears and off her shoulders as best she could while still dressed. Clelia handed her a linen square from a pile of folded clean rags left on a stool by the pump. Valentina dried herself off and dropped the rag in the basket next to the stool.

Bats swooped around them as the day turned into night and the stars appeared above them. Clelia held the torch high as she led the way through the garden to the kitchen while Valentina tried to look at the stars above and not trip over anything in the garden path.

The kitchen itself was in chaos. The back garden closest to the kitchen doors was a hive's nest of workers tending to the open pits dug into the ground and filled with blazing coals. Other workers carried out enormous boars dressed on spits, ready for cooking, and lowered them into the pits before they were covered with sheets of metal and then dirt on top.

"Preparing for tomorrow's feast," Clelia explained at Valentina's confused look. "They will be on the coals all night. Be glad you're not a cook and working all night, too."

She didn't have to tell Valentina twice. The only thing Valentina wanted nearly as much as food was rest. As soon as they'd had their meal, she was going to plead for a bed. She couldn't imagine a full night of labor still ahead.

Clelia deftly navigated their way into the busy kitchen and to the left, hugging the back wall to reach a section filled with benches and tables just off the main space. The benches were full of people of all ages, most of whom had on robes in the style of Master Silas. A few wore tunics and pants.

Placing the torch into a holder on the wall, Clelia ushered Valentina over to a table with two open spots.

A young girl with thick black hair on the far side of the table nodded at Clelia, along with a thin young man with long dreads pulled back and knotted in a complex style that spilled down between his shoulder blades, the long finely braided hair inter-woven with silk and red ribbons. He gave Valentina a brilliant smile.

"Welcome, Wiley," he said, his voice thick with an accent that Valentina could not place.

"Thank you…" she said.

"Dante," he said with a hand on his chest.

"Dante," Valentina repeated. She looked down, flustered. After the quiet of the horse barn, the noise and chaos in the kitchen was disorientating. Metal ladles banged on pots, women and men yelled commands in the kitchen, while the ever constant noise of feet running back and forth on the tiles left no quiet moment in the kitchen. Around them, the others at the tables ate from plates laden with food.

Valentina looked around the kitchen to see where the food had come from. Several smaller pots on long metal handles boiled over fires set underneath the chimneys along the long wall on the far side of the door. While Valentina watched, a kitchen maid with her hair tied back under white linen and wearing a white linen smock scooped stew from one pot into a metal bowl with a wide flat rim, placed a hunk of bread on the edge of the bowl, and then brought it over to the tables. Valentina rose to help herself, but Clelia placed a hand on her arm.

"Don't. We're forbidden from going any further into the kitchen than these tables, especially during feast preparations. We're lucky they feed us at all. The head cook has promised to chop off anyone's hands who touch a single thing in her kitchen during the spring rites preparation," Clelia explained.

Valentina nodded and slowly sat back down on the bench. She looked anxiously over at the pots, her stomach growling, and forced herself to wait until someone in the kitchen noticed them and brought them something to eat.

"They're pretty fast," the girl with black hair sitting across from Valentina said. "I'm Luno. I'm another student." She motioned to the rest of the table. "Most everybody else here is too, though many are scholars more advanced than we."

"Everyone is more advanced than you," a young man with stick-straight red hair in a wild mess in all directions said with a mouth full of food from the far end of the table. His cronies clapped him on the back.

"No one asked you, Rutgre," Clelia said, not even bothering to look at him.

Despite his rude way of saying it, Valentina had to agree with him. Most of the other people at the tables were older, some even having gray beards reaching halfway down their chests. The elder women had their white hair in tight braids that circled the top of their head like crowns. She'd never seen such a mixed array of people.

"All picked by Master Silas," Clelia leaned in and whispered in her ear.

Valentina's face flushed to realize that included her as well. Suddenly, the horse barn felt warm and comforting compared to the intimidating presence of all these people, many of whom had studied for years, and all of whom knew the school much better than she did. She didn't even know why she was here. Her mood started to sour.

Luckily, a kitchen maid picked that moment to set a plate of hot meat, stewed lentils, vegetables and even a few pieces of fruit and bread in front of her. A jug of cold water and glasses were dropped on the table along with the food.

Valentina didn't wait for anyone's permission before she grabbed her spoon and started eating. Suddenly, everything felt better. No matter what situation she was in, she could deal with it better with a full stomach.

Valentina sat on the spartan bed with her head against the wall behind it. It was a small bed, just long enough for her, and covered only with two rough blankets, but it was all her own. The room itself was small as well, even more so with Clelia, Luno, and Dante crowded in with her. Clelia had commandeered the desk chair, while Luno and Dante fit themselves onto the small rug in the middle of the room. Besides the desk and oil lamp, there was nothing else in the room except some fluttering curtains over the second-story window. It was Valentina's assigned room and she was glad to have it.

"I'll get you a trunk from somewhere tomorrow. You can't have your clothes scattered all over the floor," Clelia said. "Actually, do you have more clothes? I can't believe that's all you have with you."

Valentina bit her lip. Luno and Dante looked curious as well. She had to say something. "We didn't have much money, and I couldn't leave... I couldn't take away things from the people who need them," Valentina said. Her face flushed at the lie. They probably thought she was blushing because she was embarrassed to be so poor, which worked out just as well. It should at least discourage them from asking more questions.

But Luno and Dante only nodded with kind understanding. When Clelia didn't ask any further, Valentina felt her stomach relax and her breath slow.

"She needs something for the ceremony," Dante said in his gentle voice.

Clelia eyed Valentina critically. "That she does."

She? So much for her disguise as being a boy. Valentina looked down to hide her disappointment. How could it be so obvious, or was it just obvious to Dante?

"I have the perfect dress," Dante said.

Valentina's head flew up at that. "No, no dress!"

The three others stared at her, surprised.

"That's fine. No one is required to wear anything specific," Luno said. "But it is the High Spring Rites. You will stand out more if you don't wear something fancy."

"Or they'll ask what a gardener is doing at the ceremony," Clelia said with a smirk.

"Clelia," Dante chided. Clelia waved him off.

"I don't have to go," Valentina said.

The three of them stared at her and frowned.

Anxiety pricked at Valentina's scalp at their horrified expressions.

"Actually, you do," Luno said. "It's one of the conditions of the school. The school has protection from all the kingdoms, yet in return, the kingdoms get to inspect all the students during the High Spring Rites."

Valentina scowled. What luck. If she'd arrived just two days later, she could have hidden here for a year. Exhaustion pulled at her. She looked at the black night showing through the blowing curtains of the window. It was too late, near midnight, and she was too tired to come up with another plan now. She would have to just find a way.

She looked up at the three staring at her. Despite only being on the school grounds for half a day, and knowing them for just hours, they already felt like friends.

"Okay. Help me find something to wear, but no dress. I cannot look like a girl," Valentina said.

Dante gave her a brilliant smile, as if she had just given him the best gift of his life.

# 8

Valentina dreamed of riding an enormous horse through a dark forest, the motions of its walking rocking her back and forth in a nauseating fashion. Suddenly, the horse turned its head around and spoke to her. "Wiley, wake up." Its high-pitched voice confused Valentina until she realized she was dreaming.

Forcing her eyes open, she found she was still rocking. That was no dream. It was Clelia, shaking her roughly. The girl was barely visible in the dim light coming through the open window. The sky was a dark blue fading to a lighter color lower to the horizon. From her position on the bed, Valentina couldn't see if the sun had risen yet or not. She thought not by the dimness of the room.

"What happened? Is something wrong?" Valentina asked, her voice groggy with sleep.

"Nothing yet, but there surely will be something wrong if we aren't ready before our housemaster arrives. Everyone is to be outside and dressed at dawn."

"Dawn?" Valentina asked, then groaned. She pushed Clelia's hands away to stop the nauseating motion. "Why so early?"

"Because they can barely get all the ceremonies in as it is.

There are things planned until far past nightfall tonight. You can sleep tomorrow," Clelia said.

"She's going to have to," Dante said, peering over Clelia's shoulder. He held up a pair of scissors for Valentina to see and snapped them twice in quick succession.

Valentina focused on him slowly, then glanced at the scissors. She reached up to grab a hank of her hair. He grinned and snapped the scissors again.


Dante had insisted that Valentina go and bathe at the pump again, this time from head to foot. Clelia and Luno accompanied her to hurry her along. Valentina appreciated their help, even though she felt guilty that they had to get up so much earlier just to do so. "Don't worry about us," Luno told her. "Getting you properly prepared helps us as much as our own dress. We're responsible for you as a housemate."

After the ice-cold dousing, she had no choice but to put back on her dirty clothes for the walk back. She walked hurriedly back to the house, her teeth chattering, while Luno and Clelia held the torches to light the way.

"How can you only have one set of things to wear?" Clelia asked, incredulous.

Valentina looked away, not willing to answer the question. Instead, she focused on climbing the stairs to the second floor where Dante waited. He'd laid out a long tunic of a dark red, along with fitted pants of the same dyed linen on her desktop. Deep red leather boots rested on the floor beneath. The final piece was a large billowing matching cap with a tassel hanging off the point.

Dante grinned at her return and held the scissors up as if he had not moved since she had woke up. He repeated the snipping motion, the scissors clicking loudly in the predawn quiet.

"Lucky for you caps are acceptable headgear for the High

Spring Rites, as long as they are fashionable enough. I'd love to dress you in purple, but even I'm not that daring." He didn't explain any further.

Clelia pushed Valentina further into the room from where she had stopped in the doorway. At her confused look, she explained. "Deep purple is reserved for royalty and the emperors. You're not an emperor, are you?"

"No," Valentina answered. "I don't think so."

Luno laughed from the hall. "Be glad. We would have no peace for sure."

"We'll be back when we are ready ourselves," Clelia said to Dante and Valentina. "Hurry."

Dante nodded at Clelia's command, then turned to Valentina and motioned to the outfit on the desk. "Get dressed, then I'll get you finished up," Dante said before leaving the room to give her privacy.

Valentina gratefully shut the door, pulled off her old clothes, and dropped them into a pile in the corner. She grabbed the new set and found a thin set of undergarments underneath the top clothes. Struggling with the stickiness of her still wet skin, she managed to pull them on, then marveled at how well they fit. Dante had taken one set of measurements the night before using a long knotted string, and managed to come back before dawn with something that fit her perfectly.

The rest of the outfit followed, also tightly fitting, except for the tunic that draped luxuriously. It wasn't a robe, but gave the feel of one with just enough extra fabric.

A knock on the door pulled Valentina from her examination of the outfit. She opened the door to find Dante and his scissors waiting.

"Don't worry, I don't have to cut it all," Dante assured her as he held up a length of fabric the width of Valentina's hand and the length of her arm. Separating out the front section of her hair, he twisted the back hair and then tied it close to her head with the loose fabric, hiding the length and bulk of her tresses. Pulling the front section of her hair forward, he twisted it into curls and then cut it to frame her face. Then he pulled the cap on over her bundled hair and tied a hidden string within the band to keep it tightly on her head, resting just behind the bangs he had just cut,

With only the short front fringe of her hair showing and the rest hidden under the cap, it looked like the shorter boy's haircut favored in Valderhorn, where the heat discouraged anything longer.

"Don't worry," he said, leaning in to whisper. "At first glance, you do not look like a girl. Just don't talk."

Valentina's eyebrows knit at his confusing comment.

He laughed and imitated a high-pitched Luno. "We'll have no peace for sure."

Oh. She sounded like a girl.

"Right. No talking," Valentina said.

Dante winked at her as he disappeared out the door to finish his own dressing.

The trumpets rang out and echoed across the entire city, the sudden noise so loud, ever present, and thundering that Valentina jumped in the safety of her room.

Clelia's panicked yell came down the hall. "We're late! Run!"

Valentina looked out the door of her room and was yanked into the hall by Luno, who was now dressed in long white robes with blue trim. Luno dragged Valentina along with a firm grip. Clelia ran close behind in her army dress uniform, and Dante followed, dressed in similar white and blue robes as Luno. Other students Valentina didn't know pushed in behind them.

As a horde, they ran down the hall to the stairway and thundered down the wooden steps to pour out of the building into the plaza by the barn and the blacksmith. On her way out the door,

Valentina glanced up and saw similar crowds coming out of other buildings in the school. The trumpets continued to ring, but they sounded louder and from further away than just the school property.

It sounded as if the whole city was waking at dawn.

The students formed a long line and stood at attention. Valentina looked around in wonder at the sudden crowds out just as the sun came over the horizon. Clelia kicked her in the ankle, and Valentina snapped her head forward.

A stern faced attendant approached the group and slowly walked by each student. He had a gray beard and gray hair, topped with a woven garland of fine olive leaves. His robes were long and a full rich blue, not just the white robes with blue trim. He slowed in front of several students and adjusted their outfits, touching their collars, sometimes straightening a cape or headgear. He slowly approached. Valentina heard Clelia force her breathing to slow, and she tried to imitate the girl by focusing on her breathing and a knot in one of the wooden planks of the barn across from her. Valentina put all her concentration into disappearing and being just like everyone else.

It didn't work.

The attendant finally reached the group and came to a stop directly in front of Valentina, breaking her line of sight with the barn. She dropped her eyes.

"Who is this?" he asked in a firm voice.

No one answered.

"I asked a question," he said quietly.

Valentina looked up. Despite the stern tone of his voice, he had a twinkle in his eye.

"Wiley," she said.

He raised his eyebrows. "You look different today than I expected," he said. He waited for a response.

Valentina said nothing.

"I see," he said. He looked at her outfit from the top of her cap to her boots. "It will do for the ceremony. Well done for a newcomer."

"Thank you," Valentina said, her voice cracking.

The attendant moved on. Valentina exhaled in a rush as she heard Luno and Dante giggling to her right.

When the attendant reached the end of the house line, he looked down the row of students and gave them a smile and lifted his right arm up. Time to move. He turned and led them on the paths between buildings.

Their snaking chain of students was one of many, all twisting their way through the formal paths in the school. People of all ages and manner of dress filled the groups. Some, like their own line, were more uniform in age, either young or old. Others had all ages mixed together following a logic Valentina could not piece out. Others yet had just a few very old members, but still, they walked carefully in a line.

Valentina craned her neck to take it all in, walking straight into the student ahead of her when they paused to let another line go through before them. The girl just nodded at Valentina's apology.

Like their group, all the people out on the grounds were dressed in their finery. Many had the robes of white and blue Valentina guessed was the dress of the school, but many others had widely varying costumes—from voluminous robes to metal plates over short wool dresses, to long tunics and robes of wildly bright geometric patterns in bright colors of yellow, red, green, and blue— and decked in more jewelry than Valentina had seen in her lifetime.

Valentina turned to Clelia, who walked right behind her. "Where are we going?" Valentina asked. So much had happened so quickly, she'd not even asked what the ceremony was to be that day.

"The Forum Peti," Clelia answered. She pointed to the round structure ahead. It looked like the gigantic forum she'd seen riding in with Mercato, but scaled smaller and contained completely within the school grounds. "We start here, then have our Rite of Passage through the city in the afternoon. It gives the locals time to prepare."

"Prepare what—" Valentina started to ask, but was cut off by the ringing voice of the attendant leading. Valentina turned to face him, suddenly feeling anxious.

While this forum was smaller than the main city one, it was not small. Again, the base stones towered over Valentina. The scale of the city did not seem made for humans such as they.

They sat halfway up the sloping walls of the Forum Peti, on stone benches. Some of the older people had thought to bring pillows and Valentina envied them. The benches were hard and cold. She shifted uncomfortably on hers, seated between Luno and Clelia. The forum slowly filled, in no order that Valentina could figure out, except for each group followed a leader wearing a garland of olive leaves.

Finally, when the last person was seated, a quiet fell over the space. A silent anticipation. The squeaking echoes of the hinges filled the forum and bounced around the space as two large doors on the bottom were cranked open and the machinery of their inner workings complained. Out walked Master Silas, recognizable to Valentina even after her short time with him. He looked tiny so far away on the yellow paving stone floor at the center of the auditorium.

He spoke, projecting his voice, amazingly so, and aided even more by the clever design of the forum. His speech was as clear as if he had spoken in her ear.

He rambled a long welcome in the name of gods Valentina did not recognize. After each pause, those around her would murmur an assent and nod. Even Clelia and Luno next to her followed along in perfect time. Valentina tried to fit in, but blushed awkwardly every time her words came a moment after everyone else's.

Finally, he gave a long sweeping bow that was greeted with a roaring cheer from the crowd. He stood up again and walked back to the door still open and disappeared in the darkness, leaving the forum floor empty.

Moments later, music flowed out from the door below, followed by those responsible emerging from the dark shadows of the door, playing harps, long trumpets, and stringed instruments Valentina did not recognize. Seeing new types of instruments surprised Valentina, though it probably shouldn't have.

Their court had been isolated, but as a child it seemed every week in the warmer months a musician had been passing through, hoping to earn some coin for entertainment. Only now, after seeing Valderhorn, did Valentina question how little she knew of the world. Surely, if people had passed through the court, she would have learned more of the world outside of their tiny kingdom.

But then childhood memories came back of being swept away from the evening's entertainment by Nurse, or being kept out of the stables when visitors came, or being forbidden to speak to any stranger at all. Indeed, all together it easily explained that she never learned much of the world outside the kingdom.

Her father had always told her it was to keep her safe as he gently kissed her on the head, but now he was gone, and she knew so little of the world.

"Are you okay?" Clelia asked, her brows pulled together.

Valentina turned from the entertainment and focused on her face. "Yes, why?"

"You... looked strange." Clelia gave her a small smile.

"Uh, thanks?" Valentina said, a small laugh escaping. "I'm fine, really." Just then her stomach growled. "Well, I'm a little hungry, actually. Why exactly didn't we get breakfast?"

Clelia smirked at her. "You'll see."

That didn't sound so good.

"Do we have to—"

"Not us. Not this year," Clelia reassured her, patting Valentina's knee.

"Next year," Luno said, leaning in to join the conversation.

"Next year what?" Valentina asked, looking from face to face.

Clelia just smiled at her.


The white horses thundered onto the forum floor, their iron-shod hooves beating on the stones and their muscles flexing beautifully under the morning sun. Their bridles and saddles were decorated with streaming cloths of deep jewel colors, each one different, each one matching the rider's apparel. One was sapphire, one was ruby red, and one was a golden citrine, luminous in the bright rays shining down on the clear day.

This was the last of the student demonstrations for the morning. Some had performed plays, others sang, others performed oratory designed to convince the audience of one point or another. Valentina had to admit she had liked the funny ones the best, where the audience had laughed and blushed at the jokes and truths told by those below.

These were the students' presentation for the masters and for each other of all they had learned over the previous year, especially what they had done with their winters when the air was cold and all the world was hiding.

Valentina's group was given grace this year because so many of them had come as of recently. It was decreed at the school that no student could stay beyond three seasons without performing satisfactorily and presenting their works. This was the school's inner judgment of its students, and not the only one. Clelia had whispered into Valentina's ear of the additional tests masters gave the students one-on-one, sometimes before the High Spring Rites and sometimes after. Those tests were secret, and it was not always known why some students left abruptly, while others stayed despite not showing well in the Forum Peti.

Now the displays had moved on to the studies of war and strategy and physical skills. Clelia leaned forward in her seat, entranced with all the displays. But when the horses galloped into the center of the field, she could barely sit still and elbowed Valentina to pay attention.

"These are the favored to be the next emperor. You must have skills of Ekrute—the military—in addition to oratory and skills of state. Only the most talented reach this level," Clelia explained.

Valentina stared at those below. The white horses and their riders looked familiar, but there were only three. Why did she think there should be four?

Then she remembered. The riders who had passed her and Mercato on their journey to the city. Could these be the same ones? They had been so young though, and besides, there had been four. The one missing was the woman in amethyst.

"No women?" Valentina asked Clelia. A dark look passed over Clelia's face. "No, they claim it is for one reason or another, but I don't believe their excuses. I intend to be in that group of finalists no matter what."

"You want to be emperor?" Valentina asked, shocked. "Why?" She looked around to see who was listening, as if they were speaking treasonous thoughts.

"I don't want to be emperor," Clelia said. "I just want to be capable. At that level. With oratory skills and military training and everything. I know I can do it."

Valentina again looked down to the forum floor. The three horses galloped in a circle, the flowing pendants the riders had come out carrying discarded to the side. Now they displayed swords and twirled them in a showy fashion, the blades gleaming and sending shafts of reflected light up into the stands.

A line of straw men had been set out on stands at regular intervals on the forum floor. The riders wove back and forth between the straw figures, slicing off pieces here and there until there was nothing left of the figures but the pole stuck up the middle. The crowd cheered wildly.

The figure in orange went further. While his horse galloped at a breakneck pace, he braced himself on the saddle then slowly pulled his feet up and onto the seat. At the same even pace, he then rose to standing on the galloping horse's back, using his arms and sword to balance himself. His horse kept on, completely unfazed by the rider's new position.

The crowd stood to cheer.

The rider took one lap around the forum, then returned to repeat the slashing demonstration on the new straw men that had been placed out. He single-handedly demolished them all. The two other riders—the red and the blue—twirled their swords to get the crowd's attention, but they could not compete with the feat just demonstrated by the orange.

"All hail," Luno said under her breath as the orange rider took his victory lap.

"Show off," Clelia said, her arms folded and her chin down in disapproval.

Valentina looked between the two of them. Whoever that orange rider was, he evoked strong reactions, whether for good or for bad.

"Do you have to do horse tricks to be emperor?" Valentina asked. It didn't seem like a good way to choose a leader.

Clelia's frown broke and she burst out in to laugher. "No, but it doesn't hurt. Come, it's time for the Parade of Challenges, and then we feast!" Clelia rose with the rest of the crowd. Everyone stood and turned to the exits, waiting for those closest to leave and make room for the rest. Valentina stared at Clelia's back, pondering her words.

"Challenges?" Valentina asked Clelia. "Clelia? What challenges?" Valentina said, poking Clelia when she didn't answer right away.

Clelia shrugged, her metal plate glinting under the hot sun. "It's nothing. A formality, I think, from olden times. At least I've not seen anyone challenged." Clelia waved it off as no matter.

From behind Valentina, Luno spoke. "I heard a rumor a thief was expelled five years ago."

Clelia and Valentina both turned and stared at Luno.

"Really?" Clelia asked. "I wonder how true that is."

Luno shrugged, not claiming to know the truth, but Valentina listened with dread. Luno did not strike her as flighty, or prone to listen to unreliable people.

"So you have to be a thief to be thrown out? Are there other reasons?" Valentina asked, but Clelia and Luno had no answer. No one seemed to know.

"We are the newest of the students," Luno explained. "They don't really talk about the challenge much. With Master Silas personally choosing the students, challenging a student is the same thing as challenging him."

Valentina bit her lip as she considered this. If Master Silas had that much power, surely few would dare.

"Don't worry, you'll pass. No one will bother you," Clelia said over her shoulder as their group started to move toward the exit of the Forum Peti. Valentina felt suddenly dizzy, but had no choice but to follow her, pushed by the masses behind her heading for the stairs.

# 9

Valentina followed Clelia as they made their way from the Forum Peti, following their attendant under the high sun that beat down on the students pressing to leave the place. Around them, students tittered nervously, while others pointed to the space below, where the white riders still stood.

The smell of sweat and nervousness filled the air. The chaos of everyone talking at once pressed on Valentina, giving her the feeling of suffocating in the hot and close quarters.

Luno and Dante bumped up close behind Valentina to keep from getting separated. All formality of the lines from the morning's procession had been broken in the boisterousness of the Forum's displays as the students crowded and jostled on their way to the location of the parade start. Just getting safely down the stone stairs and out of the Forum Peti felt dangerous in the press of people.

Sweat coated Valentina's back from their hours in the Forum Peti. Once outside the building, she wanted to pull her cap off and let the sweat on her neck dry in the salty breeze coming from over the southern sea, but she didn't dare, especially if they were going out into the city proper. Instead, she just lifted her cap and allowed the air to flow over her neck.

They walked through the school grounds in a press; the whole school headed for the main building that marked the entrance to the school.

As they approached the stairs that led up to the massive building and then down again to exit the school grounds, a tremble of fear roiled in Valentina's gut. This school was supposed to be her sanctuary and here she was going outside of it the very next day.

It didn't seem smart.

It seemed the very opposite of smart, but there was no way she could see out of it. Perhaps there was some custom she could have called on to stay on the school grounds, but having only been there half a day—had it really only been half a day?—she knew next to nothing of how the place worked.

The sea of students swept her along, and she pushed her misgivings down into her gut. There were too many people out and about in the city for anyone to spy on her, she told herself, especially not anyone from as far away as her kingdom. To distract herself, she turned to Clelia. "I don't understand why the candidates for heir to the emperor are so young and so few. I would have thought the emperor's heirs would have been related by blood, or accomplished elders."

"By blood!" Clelia said, recoiling.

Luno glanced back at the exchange. She leaned in to Valentina and spoke as quietly as she could in the chaos and still be heard. "By blood is not allowed since *the time*." She nodded sagely as if what she said had made complete sense, but just confused Valentina.

What time was she talking about? Valentina opened her mouth to ask more, but Dante grabbed both of Valentina's shoulders from where he walked behind her and leaned in to whisper in her ear. "It's bad form to talk about it in public, especially on the High Holiday. Master Silas would be most displeased."

Valentina whirled at his admonishment, but he only gave her a wink and passed by her in the crowd along with Luno and Clelia. Valentina forced her feet to move from where she had stopped in shock to race after her friends before they disappeared in the chaos of the city street.

All the city folk were out it seemed. Sedan chairs even crowded into the streets, forcing those lower born on foot to push back in waves of humanity to let them through. Unlike the formality of the morning at the school and the ceremony at the Forum Peti, the city felt like a carnival. Vendors hawked pastries and grilled meats on sticks, flowers woven into complex crowns, and small ceramic gods of all shapes and sizes.

"The Goddess of War for the fine young man?" A large man in a poorly wrapped and yellowed toga stepped out in front of Valentina and blocked her path, evidently meaning her. He looked at the material of her outfit and Valentina could imagine his internal calculation that she could pay for the token idol he sold. Sweat beaded on the tight roundness of his belly that didn't quite fit within his robes and when he stepped closer, she could smell the pickled fish on his breath. "A good one to have on your side," he said in a singsong coaxing tone while holding up the idol and waggling it in front of her eyes.

The idol he hawked wasn't a fully shaped figure, unlike most of the others. This one was the profile of a woman carved on a large discus of clay. The woman had a strong nose and wore a feather headdress that pulled her hair back and gave her a hawkish beauty.

She also looked familiar.

Valentina's gaze shifted to the man's stall nearby. Some stands sold an array of idols, the God of Fire, the God of the Sea, the God of Death, as many as would fit on the makeshift tables set up on the edges of the boulevard.

This man only sold one.

More of the clay discuses with the same image littered the table, glazed in all sorts of colors, but on the back canvas walls hung paintings of the same goddess, adding more color and detail to the images. One of the portraits, the one in the center spot of honor in the stall, faced out, the painted eyes piercing into the crowd. Valentina's heart missed a beat when she saw the painting and it felt like her eyes met the eyes of the Goddess staring back at her.

He followed her gaze, then chuckled as he wiped back the sweat off his forehead with a folded cloth. "I am loyal to my goddess," he said.

Valentina nodded numbly.

The man looked more closely at Valentina, as if seeing her for the first time. "Young man,—"

"Sorry, I have to go," Valentina said in a rush, not wanting to hear what he might say next. She pushed around him, jostling into the crowd to avoid rubbing against his sweaty abdomen. Ahead, Dante's dark dreads bobbed above the heads of most others and she focused on getting to him and her friends.

But the seller did not give up, yelling out after Valentina. "Young man, if you ever need the goddess, my shop is south of the palace. Knock on my door!"

Valentina walked faster, ignoring the glares of the city folk as she pushed through to get away from the yelling vendor.


A large field had been set aside for preparing the school formation for the parade. Stubble from last year's crop still covered the ground, and hay had been sprinkled in the few puddles left from the spring thaw. They were at the edge of the city, away from the shielding of the buildings and their reflective warmth. The breeze coming in from the sea almost felt chill.

Clelia and Luno talked excitedly about the food waiting for them at the end of the parade while their attendant nudged them into formation. Valentina stood by silently, not wanting to talk and feeling a bit shaken. Dante had asked how she was, but had allowed her to only nod that she was fine without pressing her further.

Around them, other students crowded around in their own groups, much as they had in the Forum Peti. Several long wooden platforms lumbered by, keeping to the gravel laden path in the field. These held elder scholars in rich robes of a deep sea blue. They were the senior teachers from the school and were not expected to make the long walk through the city.

A jingle of horse tack alerted Valentina to look up. A huge white horse bore down on her and the others in her group, the rider in a flame orange outfit and sporting blond curls. It was one of the emperor heir candidates.

The rider set the horse to a gallop, ignoring the cries from the outraged students rushing to get out of the way of the galloping horse and the indiscriminate mud clods coming off of its hooves. He rode by Valentina so closely that her hair fluttered on her forehead. She turned away after she saw his face up close.

He'd not glanced at her at all.

Not only was he from the group of riders she'd encountered that day with Mercato, and saw on the floor of the forum just a few hours ago, he was also the same as the man she'd encountered last night in the barn.

Valentina's hands clenched. She had not made the connection until just now when she could see him more clearly.

She'd dumped hay on one of the possible heirs apparent to this city. Of the entire empire.

Just as quick as her anger rose, humiliation at her mistake mixed with anxiety in her belly at what it would mean for her future in the school, or a future anywhere. She was off to a truly terrible start, since from what Mercato had said, this school was her best hope for safety.

Unable to stop herself, Valentina turned back to watch the rider gallop all the way to the rear of the line. He looked so sure of himself and his place.

Valentina wished for the day to end so she could go back to her room and never come out again.


The march through the city felt interminable. Valentina held her head down as their group, allowed to be only three wide, walked in their place within the long formation of the school's parade. She was between Clelia and another girl with flame red hair whose name she didn't know. Dante and Luno were somewhere behind them.

Ahead and behind their small section, other groups held different formations, some wider, some only single file. Interspersed with the groups of walking students were the wagons of teachers, a few groups of students and professional musicians playing music, and jugglers.

Everyone held to their formation, walking down long boulevards. They'd taken so many twists and turns Valentina was completely confused as to where they were, and only when they'd crested a hill here or there and she could see the tall round walls of the main forum on the center hill of the city, or the sky-touching arches of the waterway, did she have a sense of where they were. Then, the street would dip down again and her world returned to the maze of white walls everywhere that was the city.

People packed the streets, from elderly grandmothers sitting on tiny makeshift stools at the end of the boulevard, surrounded by children, to burly men, also dressed in their finery, some bearing swords.

It seemed that everyone who owned a sword or a weapon had them out today. It put Valentina on edge.

All the people seemed to be looking for something, and Valentina didn't understand what. She walked closer to Clelia and whispered, "Why are they staring so intensely?"

Clelia whispered back, "It's the test."

"I thought you said it was a formality?" Valentina asked. Those people looked deadly serious. Not all of them, but enough that Valentina was starting to count the breaths until they reached the safety of the school again.

"They have to act serious, don't they?" Clelia said. "They only get one day to check out the students. They have to make the most of it, no?"

That made sense, sort of.

Still, after they passed one particularly intent man with a sword held in a sinewy bared arm and an agitated manner searching the faces of all the students, Valentina fervently wished they'd take it a bit less seriously.

Finally, after an especially long uphill trek that made Valentina's legs ache and her calves cramp from pushing up on the stones, they topped a crest and she could see the opening to the main square ahead. The main square occupied the prime spot in front of the large forum. She knew the school lay just beyond that. They were almost back.

But first they had to pass by the massive complex that compromised the palace and its massive front lawns, now packed with citizens of the city. Some had brought blankets and constructed shades of poles and fabric, others had brought makeshift chairs. It was the prime spot to watch the parade, and some looked like they'd been waiting all day.

Beyond the expansive lawns, four soaring buildings, several

stories tall, stood face out in the formation of a cross, with the inner space between them nearly completely hidden from the public. Each building alone was the size of the main school building. The four of them together, and with all the land they stood on, was larger than many cities. Valentina strained to see inside the private space formed in the gap between the four buildings, but the view was hindered by lush trees and thick bushes that the gardeners had planted in the spaces between the buildings to prevent curious eyes from spying on the rulers.

Guards stood at the edge of the walkways in front of each building. One glared at her for looking at the complex he guarded, and Valentina quickly shifted her eyes forward again.

"There are central gardens within each building. They are open to the air above and take in rain directly. That palace could withstand siege for a thousand days," Clelia said without shifting her gaze from the student ahead of her.

"How do you know?" Valentina asked, careful to keep her voice low enough that the palace guards closest to the crowded parade path could not hear them.

Clelia smirked. "The palace is a marvel of military planning. I barely know half of it," she said. She looked pleased at the opportunity to learn more in the future.

"Do you want to be emperor or captain of the palace guard?" Valentina asked.

"Either would be fine," Clelia answered.

Somehow Valentina believed her.


On the opposite side of the boulevard from the palace was an open spot normally reserved for the morning market that had been canceled that day. The semipermanent structures for farmers to display their wares had been pulled back, allowing the city citizens to get closer to the parade participants. The space was large enough that men on horseback and sedan chairs also jostled for a place to watch the parade.

To Valentina's horror, a cluster of black horses stood uneasily in the crowd, their eyes rolling and showing white at the noise and press around them. The beautiful sheen of the horses' coats and the distinctive saddles with the double pommel reminded her of the horses she remembered from home.

The horse riders struggled to control the animals. They dressed in all black, with large leather hats shielding their faces from the sun, but also making it difficult to see them. They stood out from the city's citizens dressed in their finery and more summerlike clothing.

In one way, they were similar to the city's denizens, though. Like many of the city, they too were armed, holding large curved swords, and a few with long spears.

Valentina focused on her breathing and made herself not continue to glance at the horses and their riders. The chances of them being from her kingdom were small. In any case, they would have no reason to come look for her in the parade. They probably thought she died in the woods, especially if her horse had come back with her clothing.

The parade marched closer.

Valentina gritted her teeth and stared forward.

Bolting would attract more attention but continuing on was agony. Valentina felt as if she was walking in slow motion through thick mud. The sound of the crowd faded away and all she could hear was the roaring of her blood in her ears. Clelia gave her a smile, and she tried to smile back, but it felt unnatural so she quickly looked away again. Valentina stared at the ground and counted to herself as they walked by and drew closer to the riders on the black horses. She didn't dare look in their direction.

She'd counted a hundred and ten paces in her mind when the band around her chest loosened a bit and she thought she might be safe. They had passed the black horses with no incident. Only another couple dozen paces ahead and they would turn the bend in the boulevard to go past the forum and be on their way back to the school.

Just then, some small kids of perhaps eight or nine playing with a large wheel and sticks at the edge of the street lost control of their wheel and it went flying into the students walking in the parade. Despite the parents reaching out to grab them, the kids evaded control and ran yelling into the parade, knocking into the students and laughing at the chaos as they chased their errant toy.

Valentina tried to get out of the way, backing up as one child ran toward her completely oblivious with his eyes focused on the wheel bouncing ahead of him. She didn't see the child behind her, swinging his own stick in large circles as he tried to beat the others to the toy. She only felt it when the stick of the boy behind her swung up and got caught in the tassel of her cap, and the force of his movement pulled the cap from her head entirely.

As the cap came off, her sweaty hair once trapped below it suddenly chilled as it was exposed to the breeze coming from the sea. Valentina's first thought was it felt good. Her second was panic. She put a hand to her head to verify the cap was gone, then saw the child with it swinging from his stick and ran after him.

Clelia grabbed Valentina's arm. "You can't!" she yelled, then glanced at the school elders who walked to the edge of the parade. Valentina tried to shake off Clelia's grasp, but Clelia was too strong. Valentina's hair blew wildly in the sea breeze as she struggled with Clelia.

Her simple disguise broken in the swing of a child's toy.

"Get back in line," Clelia hissed at her.

Reluctantly, Valentina did so. She kept looking to the right, hopefully away from any prying eyes of the riders on the left but it was too late.

Shouts came from that direction. "That's her. That's her!"

Denial and hope and despair flooded through Valentina that they might mean someone else, until a black horse and rider appeared to her left, dragging along a school scholar trying to stop him while the rider yelled and pointed at Valentina, anger contorting the rider's face into a hideous mask, and she could hope no longer.

# IO

The inside of the palace was nothing like what Valentina expected. Not that she'd been thinking about the inside of the palace, but when the school officials and guards had dragged her in, along with the agitated horse riders, she'd been momentarily distracted from her panic.

The tall columns that decorated the front face of the building they entered were several times as wide as she was, and reached up to the skies above, holding up a roof of stone so massive that if it fell, it would crush her and anyone else beneath it instantly. The open portico the columns rested on looked over the city, giving a clear view in all directions. But when the massive doors opened to the inner building, she did not expect the open and echoing corridor inside the building to lead to a lush jungle of live plants and water fountains in the middle of the building in a courtyard that took the entire central space of the building.

A courtyard that had no roof.

The center of the lush space lay open to the sky above, letting in both sun and rain. Food could be grown here. Rain collected.

The horse riders, who had been dragged in cursing under their breath and demanding the guards remove their hands from their persons, had also been surprised and sucked in their breath at the luxury of the inner courtyard of the building. One had long, dirty blond hair, while the other three had dark hair, so short as to be shaved. The three looked like brothers.

The blond rider twisted his arm away from the guard who held it and walked over to a fountain at the edge of the courtyard, one of many in the space, and stared at the stream of clear water tumbling down from the marble pitcher the carved woman held. He reached out a hand to touch the water. The guard that he'd escaped from grabbed his wrist before he could do so and pulled him back to the group.

The guards arranged the riders in black to one side, muttering and looking around, and Valentina and two of the school scholars on the other side, also surrounded by guards. The guard standing closest to Valentina stared intently at the riders, on edge for any sudden movement from them.

A silence fell over the group. They waited.

Dazed, Valentina thought about what had just happened and how quickly everything changed.

Out on the street, the riders had tried to grab Valentina and pull her physically away from the school parade, adding to the chaos started by the children. Clelia had grabbed the arm of the rider who'd grabbed Valentina's hair and kicked him viciously, something that only ended up getting Clelia backhanded and thrown into the laps of the nearby spectators lounging at the edge of the street.

The spectators, enraged by the violence against the girls and the danger to their children, had entered the parade to fight with the riders, whose distinct dark colors and leather hats marked them as outsiders.

The four horse riders wore no leather hats now. They were not allowed in the palace, nor were their horses, two things that had made the angry riders even more enraged.

Finally, the outside doors swung open again and more guards entered, followed by attendants and two men in the center of the circle of people: Master Silas, and another man dressed in brilliant white robes with red and purple trim on the edges, and a huge wreath of olive leaves adorned with purple berries on his head.

The emperor.

He walked quickly, his trim figure and good health radiating outwards. His black hair was combed back underneath the crown, and his jet-black eyes flashed between the groups, taking it all in. A tiny curve of his lips almost made Valentina think he was smiling. She had no idea if that was a good thing or not.

Master Silas also took in the situation, but his expression was more guarded.

"So so so," the emperor said, once he reached them and stood with his hands behind his back and rocking back on his heels like examining a fine puzzle. "We have a challenge. It has been years. I'm not entirely opposed to some excitement, although I'm sure you're not enjoying it." He spoke the last words to Valentina, who swallowed and looked down at the emperor's sudden attention. Her eyes stung, and she blinked them furiously, realizing that she'd been staring.

"Ah yes, I see my guess is right," the emperor said, not taking outward offense at Valentina's lack of a reply.

"This is no challenge," one of the riders said, taking on a demanding tone. He stepped forward, his dirty blond hair falling into his eyes. "She belongs to us—"

He stopped talking abruptly when one of the soldiers struck him in the belly with the hilt of his sword.

"I do understand you have a complaint," the emperor said coolly. He held up a hand to stop further outbursts from the riders. "We shall do this according to law, shall we not?" He looked around until one of his attendants stepped forward, scroll in hand, bowing obsequiously.

"The full decree is here, Your Imperator," the attendant said, his gray hair falling forward as he performed a bow.

"But I'm sure you know the decree by heart, don't you, Isagani?" the emperor asked with a chuckle.

"Yes, Your Highness."

The emperor turned back to face the waiting group. "There you have it. Now, let's get to the bottom of this. I have a feast and several beautiful dancers waiting for me and I hate to make beauty wait."

Valentina didn't think the riders could look any more enraged, but the emperor's cool treatment goaded them on. She shivered and felt a wave of gratitude for the guards surrounding her. How long would that last?

She stared at the riders, trying to see if she recognized any of them, but she didn't. The men all looked to be just a few years older than her. If they'd been in the court three years ago, she would have recognized them. Several had large scars on their faces, and at least one walked with a limp. They might have been in the army. If they had not exposure to the court, how then could they know who she was?

The attendant Isagani stepped forward, his voice suddenly strong and belying his frail look as he held up the scroll and read from it. "According to the laws of the Dawn Empire, and within it the School of Stanasbrisson, as decreed by the Will of the Gods and the Emperor Ramil many years ago, there is but one chance to challenge the presence of a student. That shall happen on the day of the High Spring Rites. The challenge shall be based in merit and according to the laws of the empire. False claims will be dealt with as if the challenger were guilty and the punishment as such. All shall acknowledge these conditions before making a claim."

Isagani lowered the scroll and looked at the four riders, their dirty and road-worn faces glaring back at him. "Do you acknowl-edge these conditions?" he asked.

The riders stood, looking sullen. Finally, the one with the dirty blond hair spit to one side and said, "We accept no such conditions. We are not liege to this empire, nor are we bound by its rules. She is ours and we demand her back." The three men behind him nodded their agreement and muttered curses Valentina could not understand.

The guards bristled at the man's spitting inside the palace. The emperor held up one hand to silence their agitation.

"There is a problem with that logic, my friends, because you are inside the empire. The laws will apply to you," the emperor said, still cool and unruffled.

"Our swords say they do not," one of the back three riders said, earning the stare of everyone gathered.

"Our swords can bring you out of the empire, one piece at a time," a tall guard said. Of all the guards, he stood closest to the emperor, and Valentina noticed for the first time the array of ribbons and medals hanging from his dress uniform.

"Your enthusiasm is appreciated, my good Captain Terif, but I don't think it's necessary," the emperor said to the guard. He turned and looked at the riders. "Is it?"

The riders said nothing to that question, their eyes jumping back and forth from the emperor to the guard who'd spoken, the seriousness of their situation starting to show in their eyes.

"Who is this girl to you?" the emperor asked.

The riders did not answer.

"Who is this girl to you?" the emperor asked a second time, a hint of anger in his voice for the first time. His captain pulled his sword from its sheath and the slide of metal echoed in the large space.

The blond rider pulled himself together first. He dug into a leather pouch at his waist and pulled out a brown linen wrapped package the size of a flattened apple. Unwrapping it, he pulled out a lock of hair tied with a ribbon, and a portrait drawn in ink on a bit of wood. "My king commands me to bring back this girl." He held the hair and portrait up for them to see.

The image was Valentina.

The lock her hair.

The emperor waved to a guard who ran to the blond rider and got the wood portrait and lock of hair and brought them to the emperor. The emperor took the portrait from the guard's hand, then stepped closer to Valentina. She wanted to look down, away, anything to prevent his clearly seeing her face but that would just delay the inevitable. Even she could see it was her face on that piece of wood. And not her face of three years ago. It was as she had been this past winter, with the new headpiece she'd been given against the cold in the tower. When had that image been made, and by who? Her hands clenched in frustration at the danger all around her.

Had she no one she could trust?

Apparently few in her old kingdom. Perhaps only Nurse. A stab of fear and guilt pierced her heart at the thought of the gentle old woman, but she dared not ask about her. Her care for the woman could be the woman's death sentence if they didn't already know of Nurse's role in her escape.

The emperor came closer to Valentina, the faint scent of hair oil and from the flowers in his crown washing over her. He smiled at her as he evaluated the picture and compared it to Valentina. "Yes, this is an amazing likeness." He turned back to the riders. "How did you know she was here?"

"Your city guards have excellent memories," the blond rider said with a smirk.

The emperor frowned at that. "I see."

A commotion outside with yells and banging culminated with the outer doors opening and four guards dragging in two more of the black-clothed riders and a bloody and injured Mercato. Valentina jumped.

The emperor turned back to the blond rider for explanation. "Are there any more?"

The blond rider looked sullen and did not answer. The captain moved to stand in front of the blond rider, his sword still drawn. The rider finally answered, "That is all."

"You beat up your own?" the emperor asked.

"I am not with them, sir," Mercato spoke up. His words slurred from his fat lip keeping him from speaking properly. "They attacked me at the gate."

"Captain Terif, I am starting to think we have a problem with the gate. Wouldn't you agree?" the emperor said.

Terif turned pale. "Yes, Your Imperator. I will take care of it."

"See that you do."

Mercato looked at Valentina with his good eye, the other swollen shut with bruises that covered most of his face. He shook his head minutely, warning her not to speak. Valentina bit her lip. She looked away, unable to stand it any longer.

"So so so. We have a picture of a girl and an order from a king. Who is your king, and what is your name?" the emperor asked. He waved one hand, and an attendant came running with a chair. The emperor sat. He looked around, then waved again, and another chair was brought for Master Silas, who had stood by and watched the proceedings without speaking a word.

The emperor turned back to the blond rider when his question had still not been answered after both chairs had been brought. He did not look like the kind who liked to repeat himself.

The blond man stepped forward, giving the guard who tried to stop him a foul look. "My name is Osian. We are from Cerceion, and we come in the name of King Elgar."

Valentina gasped at that. Everyone looked at her. She pretended to choke and looked down.

The blond man, Osian, stared at her, waiting to see if she would say anything. Valentina looked anywhere but at him.

"Cerceion is far from these lands and has made great pains to not be a part of my holdings, yet you have traveled all this way to kick a hornets' nest. Tell me, intruder into my city, what does your king want with Master Silas' student?" the emperor asked.

Silence fell over the gathering at the emperor's sudden bluntness. The attendants held their breath, while the guards put their palms on their weapons.

Osian clenched his jaw, the muscles flexing in the light, but he did not answer.

"What does he want?"

The blond man glanced back at his compatriots and then at the guard arranged around him.

"Tell me," the emperor said in a low voice.

Cerceion was far from the Dawn Empire, that was true, but the empire had enough strength, and perhaps enough spies, to find out if Osian lied on this day. It was not Osian's decision what was to be done about the girl, but he had not sworn an oath to lie about it. That was the fight of kings and emperors and the gods above.

"To kill her," Osian spit out.

Everyone stared at Osian in silence, the trees rustling in the gentle breeze in the courtyard the only sound.

Finally, Master Silas spoke. "And what would be her crime?" His eyes narrowed at the rider in front of him.

"She is an offense to the natural order. The gods have cursed her. If she continues to live, the danger will befall us all," Osian said.

"Says which god?" the emperor asked, tilting his head.

"The one true god," Osian said.

Hisses came from the surrounding attendants. A few of the guards shifted uneasily.

"Be careful not to offend, my friend," the emperor said, a warning in his voice. "The gods of Valderhorn are not forgiving."

Osian scowled, but gave a stiff nod. "If she lives, war will come to us all."

"Yet she is doing nothing, and you are here causing trouble," the emperor said.

Osian closed his eyes in frustration, then opened them again. "She cannot live. Test her. You'll find my king righteous in his path.

"And how shall I test her?" the emperor asked.

Valentina looked to the emperor and then back at Osian and the other riders. One of the dark three caught her looking and glared at her, his hands twitching, and Valentina stepped back. The school scholars next to her pushed her back into place.

"There is a way," Osian said. "Put her to the knife. If she brings forth the power, she is cursed."

*The knife?*

A chill ran down Valentina's back, despite the sun and warmth coming from above. Her vision grew dark around the edges. She looked at Osian and he glared back, the hatred on his face palpable and seething. If she had been within reach, he would have choked her himself.

A buzzing sensation overcame Valentina as her vision went completely dark.

She fell to the floor.

Curses reached her ears and was the last she heard.

# II

A breeze blew over Valentina. Her feet felt warm, as if stuck in an oven.

She opened her eyes.

Ahead of her, a wall full of carvings came in and out of focus. In the middle of the wall, a fire roared. Wait, the wall couldn't be on fire. She squinted, straining her eyes to see. No, the fire was in a huge firepit built into the wall.

Thin-fingered trees and bushes filled the space around her, lending to her confusion. She turned her head to see what else was there and a sting of pain shot down the back of her neck and into her right shoulder. "Ouch," she said, reaching with her left hand.

"Don't move," Mercato said gently. He leaned in so she could see him without moving. He looked terrible. Valentina winced. "Are you okay?" he asked at her expression.

"Yes, I'm fine," she said, not wanting him to ask any more questions. "Where am I?" she asked.

She looked down and found she was on a couch of soft cushions and pillows.

"We're still in the palace. They've sent for a physician. You hit your head pretty good on the floor when you fainted. Osian claimed it a trick and that you should have been tested right away anyhow," Mercato explained. He looked back to where guards stood at the doorway to the room they were in. The guards looked straight forward and were not paying any attention to him and Valentina.

"While I was unconscious?" Valentina asked.

"Yes."

"Sure that would have gone well."

"Osian would probably think so." Mercato winced as he sat back on the couch near Valentina's feet.

"Are they..." Valentina stopped her question, not even sure what she wanted to ask. She had no idea what Osian had meant by *the test*, and the fact that the emperor had asked further questions terrified her. Could the emperor be considering doing what those men wanted?

Who were those men?

Valentina pushed on the couch to sit up. Pain shot through her head. The room spun unexpectedly, and fast. With a gasp, she gave up on the getting up and let herself fall back down.

"Not so fine," Mercato said.

"No," Valentina agreed.

She lay there, staring at the ornate carvings and paintings that even decorated the ceilings of this lush room. It could not be far from the courtyard the emperor had received them in. Someone had to have carried her to this place.

Never in her most fervent imaginings could she have thought of a place like this. This entire wondrous city with its massive buildings and flowing waters, but especially this palace. What a cruel joke it would be for her to only see it because it was the end of her mortal life.

She should have appreciated her quiet existence in the tower while she had it.

99

"I'm so sorry," Mercato said. "I didn't say anything."

"What happened?" Valentina asked, even speaking those few words hurting her head even more.

"They grabbed me at the gate. The guard had told them I'd be coming back. I tried to lead them away from the school, but they knew where it was." Mercato sounded terrible. Valentina tipped her head to look at him. The bruises on his face made it difficult to see his eyes.

Quick footsteps approached the archway opening into the room, the slap of leather on marble echoing painfully in Valentina's head. She moaned and looked to the doorway. A balding man came in. He wore a long yellow tunic and red pants under a white robe that sat crooked on his shoulders and carried a large black oxhide bag.

The man came closer and looked down at Valentina. She knew she should sit up, but she was more afraid of the spinning room than the man who smiled down at her.

"Ah, good, the patient is awake. Can't have you unconscious before they kill you," the man said with a cackle as he put down his black bag.

Mercato leapt to his feet. "Kill her?" He staggered, then clumsily tried to get between the man and Valentina.

The man focused on Mercato, as if seeing him for the first time. He blinked slowly as two of the guards quickly came to stand on either side of Mercato and each grabbed one of Mercato's arms and pulled him back. Mercato was so unsteady, one guard could have done it, but then both he and the guard might have gone down in a pile.

The guards guided Mercato to a chair and gently placed him on it. He nodded at them both and shifted back into the seat and smiled at the guards until they were satisfied he would not get up again. They left him there.

"It's a saying," the man said to Mercato, still confused at his reaction. "Most of my patients think it's funny,"

"Funny?" Valentina squinted up at the man. "They really want to kill me." Her voice cracked as she said it.

"What?" the man said as he turned back to Valentina. "Oh, strange day today. I do hate going out on the High Spring Rites. Let's get this over with." The man reached down to open his bag, but his robe, not being properly settled on his shoulders, kept falling in front of his hand and blocking his fingers from working the latch on the bag. He tried to pull the fabric back several times, each time failing to reach the latch before the fabric fell down again. On the third attempt and failure, he pulled the robe off over his head and threw it down on the ground.

"Ridiculous rules," he muttered to himself, then used both hands to unlatch the bag and opened it so vigorously several items flew out, one of which slid across the floor and stopped by Valentina's head. It looked like a finger bone. She blanched. The man grabbed the things that had come out and stuffed them back in the bag, getting the bone last.

He looked deep into the bag, dug around a few times, then pulled out a thin piece of fabric and a tall delicate metal cup. Finally, he pulled a flask from his pocket and poured out three drops of water on the fabric, then walked to Valentina. "Lay back," he instructed. Since she was already laying down, she just shifted to be on her back.

Placing the fabric on her forehead, the man arranged it flat, then stood back and stared at it.

"What are you doing?" Valentina finally asked.

"Seeing if you are taken with fever," the man answered. His eyes did not leave the material.

Valentina raised a hand to touch the material. "No!" He exclaimed and moved both hands to stop her. "Let it dry. I'm timing it."

Everyone in the room watched the man, while the man stared at the fabric on Valentina's head. Finally, he picked up one corner of the material and held it overhead to examine it. "Still damp. You are not feverish, young lady."

"That's good, I guess," Valentina said.

The doctor finished up his exam by placing the cup on Valentina's sternum and then placing his ear inside the opening. He listened for a few moments and then put the cup away.

"You seem fine," he said finally.

"My head hurts," Valentina said weakly.

"Ah yes, the fall." The man leaned in and slowly felt Valentina's head. "No blood. Does anything I'm doing with my fingers hurt?"

"Not really, no."

"Your head just throbs all the time?"

Valentina nodded, then immediately regretted it. It really throbbed.

"Nothing to be done. You'll either be fine, or you'll die. We'll know in a day or two," the man said nonchalantly.

"Who are you?" Mercato asked. Even in his weakened state, he looked like he wanted to throttle the man.

The man turned to him, surprised, since he'd forgotten Mercato was there. "I'm Physician Flaraite. The royal physician"

"Who doesn't like working on holidays, but then who would?" a low voice said from the door.

Valentina twisted on the couch to look to the door. The emperor stood in the archway, along with Master Silas.

"The patient lives?" the emperor asked.

"She does, Your Majesty," Physician Flaraite said, giving a small bow.

"Good. We have some things to settle."

Valentina stared wide-eyed at Mercato. She was not ready for this. One glance at the guards told her they were just as unsettled by the sudden appearance of the emperor as she was.

A flurry of attendants brought in wide heavyset chairs for the emperor and Master Silas. A few servants moved the plants and created an open space in the room. Valentina was grateful she was allowed to remain sitting due to her dizziness. "Don't want to be called out again," Physician Flaraite said to Valentina as he left, pressing a hand to her shoulder.

The riders were brought back in. Their expressions were calmer than before. How long had she been out?

The attendant Isagani stepped forward, clutching the scroll of rules. He unrolled and cleared his throat to begin, but was stopped by a gesture from the emperor.

"I believe we all remember the rules, Isagani," the emperor said.

Isagani bowed and retreated.

The emperor faced the riders and then Master Silas.

"Master Silas, what do you know of this student?" the emperor asked.

"Little, Your Majesty. She arrived yesterday, giving a false name but true answers to my questions. I granted her a place based on that."

Valentina blushed furiously. He knew she lied, yet let her into the school without saying a word to her of her falsehood?

"A false name," the emperor said, drumming his fingers on the arm of his chair. "Is that a valid claim for expulsion, Isagani?"

"No, Your Majesty."

"I thought not." The emperor turned to Master Silas. "What is her true name?"

"That I do not know. I only know what she gave me rang false."

The emperor asked Valentina, "Why did you lie?"

Her flush grew deeper. She glanced at the riders who watched the exchange. Osian smirked at her from under his dirty blond bangs, victory seemingly in his grasp.

"I see." The emperor considered the riders. "What is your charge against her, again?" His tone was almost that of a dare.

Osian shifted his feet at the question. He hesitated before answering. "She is cursed."

"Says your god," the emperor said.

"Says our god," Osian said.

"Have you proof?" the emperor asked.

"I have my king's command," Osian said.

"That is not proof," the emperor said.

"I would not question my king," Osian said.

The two men stared at each other.

Silence pressed down on Valentina. She both wanted this to be over and yet dreaded every new word that came out. They had only spoken in circles so far, but once the emperor made a decision, her life could be done with. Or saved. She was too cynical to hope for being saved, and too much a coward to want to face her death.

Master Silas spoke. "I hear of no crimes committed by this child. Existing alone is not a crime, in my humble understanding of the law."

"If you saw what can exist, you would not speak thus," Osian said, interrupting Master Silas. "Put a knife to her throat. See what evil spirit comes out of her when her life is in danger."

"Enough!" the emperor said, his voice reverberating off the hard walls in the room. "I think I understand how your test works. Try to kill her. If it works, she was innocent. If she defends herself, she is cursed. Either way, she will end up dead."

A man in the back of the group of riders giggled. A guard walked over and kicked him in the back of the knees, sending him sprawling.

"A needless death is funny, is it?" the emperor said. "I have made my decision. This student's crime is falseness of her name, which is grave, but not a death sentence. She shall give her true name ever forward. She will tend the most menial of tasks until she understands the meaning of truth in Master Silas' eyes. To that end, she shall stay here. If your king," he turned to the riders, "is displeased with this solution, I ask that he make his way here and we shall discuss it. I have other things I wish to treat with him about in any case."

Osian glared back at the emperor but said nothing.

"If that does not satisfy, and another attempt to kidnap a citizen of my city and a student of my school is made again, my army will visit your kingdom and we shall have our discussion there. In addition, any life involved in such an attempt is forfeit, with the sentence carried out immediately. Have I made myself clear?" the emperor asked the group of riders.

Osian nodded, the thick tendons in his neck tight with anger. His followers muttered, then followed Osian's lead after the guards stepped close.

"Be grateful for your lives," the emperor said, dismissing them.

Guards escorted the riders out.

"That will not be the last of them," Master Silas said.

"No, I suppose not, but it will last for a while. Isagani," the emperor said.

"Yes, Your Majesty."

"Have all the most current maps of Cerceion brought to my study, and let the generals know I expect them tomorrow."

"Yes, Your Majesty."

The emperor turned to Valentina and studied her. She wished she could melt down between the cushions and disappear.

"So so so, what is the name of the person who has brought the threat of war to my empire?" He stared expectantly at her, waiting for an answer. All others waited too, barely breathing.

Valentina took a tiny breath, then said, "Valentina."

Master Silas closed his eyes as if pained, but the emperor ignored him and smiled.

"Of the house Venancio?" the emperor asked.

Valentina nodded.

"Ah, I see now their king's concern."

# 12

Valentina sat in her room. The tiny bed with its two thin blankets and the desk and chair looked like the sweetest belongings a person could have. It was not the marbled luxury of the palace, but it had a door, and it was hers. Her belongings were even still hidden behind the drawer of the desk where she had left them.

The sun had set while she was in the palace, and the school's scholars had escorted her from the palace and through the darkened grounds of the school now only lit by the occasional torches set in metal cages on poles to her building. She smelled of sweat and fear but was too exhausted to try to find the water pump in the gardens to wash up on her own. There had to be another way for the students to bathe, but finding out how or doing anything about it now sounded like too much work.

Her head still hurt, her stomach growled, and she wanted sleep more than anything.

After her conversation with the emperor about her house, Venancio, he had looked at her for a long moment, then simply said, "Rest." One motion from him and here she was.

She'd tried to ask about having Mercato stay at the school but

Master Silas only shook his head. "He will be taken care of, but his going to the school tonight is not possible."

Why was everything so complicated? She knew she should be grateful for the rules—they had protected her this day—but she wanted Mercato here. Those mercenaries from Cerceion might just be stupid enough to try something. Hopefully not. They knew where she was. Mercato had nothing else of value to them but that information.

Mercato had sworn he'd not shared any information about her. She believed him. After all, they'd freely discussed their plans in front of the city guards and everyone else at the gate that day. Valentina leaned forward and rested her head on her knees and groaned at her own stupidity.

A gentle knocking sounded on her door.

Valentina looked up. "Come in," she called.

The door swung open and Dante looked in. "Oh, you look awful," he said.

"Thanks," Valentina said. She was too tired to even be offended.

"Don't worry, we brought offerings," Dante said. He pushed open the door and Clelia and Luno came in behind him. They all carried dishes of food, which they put down on Valentina's desk.

Valentina stared at them, confused.

"Bring back the dishes to the kitchen, or we're all dead, or specifically, I'm dead," Clelia said. "I used up all my goodwill for you. Don't think I'm not going to be demanding repayment." She smiled, despite the warning in her voice. "We couldn't have you miss all the food from the feast."

Clelia brought over a tall glass to Valentina and pressed it into her hands. "We rarely get the spiced ale, so I thought you might like some too." Valentina took the glass, the heady smell of hops and spices filling her nose. She held it up to her mouth and drank, tasting a salty sweetness, which confused her until she realized she was tasting her own tears along with the ale.

"How did you know I'd be coming back?" Valentina asked after she ate every single thing on all three dishes. Her stomach distended painfully, causing painful prickles on her belly skin, but she didn't care. She ate like it was her last meal on earth. If those riders from Cerceion had had their way, she wouldn't have made it to even this meal.

"Of course you were coming back," Clelia said as she fussed with stacking the dishes on Valentina's desk and refused to look at Valentina.

Luno gave Valentina a shy smile. "We're glad you're back. We saw you going into the palace with the guards—"

"Nope, questions later," Dante said authoritatively. "And don't let this one," Dante said, grabbing Clelia's shoulders and pulling her away from the dishes she had stacked and restacked, "keep you up all night asking you a million questions. Tomorrow is the start of the new school year. We have the placements to get through."

"Placements?"

Clelia's face lit up and she pumped her fist. "Placements. We get to duke it out for our spot in the classes. Poor against rich, the worthy against the parasites, the holy against the unholy..." She slowly stopped and looked at Luno, Dante, and Valentina who stared at her with their mouths hanging open.

"Never mind her," Dante said to Valentina. "We just show our skills so we are not in too easy or too hard a class. Every single student in the school must go through them every year. It is nothing so dramatic as Clelia would have you think."

"You're no fun," Clelia said.

"That may be so. You're not complaining when I dress you," Dante said.

"No. And you better not stop or I won't be talking to you anymore."

"Threats, threats," Dante said as he corralled Clelia and Luno out of Valentina's room. He turned back to Valentina as he grabbed the door handle to shut the door. "Get some sleep. We have to hit the baths early, then it's rotations through the Forum Peti. I'll have something for you to wear in the morning."

Valentina nodded sleepily at him, then gratefully slid down on the bed and fell asleep, clothes and all.

Luckily, early did not mean predawn, like the morning of the High Spring Rites. The sun just peeked over the horizon when Clelia knocked on Valentina's door. She wore a long white robe that tied at the waist and held another for Valentina.

Birds chirped through the window. Valentina had left the curtains open the night before, so the light came through and filled the room with a warm glow. Even Clelia looked rosy in the early morning light. Valentina threw off her covers and looked down at her clothing. Sometime in the night, she'd woken enough to pull a blanket over herself, but not enough to take off her dirty clothes from the day before.

"Don't worry about it, but don't leave anything valuable here either," Clelia said when she saw the dirt and grime Valentina had tracked into bed. "Even us poor folk get fresh sheets from the school staff." Clelia eyed her curiously. "Do you have anything valuable?"

Valentina shook her head and fussed with the robe Clelia gave her to avoid looking the girl in the eye. "When do they come into the rooms?" Valentina asked, trying to sound casual.

"After lunch, I think. I don't know, I'm not normally here," Clelia said. "Come on, we're going to be late. We'll come back to get dressed, so just bring the robe."

Valentina gave up on trying to figure out how to get the stuff out of her desk without Clelia seeing, so turned and shrugged her shoulders that she was ready.

The baths were like nothing she'd ever seen. Positioned somewhere near the middle of the school grounds, they were two columned buildings, several stories high, on either side of a small hillock. They looked like two small temples. "Men, women," Clelia said, pointing to the two different buildings. Inside, long steel tubs of water lay arranged in a row, ending with a large cutout in the floor lined with stone and filled with steaming water.

"How?" Valentina asked. She'd never seen so much water in one place except a lake or a stream. Never in a building.

"Hot spring," Clelia said, pointing to the ground. "Come, we have to get clean first."

The series of long metal tubs of water was meant for cleaning oneself before getting into the main pool. The water was not warm and Valentina tried to climb out after a quick rinse. Clelia stopped her. "We'll both get in trouble if you put your dirty self in that pool." She held out a long-handled brush and a washing stone. "Scrub all over. I'll get your back." Valentina accepted the items. The elderly lady with white hair working as the bath house attendant watched them with narrowed eyes. Valentina got back in the tub and applied herself to do a better job.

A good scrubbing later, and a candlemark's worth of time in the steaming pool, and Valentina felt like a new person. Her face flushed red with the heat.

"Ready to go kick some aristocrat butt?" Clelia asked as she got out of the pool and pulled on her robe and tied it. She winked as she handed Valentina her robe.

The Forum Peti looked like a glowing yellow jewel in the center of campus. The early morning sun had just cleared the nearby buildings and bathed the perfectly round structure with light from the base of its large foundation stones to the top of the ornately decorated stone top ring. On regular intervals on the flat top stones, stone dragons looked down, their carved tails wrapped around their bodies.

Students went in and out of the entrances, some in groups of four or five, or by themselves. Some students emerged looking despondent, while others were elated. A few were strangely dirty, coated in yellow rock dust with not a speck of clean linen on them.

Valentina wore Dante's gift of a set of white robes trimmed with light blue, and the edging accented at regular intervals with yellow dots. "A little sunshine for you," Dante had said when he'd dropped off the clothes for her. "These are custom modified. I have a feeling you might need them."

Valentina didn't know what he meant until she saw the pants that fit under the outer robe. Their neat construction held over half a dozen pockets all over, but sewed so cleverly that the pockets were not visible unless you knew exactly where to look. There were even small pockets in the folds of the robes themselves. With a sigh of relief, Valentina stuffed the wooden medallion from Mercato in one of the larger pants pockets near the ankle that could be tied snug close to her leg. She put her knife in a higher pocket she could easily get to through an opening in the overtunic.

Most of the students wore similar clothing to Valentina, in what she was coming to recognize as a school uniform of sorts—white robes trimmed in a lighter blue than worn by the instructors. A few students wore rich garments of other colors, mostly jewel tones of reds, blues, and greens. Clelia had sneered at a few of these students after they'd crossed paths with them.

"Do you really hate them?" Valentina asked after the third such incident after breakfast.

Clelia looked at her in surprise. "No, of course not. Doesn't

THE QUEEN OF WAR

mean I'm not going to humiliate them into next week. Shame is a great lesson for those spoilt ones."

Valentina covered her mouth to hide a laugh. Thank the goddess Clelia had no inkling who she was.

Yet. The mirth left Valentina when she realized Clelia might find out sooner rather than later, along with everyone else at the school. The emperor had commanded *'she shall give her true name ever forward.'* Did that mean last night too? Was she breaking the rules by not telling Clelia and the others?

"Clelia," Valentina said as she turned to face the girl. "I have something to tell you—"

A booming voice interrupted Valentina. She turned to find Master Silas himself bearing down on them.

"Valentina, I need you to come with me," Master Silas said as he reached out and grabbed Valentina's hand, pulling her after him. He nodded at Clelia as they bustled past her.

Valentina turned to Clelia as she was dragged away. Clelia's mouth formed a perfect circle. She looked bewildered at what had just happened. Valentina cursed herself for not thinking to tell Clelia right away.

Master Silas bustled her into the Forum Peti through a back entrance that snaked and tunneled under the vast structure. The same yellow stone lined the floor, but the walls were close and the ceiling low. They walked into the network of passages beneath the sloped seating above.

"Aren't I supposed to test with the other students?" Valentina asked after she couldn't take the silence any longer. Master Silas had said nothing to her the entire time after having retrieved her from Clelia's company.

"You are. I apologize for not getting you in time this morning. There was some, um, confusion," Master Silas said as he dropped her hand. She rushed to catch up to him, losing some momentum from him no longer dragging her.

"I am? Not with Clelia?" Valentina asked.

"No, not yet anyway. In the beginning things are sorted by royal hierarchy. It must be done this way to keep the kingdoms from claiming insult to their kin," Master Silas said as he rushed through the tunnels.

Did he mean the royals attending here? Those in the fancy colorful clothes and having beautiful horses. Dread filled Valentina. She did not want to be thrown in with those people. She knew nothing of their kingdoms and even less of how to act round them.

"No, I don't need that. I'm fine working in the stables and testing with those in my house. Please stop, no." Valentina wanted to grab him and stop his furious pace, but she didn't dare. Instead, she stopped and watched him walk off, his footsteps echoing down the long hallway.

He stopped after a half dozen paces and turned to her, surprise on his face at her distance. He stomped back. "Do you dare defy the order of the emperor?"

The emperor? The one in the fancy palace on the hill that saved her life. Valentina's stomach dropped. "No, of course not," she said in a whisper.

"Were you to always give your true name ever forward?" he asked.

"Yes."

He looked thunderous. "What do you think that means?"

"That I say—"

He cut her off. "You think it is words only?"

Valentina bit her lips. She didn't know what he meant and feared anything she said would only make him madder. This man had let her lie and not told her. What other error would he let her make that could cost her dearly later?

Silence hung between them for a moment. He glanced back down the hall in the direction they had been walking, then turned back and stepped closer to Valentina.

He spoke, his words softer this time. "A name is more than words. It is a place and a responsibility. Part of being of a royal house is announcing yourself to the others for judgment, and judging anon in your own part," he said. "There will be no hiding in the masses. Is that clear?"

Valentina opened her mouth to protest, but then thought better of it and firmly closed it again. She had one glorious day of quiet with the other common students, and would have loved more, but even she was not so bold as to dare challenge the master of the school, much less the emperor of the realm.

She nodded.

Satisfied, he turned from her and made his way down the corridor.

Valentina hurried after him.

The tunnel grew lighter, sunshine flooding the tunnel ahead. She squinted to see clearly. The vast spaces beneath the Forum Peti had seemed like they'd never end, but suddenly they were behind her as she emerged into the sunlight.

Blinded by the glare, she didn't notice Master Silas stopped to her right and nearly walked into a broad back clothed in a rich jewel orange fabric with a complicated pattern of gold woven through it. The person wearing the fabric turned and scowled at Valentina. She blinked.

"You" he said.

"Horse guy," Valentina whispered to herself.

"This is Prince Hayden," Master Silas announced to Valentina.

# 13

Valentina's eyes adjusted to the bright lighting shining into the interior of the Forum Peti. The sun was still only halfway up to the top of the sky, but the section of the forum they stood in was in full sun.

A light cloud of yellow rock dust floated in the air across the wide floor of the forum from the skirmishes of students with swords on the other side. The clang of metal hitting metal bounced off the mostly empty hard stone seats rising up around them. Distant yells told of spectators taking sides. Yells and a cry of pain signaled the end of the match.

The hair on Valentina's arms rose at the sounds of battle, pretend or not.

It did nothing to calm her stomach as she faced roughly a dozen students, all of them dressed in the brilliant jewel colors of the aristocratic students. There was every jewel she could think of, from rubies to emeralds to shades of topaz. The girls dressed in flowing half robes over pants, each wearing a complicated headpiece that matched their clothing color. The boys wore tunics and pants.

They looked rich, beautiful, and terrifying.

Master Silas cleared his throat, trying to get Valentina's attention. She knew she should look to the master, but Prince Hayden stood right in front of her, his gold hair backlit by the sun. Her brain felt frozen.

"Valentina," Master Silas repeated, his voice seemingly coming from far away.

She reluctantly looked at the master.

"This is Prince Hayden. He will introduce you to the others."

Valentina looked back at Prince Hayden. He stared down at her from the height of his sharp cheekbones. He looked more confused than haughty, but Valentina looked away so she wouldn't have to witness his expression change when he figured out who she was.

"Introduce who?" Hayden asked after a moment.

The other students drew near, curious as to what Master Silas wanted. They looked curiously at Valentina.

One boy in red came closer to Valentina, then laughed an ugly laugh that held no mirth. His green eyes looked to Master Silas, then back at Valentina. "What is this one doing here?" he asked the master. "She claims to know no royalty."

"Prince Genedron, you know this one?" Master Silas asked with exaggerated politeness. Valentina sucked in her breath. Most of the others students didn't notice the danger.

Genedron looked at Valentina, making sure she knew he had examined her clothing, her sandals, all of her, and found her wanting. "We met on the road. She was not someone I'd ever thought to meet in The Stanasbrisson, much less in the Forum Peti with us. Is she to sweep the floors when we are done?"

"If she were, I know you would show her the same consideration that you show all the retainers and attendants at Stanasbrisson," Master Silas said with a formal nod.

Genedron hesitated, then went on, "I would." He tried to smirk, but the smile would not stay on his face. One of the other boys in the back coughed. Valentina could have sworn it was someone holding back a laugh, but when she scanned the others, they were either looking politely at Master Silas or down at their feet.

Nereen walked closer to stand possessively close to Hayden. Instead of an amethyst dress and flowing red hair, she wore fitted lavender pants under her three quarter robe. Her hair was pulled back under a snug headpiece and flowed down her back. A long curved shooting bow hung from her hands, the carved handle gleaming in the sun.

Valentina forced herself to stand up straighter, rather than slink away as she wanted to. "I'm Valentina, of the House Venancio, of the kingdom of Cerceion." Ignoring her thundering heart, she met the eyes of each one of the royal students gathered there. Most were simply curious, but Hayden frowned, and Nereen and Genedron scowled in open fury.

A laugh rumbled from the back. Alcorn. His black eyes danced in honest merriment, exactly the same way they'd done the first time she'd met the four royals on the road. Valentina nodded at him. She couldn't help it. Somehow she knew his laughter was not at her expense.

Alcorn nodded back. "We meet again. You are most fun."

Valentina blushed at the comment, not sure how to take it.

"You said you saw no royalty with your mother," Genedron said in a growl, ignoring the disapproving look from Master Silas.

"I said we saw none such as you," Valentina said, correcting him. "That was true."

"The intent was a lie," Genedron said. He stepped closer. Despite his face still having the fullness of youth, his height was already that of a man. Valentina barely reached his chin.

She glared back at him and refused to give way. He could come close enough to push her over, but she would not take one step back.

Valentina lifted her chin. "It was."

Genedron exhaled a fury of air, then turned to Master Silas. The master lifted one hand, forestalling any complaint by Genedron. "She is here per the emperor's instruction."

Silence fell over the group at the mention of the emperor.

Hayden studied Valentina. Feeling his eyes, she turned to look at him. He returned her look with an intensity that frightened her, then smiled with a smile that did not reach his eyes. "Nice to meet you, Valentina of Venancio, the former house of the rulers of Cerceion."

The air rushed out of Valentina's lungs. Facing a lie was one thing. Finding someone who knew about her house was another.

"How do you—"

"My father would have the head of any tutor who failed to educate me in all the houses in the land," Hayden said smoothly.

Bitterness filled Valentina. What would her father have done, if he could have done anything at all? Or her mother?

Another question nagged at Valentina. What sort of house did Hayden come from to know so much about a tiny kingdom outside of the empire? She didn't dare risk the weakness of showing her ignorance by asking.

Valentina wasn't the only one surprised by Hayden. Nereen stared at him, not quick enough to hide the shock on her own face.

"Former house of the rulers," Genedron said. "So, perhaps you weren't lying about being nobody after all."

"She is still from the Artis class," Master Silas said, as if nothing untoward had happened at all. He clapped his hands. "Since it is her first year, she will be tested in all the arts. Weapons are today. Good luck to you all. Master Chendris will be along shortly."

Master Silas whirled away and left before Valentina could ask another question.

Genedron smiled at Valentina menacingly. "Good luck." He certainly didn't mean it, unless he meant good luck getting killed.

.   .   .

Most of the other students wandered off, leaving Valentina and Hayden together. Hayden held a large double-sided sword that Valentina just noticed. It had the same golden glow as his hair.

During their talk with Master Silas, more students had filed into the Forum Peti. Some did weapons exercises on the floor—javelin throwing for accuracy, spear combat, short sword and even daggers came out—but most of them sat in the stands to watch, white robes fluttering in the breeze.

The Artis Placement Tests were as much entertainment as practical.

Valentina paled as she watched the other students warming up. Did she have to know all these weapons?

A javelin flew across a quarter of the length of the forum and landed in a straw man with a sickening thud, neatly hitting the center of the target drawn on its back.

These students were no beginners.

Out of habit, she felt for her small knife tucked within her pants. Not that a tiny knife would do much against a sword the length of her body.

Unsure where to go, she watched the students practicing. Most of the students with swords held wooden practice ones, unlike Hayden's brilliant blade.

She exhaled a whoosh of relief. She might survive this after all.

Hayden watched her, bemused. She turned to him, ready for an attack.

"You can still save yourself by leaving. No one is forced to study at Stanasbrisson," he said, then corrected himself. "At least almost nobody."

Okay, maybe not ready for that.

"You are forced to study here?" Valentina asked.

He scowled at her.

"Why tell me such a thing if you didn't want me to know?" Valentina asked.

"I told you no such thing. You should take a care. This is a lot harder than not dropping hay on someone, and we both know how well you do that." He stepped back from her, then swung his sword in a series of warm-up exercises, dismissing her.

She put her hands on her hips. Fine. She didn't need his help anyhow. So much for his introducing her to the others.

Shielding her eyes, she scanned the inner walls of the forum for a weapons rack. Seeing the bright blades of one such, she set off for it with purpose.

"Practice blades are that way," Hayden called after her, pointing in a different direction.

Valentina glared at him, then corrected her path to the wooden practice blades.

She was going to defeat him and all the rest in these tests if it was the last thing she did.

The wooden blade was heavier than it looked. Valentina stood off to the side, swinging it in attempts to imitate the others. Her hands stung from thin slivers raised from the rough handle. It would be her luck to pick a relatively new blade. Most of these students were so rich they probably traveled to the school with their own well used practice blades.

And private instructors.

This was ridiculous. What was she trying to prove?

Valentina looked around at the other students sweating under the morning sun. Most were her age or a little older. Three of these students had already shown their skills in the parade yesterday as the known heirs apparent to the emperor. They were so far out of her league, even being here felt dangerous. Artis class student or not, she had not been trained, not that she could remember.

Nereen caught Valentina looking and neatly turned her body away from Valentina to hide her movements, then leaned in to whisper into Genedron's ear. They both looked at Valentina. Valentina dropped her eyes first and went back to swinging her sword.

After several minutes, Valentina stopped. She might as well conserve her energy. If she was going to get beaten, she might as well put in a good show with some strength.

A young man in school robes approached. He had the olive leaf crown of the school masters atop his short brown hair. He walked like a soldier, with strong legs and thick arm muscles. He must be their Ekrute, or military skills instructor. Coming close, he clapped his hands for their attention.

"Greetings, I am Master Chendris, as some of you already know. We are here to do The Tests. Since you have all been here for other seasons, this is a mere formality."

Genedron cleared his throat and flicked his head at Valentina when Master Chendris looked.

Master Chendris smiled at Valentina. "Ah yes, we do have a newcomer. A real test it is then."

A real test?

This did not sound good. Valentina straightened and glared back at Genedron as she said, "I'm ready."

Genedron smiled wickedly at Valentina.


At first things went well. Valentina actually hit the target with the javelin, and while she was clumsy with a spear, she did manage to knock down several of the targets swinging from the practice frame.

A few of the students even clapped politely for her. Only Alcorn smiled a real smile at her. At least she had that. Valentina smiled back at the effortlessly handsome royal, and held her smile for just a second longer than she had to, trying to make sure Nereen saw it. Nereen scowled at Valentina, letting her know she'd scored a hit.

The sun stood directly overhead now. Valentina sweated under its warmth. Nowhere in the forum offered any shade except the tunnels beneath it. No students rested in the shade of the tunnels, so Valentina didn't either. She didn't want to show any weakness. The Test would be over before it even started.

"Now swords," Master Chendris said. "This is the main weapon you are expected to know, both for military strategy, but also self-protection. You can plan your offensives and tactics only by knowing all the weapons, but the sword and the dagger are the two you need to know for self-defense. You cannot always rely on your guard."

"What use are they then?" Genedron asked, trying to play it off as a joke.

"They save your lives, but they, too, are only men. Your life is your own responsibility in the end. You must care for it," Master Chendris said, not breaking a smile for Genedron.

The master motioned for Valentina to enter the makeshift ring drawn in chalk in the center of the floor.

"The rules are simple," Master Chendris said. "Stay within the ring. Disable your opponent." He looked around the group of students and added one final instruction. "Try to not kill each other."

Chendris motioned for Nereen to enter the ring.

Genedron stepped forward, blocking her. "How about a real test? Put one of the chosen in with her. She may be capable, but we will only know her full skills if she is tested."

The words echoed in Valentina's head. *Put her to the test.* Osian's sneering face floated in her mind.

Valentina shook her head to rid herself of the vision. These people didn't want her dead.

Most likely.

Master Chendris stared at Genedron, then at Valentina. "Very well. But not you, Genedron." The teacher looked around at the students. Alcorn almost seemed to be volunteering for it, but Chendris stopped in front of Hayden. "You. Prove your skills by disabling your opponent."

"Too easy," Genedron complained, but even the other students hushed him, tired of the interruptions.

Hayden nodded at the instructor and stepped into the ring to face Valentina. She backed up. He was taller, had a longer reach, and knew what he was doing. This was going to be ugly, but she was going to make it as hard for him as she could.

Hayden got into position. Valentina did her best imitation of the starting position she'd seen the other students use. Then her mind froze and she moved on pure instinct as Hayden came at her in a flurry of movements, faster than she thought anyone of that size could move. She blocked the first one, then just moved instinctively, beating back each one of his attacks, her wooden sword just getting into position in time.

The muscles in her arms and back burned. She wasn't used to carrying a heavy sword around, much less wielding it around so fast. Sweat soaked her back.

Then, just as quickly as it started, the attack stopped and Hayden pulled back. Valentina noted with some satisfaction that he, too, was breathing heavily.

Not a sound came from the students watching them. Valentina realized no one had expected her to survive even the first round.

A second round of attacks came, as intense as the first, if shorter. She was not the only one getting tired. Sweat dripped from Hayden's hair and down the side of his face. His tunic darkened.

Valentina managed to deflect all the blows, but on the last one, he twisted her sword and managed to loosen it from her grip and fling it away from her.

Students scrambled to get out of the way as the blade flipped end over handle, then skittered away on the yellow stones.

"Yield," Hayden demanded.

"Never," Valentina said.

Her sword lay far outside the test ring's boundaries. She looked to see if she could steal one from one of the students standing close by, but none were within reach.

"Yield," Hayden said again. "I see no point in hurting you just to win."

"You won't win," Valentina said. She backed away and circled along the edge of the ring. Perhaps she could get him to run outside of it.

Hayden glanced at the ring's edge, then at Valentina. He laughed. "I am not so novice as that," he said.

"So say you," Valentina said.

"So say I," he said, a growl in his voice. He raised his sword and came at her from the side, angling his attack so he would run near parallel to the boundary of the ring and not out of it.

Valentina danced out of the way. The tip of his blade flew by her eye, the wind of its passage flying over her sweaty hair.

She ran to the far edge of the ring, once again placing herself in a hard to attack spot.

"You have to disable me to win," Hayden said between sucking in air. "Just avoiding me only delays the inevitable."

"You talk too much," Valentina said. She put her hand to her side, slipping it inside the opening in her tunic, as if pushing in on a cramp.

Someone tittered in the crowd, distracting Valentina.

Hayden took the opportunity to charge her once again, trying the same angled attack as last time. He could risk more speed that way.

Valentina knew his path this time.

She backed up just a bit, getting perilously close to the edge of the ring, but it gave her room to pull her hand back out of her tunic. She held the tiny knife. Its three rubies gleamed in the sunlight.

Dropping suddenly, she felt Hayden swing over her head and miss. She stabbed at his foot as he passed, feeling the blade easily penetrate the leather of his sandal.

He jerked his foot, then lost his balance and stumbled forward, his practice sword twisting from his hands.

Valentina leapt to his back and wrapped an arm around his neck, her blade to his throat.

"Yield," she whispered in his ear.

# 14

Absolute silence filled Valentina's ears. She looked up. Dust moats floated lazily down in the brilliant sunshine, moving as slow as molasses on a cold winter's morning. The students in their deeply dyed linen and exotic headpieces stared, their eyes rounded, some with mouths open as if in mid-yell.

No sound reached Valentina.

She looked the other way. Master Chendris also stood with his mouth open, surprise and another emotion she could not decipher clear on his features, but he did not move. No one moved, or if they did, it was too slow for Valentina to notice.

Beneath her, Hayden didn't stir either. He should be breathing, or struggling, or yelling, but nothing. Valentina could not even feel a heartbeat in his neck, nor see one in the bulging vein in his throat where she held her knife.

Even the bead of sweat on his brow hung immobile, just on the edge of letting go and falling to the yellow stone beneath them, but never doing so.

Valentina exhaled.

As if setting off an alarm, everything moved again.

Hayden moved to throw her off, then stopped as he felt the bite of the knife in his neck.

The students yelled, their shrieks and screams a deafening wave washing over her.

Master Chendris leaned closer to bark directions in Valentina's ear.

Genedron grabbed Valentina around her waist to pull her off, only to be stopped by the others students who grabbed him in turn and pointed to the knife in her hands, poised to take the life of their head student.

The sweat fell from Hayden's brow. A single drop glistening in the sun. He lowered his head just a fraction. "I yield."

With that, Valentina lowered her knife. She didn't have a chance to stand before Genedron lifted her by her waist and threw her across the floor of the forum. Valentina rolled in a tumble, yellow dust thrown up with her impact and filling the air. She coughed as the dust came into her lungs.

Looking down in a panic, she saw the knife still in her hands. The rubies glowed as if alive. She used the seconds she had before the students came upon her to pull the ticking from her pocket and wrap the knife again and put it back in its hidden place. She needed a sheath.

Then again, looking at the students coming for her blood, she might need an army.

Master Chendris came with the group. He looked as if he was struggling to pull himself together.

"That was not a sword fight!" Genedron roared at Valentina when he finally got to her.

She looked up at him and the others. Slowly, she got to her feet and dusted off her pants and tunic. It did little good, only adding more yellow dust to the air. "It was for most of the time," she finally said. She looked at Master Chendris as she said, "The rules said nothing about disabling with a sword."

As a one, all the students turned to look at Master Chendris. He opened his mouth to talk, then stopped, then started again, and stopped again. Finally, he cleared his throat. "That's correct."

"What?!" yelled Genedron.

"Stop," a quiet voice said. The crowd parted, and Hayden came into the circle of students around Valentina. "She won."

"That was not a sword fight," Genedron said, stepping in front of Hayden.

"It was a fight for survival." Hayden looked at Chendris. "Is that not what you said? We cannot always rely on our guard. Our lives are ours to caretake."

"It is," Chendris said. "She broke no rules in that test."

"She nearly killed him," Nereen said. Hatred blazed out of her eyes at Valentina.

Valentina forced herself to not recoil from it.

"Wouldn't that be Genedron, who stepped into the ring and grabbed me?" Valentina said. "He might as well have pulled the knife across Hayden's throat with his own hand. I'm sure there are rules about *that*."

Nereen hissed at Valentina.

Master Chendris stepped between the two of them. "Yes, well, that is a good reminder to not interfere with a test. There *are* rules about that. If anyone needs to step in, it will be me. I am more than capable." He was the most experienced of all the group, and his thickly muscled limbs were built like he practiced the military arts for hours a day. No one argued with him.

Chendris checked the position of the sun, and in so doing noticed the crowds of students in the stands. None were seated. All stared at their group, concern and curiosity writ large on their faces.

"Let's call it a day. We shall complete the military tests another time. Lunch and then whatever Master Silas has for you today." He clapped his hands, dismissing them.

Valentina backed up from the group, getting out of the circle, then turned and walked to a tunnel entrance alone. She felt hot and tired. Her face burned from the sun. She was in no mood to talk to any of the other students, even for something as simple as getting directions out of the Forum Peti. They could hang for all she cared.

Clelia found her at the water pump in the kitchen gardens. The school workers had not challenged Valentina when she'd picked her way on the neat paths between the rows of plants and pumped the handle of the water pump until the water gushed from its metal mouth in a torrent, sending a thick river of brown water through the rows of carrots and turnips. Once she could not bring forth the water any faster, she released the pump handle, then thrust her head under the flow of ice-cold water. The water chilled her scalp into an icy numbness. It flowed down her back and soaked her clothing, the white robes dirty with yellow dust, now also soaked through.

She didn't care.

Not a cloud hung in the sky above. The school, like the city itself, hung onto the heat of the sun, and amplified it everywhere with the reflective white buildings. Valentina thought she'd be cooked from the inside out. Someone should have told her in that winter chilled tower to be careful what favor you ask of the gods.

"Are you alright?" Clelia asked.

Valentina stood, letting the water pour from her hair down her back and shoulders.

"I am. Why wouldn't I be?" Valentina's stomach growled.

Clelia looked at Valentina's stomach. "You missed lunch, or nearly so, but it sounds like you know that."

"How did you know I missed lunch?" Valentina said.

Clelia folded her arms and stared at Valentina. "You are decidedly not alright. After he dragged you away, I got some information on where you were... with those wretched royals. Then, they showed up at the dining hall for lunch and you were nowhere to be found. What happened?"

Valentina grabbed one of the small rags by the pump. It was nowhere near large enough for what she needed, but it would have to do. She pressed it into her face and neck. "Nothing happened." She tossed the rag into the basket for used ones and grabbed another. Just for her face. The rest of her would have to dry out under the sun.

"Nothing happened?" Clelia asked. She narrowed her eyes at Valentina. "Fine, that is two explanations you owe me, but I'll collect later. We have to get to the dining hall or you will be sorry. Dinner is not for hours." Clelia grabbed Valentina by the wrist and pulled.

What was it with the folk of this city and pulling people along like dolls?

But Valentina was hungry enough to go along with Clelia, so she only gave token resistance as Clelia dragged her in the direction of the bathhouses.


"A bath would be nice, but I don't think we have the time," Valentina said. Clelia had let go of her arm as soon as she was satisfied Valentina would keep walking with her on her own.

"We're going to the dining hall," Clelia added. Clelia turned to walk backwards and look at Valentina. "You look awful."

"Thanks," Valentina said, too tired to take offense. "Will they not let me in?"

"I think you're okay. But don't sit on the same bench as me. You're dripping."

They walked past the baths to the gigantic building on the far side. "Going through the kitchen is faster, but technically we're not allowed." Clelia said. Valentina arched one eyebrow but refused to bite and ask how Clelia knew that.

The dining hall was a large rectangular building. Instead of columns and white marble walls, this building had a triangle shaped peak in the middle of the front face, rising high above the ground. Instead of stone, stained glass windows filled the front of the triangle. It was imposing and beautiful.

Valentina gaped as she stared up at the scenes above, painstakingly created in pieces of colored glass.

"They have ceremonies here," Clelia said. She grabbed Valentina's wrist. "Come on. They're not open all day."

Reluctantly, Valentina allowed her inspection to be cut short.

They entered the massive building through the large wooden double doors.

Inside, rows of large tables and benches, six wide and six deep, filled the cavernous open space. Students filled the central tables, while older people sat on a raised section to the right—either students or faculty—eating and overlooking the rest.

A cluster of brightly dressed students sat at two tables at the far end of the room. At those primely positioned tables, no one could sit behind them, and they had an uninterrupted view of the room. Of course it was the Artis class students.

Valentina purposefully looked away from that group. She had no interest in spending another moment with them.

Silence crept over the dining hall, starting first with the students by the doors noticing Valentina. Whispers between students traveled faster than a person could walk.

Clelia took it all in with wild eyes. She pointedly looked at the royals, almost daring them to make her stop. Finally, she turned back to Valentina.

"What *happened*?" Clelia asked again. "They are all glaring at you. Well, most."

"Nothing," Valentina said, avoiding everyone's eyes. It was difficult since the whole place was looking at her. Her stomach rumbled again. "Food," she croaked out, all thoughts of fitting in gone. She wanted lunch, then to get out of this space as quickly as possible.

Clelia hesitated, then gave in. She grabbed Valentina's wrist once again and pulled her to the side room where the cooks served out the meals. Servers were only employed during high ceremonies and the students were not waited on as a normal course, which the head cook loved to drill into the new batch of students every year.

Valentina grabbed a tray, but exhaustion and stress made it difficult to concentrate on her choices. Exasperated, Clelia took over and got bowls of food for both of them, filling Valentina's tray to a gratifying amount.

When they emerged from the small space, they looked for a spot to sit. Despite all the tables being full, the moment they walked toward a table, the students there moved aside and compacted to leave room for Clelia and Valentina to join them. The other students assiduously looked away, but Valentina knew they would hang on to every word she and Clelia would say.

Let them. She wasn't going to talk, at least not about anything important.

She picked up a piece of bread and chewed, watching Clelia fight back the urge to ask more questions.


The entire campus had two free hours after lunch, during the heat of the day, as the sun beat down on the whitewashed buildings and the light was so blinding it was hard to look anywhere without squinting. The experienced students took that time to go back to their rooms and rest, while newer ones foolishly wandered around the school and guaranteed themselves a poor showing in the afternoon tests.

Clelia prevented Valentina from making that mistake.

Valentina wanted to change into dry clothes anyhow. They'd made it back to their rooming house and retreated to their cool rooms in the darkened structure. It was too hot and too bright to even light a candle.

After giving Valentina time to change, Clelia knocked on her door, and then cracked it open without an invitation. So much for taking a nap.

"You can't wear that," Clelia said when she saw Valentina's green and brown pants and tunic that she'd come to the school wearing—the clothes that Nurse had given her the day of her escape. "Students wear the prescribed robes."

"Not all of them," Valentina said. She hadn't bothered putting on the boots yet. The heavy thick leather would be miserable in the heat, but they were dry. Her sandals were not, and probably would no longer fit if she kept wearing them while wet. She felt bad for Dante, who had made her clothes for her, or at least modified them.

"All of us do," Clelia said, resentment brimming.

Right. Only the royals didn't.

And that included Valentina too.

"Clelia—" Valentina started, but Dante popped into the room, followed by Luno, interrupting her overdue explanation.

"What happened?" he asked. Spying her wet clothes hanging on the ledge of the open window, he went to them and gingerly touched the stained and wet fabric.

"Sorry, Dante. I didn't do it on purpose," Valentina said. Her face flushed. Ruining his gift so quickly just added to the misery of the day.

He looked up from the material. "I didn't think you had."

"You saved me, or perhaps ruined me, depending on who you asked," Valentina said to Dante, confusing Clelia and Luno, who had no idea about the secret pockets he'd sewn into the clothes for her.

"I'd heard something to that effect," Dante said.

"Do you do leather?" Valentina asked. She pulled out her ticking-wrapped knife and unwound it from the canvas. Dante stared at the blade but did not reach out to grab it, which Valentina appreciated. She did not like to let go of it, even temporarily, to anyone else.

"A sheath?" he asked.

Valentina nodded.

"Yes, but that will take a little longer. I don't have the right needles or tools here. But I'll get that for you," he said.

"Thank you," Valentina said. She wrapped the blade again and placed it on her desk.

"What was that?" Clelia asked. Valentina had to suppress a laugh, the first one of the day, at Clelia's hands twitching in their eagerness to touch Valentina's weapon. The girl definitely had a thing for military stuff of all types.

"Nothing," Valentina said, the mirth showing in her voice.

"You know, I am coming to hate that word, especially from you," Clelia said.

"I'm so confused," Luno said, having considered and thrown away several questions already.

"Where were you two?" Clelia asked, turning an accusing look at Dante and Luno. "Lunch was something else, and you two were nowhere to be seen."

"We had a history test that ran long. They'd warned us it might. We'd brought our lunches with us," Dante said, trying to smooth things over.

"History?"

"All fashion is cyclical, you know that," Dante said. "Military strategies and weapons, too. Maybe you should consider that course?" He smiled at Clelia, mocking her consternation.

"No, never. Too much time inside. I like keeping my vision sharp, unlike you two, who are always spending your time indoors looking at those ridiculous and smelly scrolls."

Dante retorted, but Valentina didn't hear it, having laid back on her bed and closed her eyes. Sleep snuck up on her, soothed by the sounds of her classmates bickering in her room.

Valentina woke up to a soft touch on her shoulder. She opened her eyes to a stranger's face looking down at her. An attendant with light brown hair the color of buckwheat honey shook her awake. The girl looked no older than Valentina.

"Artis, you must waken. Master Silas calls for you," the girl said.

It was still afternoon out. The sunlight streamed in her window. Valentina's clothes felt damp with sweat. She marveled she could have slept at all.

Artis? Oh, right, her new class status in the school. A very unwanted status, and whose members wanted her even less.

"Where is everyone?" Valentina asked rather incoherently. There was no reason for this attendant to know where her house-mates had gone to.

"Afternoon tests. You must hurry. You are very late."

Valentina rose from the bed and tried to rub the sleep from her eyes. She pulled on her boots and followed the attendant out of the house.

They wended their way through the school until they reached the base of the massive building that Valentina had seen on the first day—the one that marked the demarcation between the city and the grounds of the school itself. It rose high atop the steeply inclined steps. Valentina had been in awe of the beautiful and ornate pillars that surrounded the building and the sheer scale of everything about it.

It impressed her no less seeing it again this day.

Despite her sour mood, excitement pricked at Valentina. She'd wanted to see the inside of this building since the first moment she'd seen it. Now she and the attendant climbed the long steps, bringing her unexpectedly close to her goal.

They reached the top. The guards nodded at the attendant and ignored Valentina. Or didn't dare look at her, she couldn't tell which. The effect was the same; it was as if she didn't exist.

She wished for more of the same the minute they opened the doors and she faced a room of students sitting at long desks in the center space of the atrium of the building. The desks looked as if they did not normally sit in that space and had only been brought in for that day.

The students looked equally out of place. It was the group of royalty students in all their finery, sitting at the plain wooden benches, with Master Silas at the front. They all looked at Valentina as she entered, the attendant who had just moments before been at her side, withdrawing the moment they opened the doors.

"Welcome, Valentina," Master Silas said. "Thanks to you, we are having a history lesson much sooner than we planned this year." He smiled at her in a seemingly sincere way.

No one else did.

# 15

The dimensions of the vast room defied Valentina's senses. The roof so high, and the walls so far apart, she could have been in a field outside, instead of within a building with a roof and walls. The ceiling was painted blue, with white clouds and faint images of men and gods. A regular geometric pattern overlaid it all, making her eyes hurt trying to focus on either the pattern or the fake sky painted beyond it.

Complex patterns of paint and tile filled the edges of the walls and floor, with the centermost space reserved for fantastical painted scenes. Iron torch holders dotted the walls at regular intervals, the artwork behind them cleverly crafted to hide the blackened walls from the soot of the torches.

Guards stood at attention inside the space, fully armed with swords and wearing plated armor matching those of the school guards. While this building stood at the edge of the school grounds proper, it was as elsewhere on the boundaries with the school guards keeping watch.

Even in a city this size, it seemed no one felt completely at ease.

In the center of the space, in a cluster dwarfed by the vastness of the room, around twenty students sat, each wearing more finery than a small village, but looking out of place on the flat unpadded benches and long tables. Riches of vellum paper, quills, and ink pots filled the tables, but few students used them.

Probably used to their servants taking notes for them, Valentina thought bitterly.

Nereen, Alcorn, Genedron, and Hayden all sat in one group at the rearmost table in the atrium, with Hayden at the center. Nereen leaned in to Hayden, but he sat stiffly upright, ignoring her.

Valentina didn't know where to sit. There was one large open section right in front of the very last table, where Hayden and his group sat. It was probably left open out of respect for them. Well, she needed a place to sit, so she was going to have to take it.

She pulled out the heavy bench and sat on the edge. Taking the middle of the bench would have been more of a statement, but she could not stand the thought of having the lot of them directly behind her. At least this way, they were in her peripheral vision.

Behind her, Nereen tittered and made a mostly inaudible comment about "letting the gardener in." Valentina flushed but refused to look behind her. She knew her brown and green simple tunic was closer to the garb of the gardeners outside than anything these rich students wore. It was dry, and that was all she cared about at the moment. At least that was what she kept telling herself.

"Welcome, all," Master Silas said. He smiled broadly, as if completely unaware of the tension in the room. His eyes met every student's in the room, lingering on Valentina, then the table behind her. If he hadn't already told the other students this special class was her fault, they would have known it then.

Valentina's stomach curdled at the attention. She dreaded a lecture for what she had done to protect herself. Would the rules change now that Hayden, the favorite, had been bested? Being an outsider was bad enough. Being an outsider who is suddenly higher in rank, and skilled enough to surprise their chosen one, would guarantee her no friends and plenty of enemies.

She remembered how ill Master Silas had looked when he heard the name of her house during her discussion with the emperor. Perhaps now that he'd had a day to work through it, he'd come up with a solution to that which concerned him.

Not that he'd shared any of his concerns with Valentina.

Forcing herself to sit upright, Valentina smiled back at Master Silas. He would not see her squirm, no matter what. None of them would.

But his lecture was not what she expected.

*When the Great Emperor Valder, honor to him always, formed the Dawn Empire of which we now live in the splendid capital city of Valderhorn, he did so for one reason.*

*He hated surprises.*

*Surprises begot wars. And famine. And worst of all to Emperor Valder, it begot ignorance. Of all the sins of the world, Emperor Valder hated ignorance the most, the legacy of which has led to this magnificent school, but I am getting ahead of myself.*

*When the emperor was a small child, and long before anyone in these lands was called emperor, the kingdoms of Winsterson, Brehallan, Anavere, and Zanders fought constantly, and had for many decades of years, if not millennium, since continents split asunder and created the southern sea, pulling the southern Thanders lands from this golden place.*

*Each generation of people in these separate kingdoms grew up in fear of their rivals, and afraid of their strange ways. What was different was bad, for it could kill in surprising and terrible ways. Even the kings killed their criminals in different ways, and for different things, for what would be a terrible crime in one land could earn royal praise in another. The people were afraid of each other, and afraid to travel from land to land, and rightly so.*

*Emperor Valder's mother, the Great Shashis, a noble lady of the court of the kingdom of Anavere, was remarkable for many things, but the most remarkable of them all was her manner of living in the latter half of her life.*

*Her husband had come from the lands of Zanders, the kingdom to the east and facing the vast black seas. They had some strange habits in Zanders that Shashis had always commented on, and when her husband passed, she decided to see them for herself.*

*So she left court life, claiming fragility and poor health, and retired to the countryside, only in reality to travel the lands as men claimed no lady should.*

*The Great Shashis called this journeying "The Tourica." It was her education for her son, for all the things the fragile and beautiful court could not show him.*

*Despite being brought up with baths hand-drawn for her and many silken dresses, and jewels and always having more than enough to eat, she chose to travel unknown to all as a wanderer in great covered wagons, bringing along musicians and laborers and cup makers. All the things a good house of any village could want. They helped all and talked to all, making especial pains to help the maids and manservants of all the great houses, doing special favors to learn more of the servants' lives, and incidentally of their masters.*

*All of these things her son took in, and judged no one. He learned of the struggles of the common man, and the worries of the rich men, and saw the crimes of all were more often than not rooted themselves in the fertile grounds of ignorance, and its sibling, fear. This was his education from the time of ten until sixteen.*

*He used that time well.*

*When his manhood approached, his mother asked what he had learned, and he told her; she judged him ready to return to his place in their kingdom in the north and make his mark.*

*Using all the knowledge he gained in his journeys, he returned to the kingdom of Anavere and soon became an indispensable advisor to the wise but old king. When the king's sole heir died in a hunting accident, Valders had made himself so useful, and so well loved, he became the natural heir to the throne. When the old king died, Valder was enthroned and the people were glad.*

*Thus began a fifty-year peaceful rule to the kingdom of Anavere, and the gradual helping of their neighbors and new way of ruling that ended with the formation of this empire and a new era.*

"Weren't there some wars in there?" Genedron asked grumpily, interrupting Master Silas' flow.

Silas focused his eyes on the group, as if coming out of a dream. "Well, yes, but they are rather incidental to *this* story, and your histories class will go into more detail."

One of the shyer students in front raised their hand for attention, then said, "This is common lore in the city. We all know this. Why are you speaking of it now?"

"Do you know this?" Master Silas responded. "Do you know the meaning, and not just the words?"

No one said anything.

Valentina had known none of that, but she wasn't sure what particular piece of information Master Silas was so concerned about, so she wasn't going to speak up. It wasn't a lecture on abusing those in power—not that she had thought she'd done such a thing, but you never know how someone will take to having their favorite bested—so it was a win for her.

Not that she'd bested him, truly. Just a little.

Valentina snuck a look back at the students behind her. Nereen made no effort to hide her glare, but Alcorn, Genedron, and Hayden stared steadfastly forward, ignoring her. A muscle twitched on Hayden's cheek and for some reason that made Valentina want to smile.

Master Silas clapped his hands for their attention, then cleared his throat. "I see this lesson might take some time to sink in. You will all have your regular schedule tomorrow. Valentina, an attendant will bring you yours so you will not be late again. Is that clear?"

Valentina nodded, feeling unjustly singled out. It hadn't been her fault no one had told her where to go.

"You'll be staying where you are now, per the emperor's order," Master Silas said just before he left through the large double doors. A guard closed the door after him.

A flurry of whispers sprung up around the room. Apparently this select group of students had not heard all the gossip just yet about the events of the parade. Valentina looked down and smiled. Perhaps there was something to be said for running around with the common folk.

Valentina took her time walking back to her room. She was starting to not get so lost in the maze of white buildings that all looked the same and the endless lawns of green and bushes trimmed to tight bundles of greenery.

As she walked by, one gardener glanced back and ordered her to pick up the bundle of twigs round the back of the next building so they could cart it away. Valentina knew his mistake, but went and got the bundle anyway and greatly enjoyed the surprise on his face when she came back with it and he finally focused on her face.

His true assistant watched with much confusion as the gardener apologized to Valentina profusely and tried to take the sticks away from her. She refused and insisted on carrying them to the gardening wagon waiting nearby.

It felt good to do the work. Mayhaps she had more of Clelia in her than Dante and Luno. Studying inside was exhausting. Besides, she'd been cooped up inside against her will for three years. Being outside was better.

When she returned to her room, the hallways of the house were quiet. None of the other students were back yet. Master Silas must have dismissed them early. Valentina looked around her room, but she had too much energy to nap again, and there were no books or things of interest in her room.

She went back outside and found her way back to the horse barn. This time the stalls were full. The horses that had been elsewhere on her first night had returned. With the sun soon to set, they'd been brought in from whatever pasture they might get set to in the daytime. Despite the crowding, several workers raked the stalls and carried feed.

Valentina motioned to one that she would like to help. The woman nodded gratefully and pointed to the rack of shovels and pitchforks.

The stalls all needed attention and Valentina worked well and quickly, trying to get to the one at the end. The other workers laughed at her, but did not argue.

She lingered there far too long, arranging the hay just so, and giving the enormous horse there a special pat on her forehead.

Finally, she had to admit it was time to go or miss dinner. She told herself her disappointment had nothing to do with a certain person who failed to come check on their horse.

"Again?" Clelia asked, her hand on her hip.

She stood in the doorway to Valentina's room. Valentina had returned from the kitchen pump with a pitcher of water and was trying to clean herself with a rag in her room, instead of out in the open in the garden. Her robes from Dante still hung in the window, now dry but still dirty. Working in the horse barn had done no favors for her only other set of clothing besides the fancy parade clothing.

If she didn't start washing some of these things, soon she'd have nothing to wear.

"My brother doesn't make such a mess of himself, and he's three," Clelia said.

Valentina snorted as she grabbed the clothing from the windows and considered the small basin she'd used to wash her face in. Would they fit in there? Probably not. "Your brother probably doesn't have to have sword fights," Valentina said.

Clelia grimaced.

"Sorry, did I say something?" Valentina asked.

"No, he's three. What could you have said?" Clelia said, waving it away like it was nothing. Valentina decided not to press it, though she thought Clelia was not telling her everything.

"So," Clelia said, pointedly changing the subject, "you owe me several explanations. Which would you like to give first?" She sat on Valentina's bed and crossed her arms.

"Several?"

"Several." She held out a hand, flicking out a finger for each item. "One, your name, *Wiley*. Two, what did you do to get so dirty and get those Artis kids so mad, and three, why are you still cleaning out the horse barn?" She narrowed her eyes at Valentina.

"All that?"

"Yes, though I must admit a special fondness for wanting to know what you did to those Artis snobs. Oh yeah, how could I forget—number 4, which should be number 1—what the heck happened with the emperor? We heard you saw him personally, and he's given orders for you." Clelia put both hands on her hips and glared at Valentina. "Who the heck are you and how can you help me in this school?"

Valentina stared at Clelia, then burst out laughing. "You're not subtle."

"No. I'm not. That's why I like the war stuff."

"I bet you're good at it," Valentina said as she gave up on cleaning and sat on the floor in front of Clelia to keep the blankets from getting dirty.

"I am. Which is why you should be happy to be my friend," Clelia said. "Oh yes, another question. What test did you have this afternoon?"

Valentina furrowed her brows. "We didn't have a test. Master Silas—"

"Master Silas?" Clelia asked, interrupting Valentina. She sat upright. "Are you telling me you had Master Silas for two classes today, and you didn't have an afternoon test?"

After a hesitation, Valentina said, "Yes. Is that bad?"

"Is that bad? Are you jesting with me? He's the top guy in the school. Most students are lucky to have a class with him after years of study. What *did* you do?" Clelia asked.

"He told us a story," Valentina said, pretending to misunderstand the question. She wasn't ready to talk about anything from the morning, not yet.

"That's all you're going to tell me? What story did he tell you?"

"About Emperor Valder's childhood and wandering and stuff." Valentina scowled. There must have been something important about that story, but the obvious message was to learn new things. He couldn't have possibly told that story just because of her.

"That's it." Clelia drummed her fingers on her knee.

"It was long. I don't remember it all," Valentina said, then stretched. Her stomach took that opportunity to rumble. "So, when's dinner?"

"After you answer all my questions, and better than that response."

Valentina laughed at Clelia's exaggerated expression. "How about I tell you my name, because I have to now, or else, and then the rest when everyone is back?"

"Or else?"

Valentina nodded. "Part of the story coming later, I promise."

Clelia weighed the offer, then finally gave in. "Well, you'll ruin my fun in telling everyone else, but okay, deal. I'm actually hungry too."

"Excellent," Valentina said as she rose from the floor. "My name is Valentina, from the house of Venancio, of the kingdom of Cerceion. Nice to meet you." She gave Clelia a version of the bow she'd seen the boys do at court. Trying to do a curtsey in pants just didn't seem right.

Clelia's mouth dropped open. "You're one of *them*."

# 16

"Do I really have to wear this? I feel ridiculous," Valentina said. She wore a light green linen tunic of material so fine it was almost translucent, which was why the material was sewn doubled over and not in the usual style. It was paired with yellow pants. The whole ensemble was so beautiful, she felt bad wearing it. With her past record with clothing, it would be dirty and stained by morning.

Dante, Luno and Clelia walked with her through the darkening school grounds toward the dinner hall. School attendants ran through the grounds, lighting the torches set in metal pikes around the school. The flames flickered into the night, with moths and insects flying around them and sometimes misjudging the fire to die a quick death.

Larger insects scuttled across the paving stones ahead of them. A chill ran over Valentina and she decided to stop looking down quite so much and to let Clelia lead them.

Dinner was pushed back several hours on the first day of the term due to all the testing. It was the last big event before the hard work of the school started for the summer.

Despite Valentina's finery, Dante, Luno and Clelia wore much more subdued clothing. Luno seemed to always wear the standard student robes, as did Dante. Only Clelia tried something daring with a plated metal belt like those the soldiers wore. "Can't wear the whole uniform on a non-parade day," Clelia had admitted, looking a bit sad about it.

Clelia turned around from her position ahead of the group on the path and gave Valentina a quick meaningful look. "Yes, you have to wear that," she said, then turned back to navigate the narrow path. The torches were not nearly bright enough to fight off the quickly coming night.

"You're Artis." Clelia's words floated back to Valentina. "You must show it in your clothing. Not showing it is like lying. You can catch other people off guard."

"That seems silly. Just treat me like anyone else," Valentina protested to Clelia's back.

"It's for other people, not for you," Dante said, squeezing himself next to Valentina on the narrow path. He'd been the one responsible for the clothing, despite never wearing anything too extravagant himself.

"The consequences for doing something against an Artis are higher than against others—"

"That's not fair," Valentina said.

Dante held up a hand. "Fair or not, you are being cruel to others by not announcing yourself. Besides, I am enjoying the chance to play dress-up."

His eyes had lit up when he pulled the outfit out for Valentina for dinner, rushing into her room with the set already laid out in his arms. "This is perfect. I could not give you too much finery before, but now... now I can go all out." And he looked thrilled to do it.

"Why spend all your precious coins on fabric for someone else?" Valentina asked as she touched the unreal lightness of the green top. "If you can create all these wonderful things to wear, why don't you wear some of them?"

Luno, Dante, and Clelia stared at her like she was a crazy country idiot, which fair enough, it seemed like she was when it came to customs in the capital. Luno and Clelia had come into her room to see Dante's candidates for what Valentina would wear for dinner.

"I can't," Dante said dramatically with a hand to his chest. "I'm nobody. Yet." His eyes twinkled. "If I can dress enough people and get someone important's attention, then I can because a Dressier. And then, if I'm famous and rich enough, I can wear whatever I want as a merchant class. But until then, I'm just another poor student."

He pursed his lips and evaluated Valentina. "Now, turn. Are you sure I can't get you into a dress? All my best material is in the dresses."

Valentina shook her head and backed up for good measure. No dresses. No women's stola.

Dante frowned. Behind him, Clelia gave Valentina a look like she understood. At least that was one person.

They were almost at the dining hall. The inside must be full of torches because the light spilled out from the large stained glass window of the front face and lit up the whole stone paved area in front of it like a sunrise coming up. Students and faculty and atten-dants poured into the front door, coming from all the different paths of the school. Even in the few minutes they'd been approaching the front door, it seemed like more people had gone in than should fit.

Valentina stared. All the colorful Artis students from the day wore some variation of what she had on. Actually, most of the boys did. The female Artis students had flowing layers and layers of fine linen, and ribbons in their hairs. They stood out like jewels twin-kling in the dim light. They all looked so beautiful.

Not a one of them had ever spent much time being hungry, Valentina guessed. Having enough to eat does wonders for someone's looks.

She knew, because she'd seen enough of the ones who didn't get enough to eat, the hungry kids from the villages around her tower back home. Sometimes they'd sneak past the guards and throw rocks at the tapestry over her window. Whenever she came to look out, they'd run away screaming like she was going to fly down from the tower and eat them.

Honestly, she had wished they'd stayed. Even looking at someone else her own age would have been better than all that awful time alone in that cold tower in the shadow of the Forbidden Woods.

But now she was here, and Dante had dressed her perfectly to fit in with the kids that all hated her, but for a different reason.

"Do you have to move in with them?" Luno asked Valentina, motioning to the brightly colored Artis kids ahead going into the dining hall.

"No!" Valentina said before she really thought about it. "I mean, I was told to keep doing the chores and stuff to learn a lesson."

"Master Silas told you that?" Clelia turned around to ask.

Valentina looked down, her face flushing. "No."

Clelia stopped walking. Dante followed suit and soon Valentina was neatly stuck between the three students.

"No, Master Silas didn't tell you that, but you're still cleaning out the horse barn? Who told you to do so?" Clelia asked.

"The emperor," Valentina said so quietly she was almost mumbling.

"The emperor!" Clelia said, nearly yelling.

Valentina glared at her. "Quiet. Not everyone has to know. I'll not tell you anything else if you shout it to everyone. I barely know you."

Clelia's eyes widened at the words "barely know." Valentina instantly felt bad but she was too mad to try to fix it.

Luckily Dante wanted dinner enough to play peacekeeper. "Come on. We shouldn't be talking about any of this here anyhow." He looked around meaningfully and everyone took the hint.

They got closer to the dining hall and then slipped inside along with the crowd.

Just inside the door, an elderly man sat on a stool and nodded at everyone coming in. He seemed friendly, but Valentina caught him evaluating her outfit with pursed lips. No doubt he felt perfectly within his rights to throw out anyone who didn't pass his standards. She lifted her chin as they walked past.

Valentina walked toward the kitchen area where they'd picked up their food before, but Clelia grabbed her arm and stopped her. "Not tonight. They bring the food out to make it quicker because everyone eats at once."

The four of them pushed through the crowds to find a spot at the end of one table. Valentina recognized some of the others at the table as also living in their house. She stuck out badly with the group of students who all wore the school robes. At least she was sitting at the end, partially hidden by Luno, so the rest of the students couldn't stare at her as easily.

All the students she actually looked like tonight sat at the back of the hall. Valentina could almost feel their stares and glares at the back of her neck. She snuck a glance back, looking for blond curls and a citron tunic, but didn't see him.

Maybe he's not here yet.

She checked the door, but the stream of students coming in had slowed to just a few scrambling in.

School attendants walked between the rows of students, going so fast as to nearly be running, setting out drinks and bowls of nuts.

One large bowl landed in front of them and Clelia immediately stuck one hand in and pulled out a salty oily mess of nuts and shoved them in her mouth. "What?" she asked at Dante's glare. "I worked hard today."

"We all did," Dante said, and pulled the bowl away from Clelia and handed her a square of linen from his pocket. She took it with a sullen look and wiped her hands.

Luno leaned in to Valentina. "We don't usually get nuts. Or that much salt even." Luno licked off the salt from the walnut she'd plucked from the bowl before popping the whole thing in her mouth.

Valentina took a long drink of water, using it as an excuse to look around.

The students seemed to have sorted themselves by age.

Their row of tables was all about the same age. Another row forward looked younger and smaller. The elder students sat behind them, some tables quite old with gray hair and beards, followed last by the Artis students who all seemed close to Valentina's age, some a little younger, some just a little older. Maybe they didn't stay at the school all that long, having vast estates and court positions to go to instead.

Along the sides of the room, long tables faced out. The fancier robes of the men and women eating there and ornate silver candlesticks on their tables marked them as the teachers and advanced scholars of the school. Master Silas sat exactly in the middle of the largest side table and seemed to be enjoying talking to those seated next to him.

"Is it like this every night?" Valentina asked Clelia. She motioned to the teachers and Master Silas and everything.

"No, only a few times a year," Clelia said. "It's our chance to see all the teachers. Usually, we don't even have to sit through speeches."

Valentina was glad to hear that. It had been a long few days and she was already feeling sleepy.

Roast boar and root vegetables came out, followed by fish dishes. Valentina had never eaten so much in one sitting in her life. She looked down at the table. A lot of the other students had glassy looks in their eyes, but they didn't stop eating either. She was not the only one taking advantage of the feast in front of them.

Out of the corner of her eye, Valentina saw Genedron and Nereen walking down the side aisle of the room toward her. No other students were standing, except for the few that scurried off to the bathrooms tucked behind the building, racing back to not miss any of the dishes.

A crash came from the other end of her long table, down another aisle that ran between the tables, where two other Artis students had collided with a server, sending roast meat and gravy flying, and ceramic dishes crashing to the stone floor. Sharp pieces of pottery struck the ankles of several nearby seated students who cried out, adding to the chaos. One of the Artis students had a slice of boar hanging from his jet-black hair and he looked fire at the school attendant bowing and profusely apologizing.

It was a huge scene, and the perfect distraction for Genedron to slam a thick knife as long as his forearm down and dig it into the table, swinging the blade inches from Valentina's face. Valentina tried to lean back, but the warm body of another student stopped her. She couldn't see the student's face, only the pure red of the fine linen of his robe. Another Artis student.

Genedron bent down and leaned in close to Valentina, his breath thick with wine. "We do not tolerate cheats."

Over his shoulder, Valentina saw Nereen smirking at her. Another Artis boy came up behind Nereen and wrapped his arm around Nereen's waist and smiled down at Valentina like she was a toy for their amusement.

Across from the table, Clelia wound up as if to strike Genedron, but Valentina shook her head minutely to stop the girl. This was not the place. Clelia hesitated, still tense. Dante wrapped his arm around Clelia, acting casual, but the muscles in his arms bunched at the effort of squeezing Clelia close.

Next to Valentina, Luno held her breath.

"Do you understand, Valentina of the mud soaked hills?" Genedron asked, not satisfied with Valentina's reaction.

Valentina looked into his green eyes. They had flecks of yellow in them, she thought inanely. Finally, she forced herself to inhale and then sigh with exaggerated effect. "No one cheated, Genedron. And it's the house Venancio, of the kingdom Cerceion."

"It is not the empire, which means it's nothing," Genedron said. "We will not tolerate what you think you are getting away with here." He leaned in even further.

Valentina coughed on the fumes of his breath, ruining her effect of acting unconcerned. Luckily, he could not hear the pounding of her heart and the blood rushing in her own ears.

"Go away, you bully Artis creep," Clelia said, unable to restrain herself. Genedron turned to look at her and lifted one lip in a sneer. Clelia tried to punch him, stopped by Dante's arms around her.

"We'll deal with you later, if we have to, you landless pest," Genedron said to Clelia.

He then stood up and pulled the knife from the table and slipped it into a holder within his robes. He smoothed down his clothing and gave Valentina a sickly sweet smile while turning to make sure the teachers on the long tables on the edge of the room could see it, before waving to his friends to come along with him as he left. At the other end of the table, the chaos of the crashed tray was just getting settled, the Artis kids who no doubt caused the accident already gone.

Genedron had timed it perfectly. They'd created that distraction just so he could threaten her, right there out in the open. The brazenness of it was part of the tactic. They wanted her to know she wasn't safe anywhere.

155

Valentina shivered, then forced herself to sit upright. She plastered a smile on her face.

"Don't worry, we won't let them disappear you like the others," Clelia said through clenched teeth as she watched the Artis students wend their way back to their privileged tables.

"Disappear? The others?" Valentina asked.

Dante put his face in his right hand, as if he wanted to disappear himself.

"What haven't you told me?" Valentina asked Clelia again. Clelia blanched at what she'd said and looked like she wanted to slide under the table and into the ground.

# 17

"I still don't understand what you mean by disappeared," Valentina said. She sat on her bed, her back to the wall and her legs stretched out in front of her. Dante and Luno sat next to her on the bed and Clelia sat in the desk chair. They'd decided to talk in Valentina's room, and Clelia had insisted on checking out the window and down the hall first to make sure no eavesdroppers lurked.

"They drive them away," Clelia said. "Usually the fights are in the Artis crowd, so we only hear about them through gossip, but sometimes a lower student gets too influential, and they..."

"Make them less influential, usually by driving them out," Dante finished for Clelia.

"One killed himself off the aqueduct," Luno said with a whisper.

"Oh," Valentina said, taking it in. "I thought you meant something worse, like killings and stuff."

Clelia pulled up her legs and hugged them. "Sure they'd threaten to kill us if we talked about it. It's why I can't stand those Artis kids. I think they're responsible."

"Genedron didn't act shy about threatening me," Valentina said, agreeing.

"Yes, what happened?" Clelia asked. "You've only been here a few days and already they're honing in on you."

Valentina closed her eyes. "That was probably my fault."

"How?" Clelia asked.

Valentina told them about the sword match that morning and how she'd bested Hayden even after getting disarmed, leaving out the part where everything went still and quiet around her. That part almost seemed a dream, and something inside her kept her from talking about it.

"Wow, I would have loved to have seen that," Clelia said. "Or done it myself to one of those arrogant ones."

"I didn't see Hayden tonight," Dante said.

"No. Do they always come to dinner?" Valentina asked.

"These big dinners? Of course they do. It has to be something unusual for them to be gone. Are you sure you didn't slice him or something?" Clelia asked.

Valentina laughed at the glint in the girl's eyes.


Valentina lay on her bed, stretching out on the thin blankets. She'd hung up her new clothes from the hook and line that Dante had instructed the attendants to install. It matched the one in his room where he hung the clothing he was working on. On Valentina's line hung her new clothing of green and yellow from that dinner and the newly washed robes he'd made, as well as her plain clothing of green and brown.

It was a shocking array of riches in the little room. She even had on a shift he'd given her for sleeping in. She would have been lost without his help.

A knock sounded at her door.

"Come in," Valentina called. Dante opened the door and stuck his head in the room.

Valentina sat up and made room for him to sit on the bed along with her, their backs to the wall.

"Thank you for all the clothes. I'm sorry I don't have anything to give you to pay for any of this," Valentina said.

He laughed, then shrugged. "Just tell people who dressed you if anyone asks. Tell them even if they don't ask."

Valentina nodded.

"I have one more thing for you. After your story tonight, I was glad I worked on it this afternoon." He pulled out a small leather sheath for a knife. The leather was thick and sturdy, the color a light brown, almost the right color to blend in with Valentina's skin or most clothing.

She clapped her hands. "Oh, that's beautiful."

"And hopefully, functional." He handed it over to her. It looked the right size for her knife. She pulled the blade out from beneath her pillow where she'd stashed it after changing. "Don't tell anyone," she mock whispered to Dante. He nodded.

The blade fit perfectly within the slot, having a slight click when fully inserted. "How did you size it so perfectly?" Valentina asked.

"Luck. I had to go by memory."

Valentina stared at the holder for her knife. It would be much better than dealing with a loose blade or cumbersome wrappings, especially if she was going to be having to deal with threats from Genedron and his friends.

The next few weeks passed in a blur. The morning after the high dinner, an attendant had slipped a precious piece of vellum with Valentina's schedule written on it under her door and every moment of her week was accounted for. Each morning was weapons drills and practice in the Forum Peti with the Artis kids. The instructors drilled them in the basic sword fighting forms over and over again so many times Valentina thought her arm would fall off. Then they made them switch arms.

The mornings not spent on the sword work covered the other weapons of war: the javelin, shield work and formations, and archery. When it rained, the instructors lectured on the basics of sieges, hand-to-hand combat, supply lines, and special weapons such as flaming arrows.

Demonstrations of the special weapons happened at a large field near the back end of the school. Valentina appreciated the chance to walk through the buildings of the school and see more of the grounds. They passed many older students, and she wanted to learn more of them but didn't feel close enough to the unfriendly Artis students to dare ask them questions about how the school worked, especially since on the few chances they had to spar with her, they'd taken pains to make as many direct hits on her as they could, sending their wooden practice swords crashing into her body. She'd gotten much better at defense quickly.

Genedron watched her constantly. It seemed every time Valentina saw him, he stared at her with narrowed eyes as if daring her to pull out her knife again so he could come over and stab her with his own much larger knife. She tried to ignore him but the skin on her back crawled as she imagined him looking at her.

Hayden had returned after a few days and joined in the morning classes. Half of his face had a light purple and green tinge to it, like that from an old bruise. Valentina had not remembered hitting him in the face, but perhaps she had. Much of the morning of the test was a blur.

Unlike Genedron, he never looked at her. It was as if she didn't exist. The instructor had never paired them together, so she didn't see what he would do if forced to face her.

The afternoons were away from the Artis students. Apparently she was so behind on studies of the empire that she was thrown in with a bunch of much younger students who all wore the uniform of the school, the white robes with blue trim. They avoided her, but for a different reason than the Artis kids, scooting away as if she was going to lash out and strike one of them for no reason. It was difficult to even make eye contact with one of them, and when Valentina did manage the feat, the kid would look down and away as if they'd made a grave mistake.

Was that how all the Artis students were treated? It felt horrible to Valentina, but she could see now how they acted so high and mighty. Everyone was too afraid of them to challenge them on anything.

The curriculum was mostly reading and writing, with some poetry thrown in. More than once, a teacher had complained under their breath that Valentina should be studying rhetoric or law by now, but the head writing teacher had only stroked his beard and proclaimed she was where she should be. Many of the words they used were slightly different than in Valentina's home, which led the teachers to think she needed remedial schooling. She didn't protest, because even with the younger kids afraid of her, it was still better than the unpleasant company of the Artis ones.

Every eight days all the classes were excused to allow for the grand markets in the streets of Valderhorn, where the students could attend if they chose. The first such break Valentina had, she slept the entire day, unaware of anything except she had a day of no classes, not realizing she was missing the chance to go do something fun within the city proper. Only later did she find out that students took the day to go into the city in groups and buy needed items, or special treats if their funds allowed. Valentina had no coin to buy anything, but she'd wanted to see if she could find Mercato, if indeed he was still within the city.

The second time market day came around, she was ready, even asking Clelia to wait for her before leaving. Valentina had been through the city streets exactly twice, once on the way to the school for the first time, and once for the parade. The second time had not been a great experience, so having some company seemed like a good idea.

She got up early that day and ran down to the kitchen pump, forgoing the long process of bathing at the bathhouse. She wanted to get into the city and was sure that Clelia would too. She brought a pitcher she'd found at the house so she could share her wash water with Clelia and the others. She brought the heavy pitcher back, trying not to slosh too much of the water as she carried it in the cool morning. It was so quiet on campus that only a single gardener roamed the grounds, also enjoying the peace.

She went to the washroom and poured some water into the basin there just for that purpose, setting the rest of the pitcher aside for the other students. It was quick work to wash her face and neck.

Unsure how to dress in the city, Valentina chose one of the plainest outfit she had: the plain brown and green outfit her nurse had given her. It wasn't the robes of the school, so no one could complain she was hiding her Artis status, but it wasn't the lightest and the fanciest of tunics that Dante had given her either. She still didn't know the customs of the city all that well and wanted to blend in as a boring nobody, and not someone that people had to worry about offending.

Wanting to disguise herself a bit more, Valentina grabbed the deep red cap of the first outfit Dante had ever given her. A slight fear gripped her as she handled it. This was from the same outfit the black riders from Cerceion had seen her in when they'd tried to capture her and take her back.

If they had taken the emperor's orders seriously, they would be gone.

Just the same, Valentina carefully checked the sling she'd made for her knife within her tunic, making sure the blade was easily reachable. Dante had thoughtfully added pockets to the pants so she could stow her gift from Mercato there, inside a cleverly made inseam to protect against the pickpockets that were the scourge of the city.

"Here," Clelia said as she came into Valentina's room and handed her a thin linen bag with a long strap that could go over her shoulder. "I'm not carrying your lunch for you."

Valentina took it.

"It's empty," Valentina said. "What lunch?"

"We have to go get it in the dining hall," Clelia said, as if Valentina should know such a thing.

"You look ridiculous," Clelia said, motioning to Valentina's outfit of clashing colors.

"Am I breaking any city rules?"

Clelia bit her lip, then finally said, "No, but do you have to look so weird?"

Valentina laughed. "If I had a green cap, I'd wear that instead. Just think how good you'll look by comparison."

"There is that," Clelia said.

"Are Dante and Luno coming too?"

"Dante has a long list of clothing shops he is visiting and plans with another Dressier friend, so we are out, and Luno claims she has to catch up on her studying, leaving just the two of us." Clelia waved as she left and headed to the washroom so she could do her own cleaning.

Only a few students sat eating breakfast in the dining hall, leaving it feeling strangely empty. Few attendants worked as well, but they had set out loaves of bread, cheeses, nuts, and fruits for the students to take for lunches. The dining hall closed early on market day and did not reopen until a late dinner.

Valentina stuff her bag with as much food as would fit, studiously ignoring the glare of the school attendant behind the counter. Clelia chuckled, but took only a tiny bit less than Valentina did.

They headed out to the large building that marked the front entrance of the school grounds, and soon they had passed the guards and were out in the city proper.

Out in the public streets, various robes and stolas replaced the uniform robes of the school grounds. Valentina pulled her cap down, checking to make sure her hair was still tucked inside. Clelia wore a more traditional robe of light blue, closer to the complex pleatings of a stola, which had surprised Valentina. She was used to seeing her friend in an outfit closer to that of the guards.

"Sometimes it's good to fit in," Clelia had said with a wink at Valentina's shock.

Crowds packed the city streets. They'd missed the morning influx of wagons that had already dropped their loads off at the market proper, and now they just shuffled through the crowd of pedestrians. Many of them were obviously servants in their plain dress, but the occasional sedan chair made its way through the crowds, forcing everyone else to back up quickly and pack along the walls of the narrow streets to avoid the wrath of the lead runner.

In the city center, most of the buildings stood close together, unlike the walled compounds of the private villas that hugged the outer edge of the city. Small buildings, with six columns along the side and four on the front face, were the exception, set on small hills surrounded by expansive grounds and guards in splendid uniforms of different shades of richly dyed linens.

"What are those places?" Valentina asked Clelia, pointing to one such building whose guards wore green uniforms.

"Temples. That one is for the goddess of the harvest. Good day for it too. Farmers coming in and giving their tribute and thanks, especially if the crops went well this year.

"Or if they didn't go well," Valentina said.

Clelia laughed and nodded at that. "That too. Can't be too stingy for your patron god."

Valentina searched the crowds, looking for the riders from Cerceion, or Mercato. Horses were rare. It was easier to look out for those, since both the visitors and Mercato might have them, but she saw no one familiar.

But then again, it had been more than half a month since she'd first arrived at the city. Mercato could be anywhere, even if he'd found a way to survive in the city. The riders had been told in no uncertain terms to go by the emperor, but they hadn't seemed particularly respectful of the ruler's authority.

"We'll go to the main market. It's by the large forum," Clelia said, pulling Valentina from her thoughts. She motioned for Valentina to follow as she plunged fearlessly into the crowds. Valentina wished Clelia would be more cautious with so many around them, but trying to restrain the girl was like trying to hold in the wind. She had no choice but to hustle into the crowd behind Clelia.

They'd gone near a block, finally trapped behind one of the straggler wagons, when Valentina spied two older boys harassing a pair of children, a girl and a boy about ten years old. She wasn't sure what was going on until one of the boys smacked the younger boy on the head and then reached down and pulled at a small purse of coins in the younger boy's hand.

The young boy struggled to hold on to the purse, but the older boy yanked at it so hard the young boy was toppled into the dirt, still clutching the prize.

"Look!" Valentina said as she pointed out the group to Clelia.

Clelia took one look and bolted for the boys harassing the children, pushing around the back of the wagon.

Surprised, Valentina gaped, then raced after Clelia, leaping onto the empty bed of the wagon itself and running over it to leap off the other side, much to the driver's surprise.

Old women yelled at Clelia and Valentina as they ran ahead. One tried to swat at Valentina's head for being so rude as to touch her when brushing by, but Valentina dodged out of the way.

The two older boys looked at the commotion of Valentina and Clelia running at them. The one trying to get the purse kicked the young boy savagely in the legs and got him to release it. The older boy smirked at Valentina as he stashed the bag and then he and his friend ran off.

Valentina growled at his arrogance. He thought there was no chance of getting caught. It only made her run harder.

The two older boys split directions. Clelia ran after the one who went to the right, and Valentina took the one on the left, only concentrating on the back of the running boy as she went deeper and deeper into the crowd on her own.

# 18

The crowds ahead seemed endless. Valentina squinted her eyes against the glare of so much white linen clothing, filling the streets between whitewashed buildings, and underneath the brilliant blue early morning sky. Old people, young ones, servants walking fast and carrying large baskets. Slower walking ladies, enjoying the morning and the possibilities of new wares at the market.

All in the way of Valentina getting the boy running from her.

She cursed under her breath, repeating an old saying they'd had amongst the court children that referenced the black tower.

Ahead, the boy jostled and ran through the crowd. The further he got from her, the harder it was to see him. Soon she only knew where he was by the movement of people around him parting like the sea.

Valentina pressed on, pressing a hand on the stitch in her side. Of all the weapons training they'd done in the mornings, none had included running.

The boy headed for the large market building, itself several stories tall and looking exactly as Clelia had described it, new and decadent with several arches and terraces. If he ran in there, it would be near impossible to find him. There would be so many places he could duck out of sight and hide.

Spying a shortcut to the entrance of the market building through the back court of a large eatery, Valentina ran into the place, keeping her head low and doing her best to avoid the ladies inside conversing in the shade, and then ran out the back and into the courtyard.

She ran weaving through the tables and then jumped the low decorative fence that separated it from the next boulevard. To her left, she could see the boy pushing through the thicker crowds on the main street. He was headed for the market entrance.

Willing herself to run faster, Valentina pushed ahead while keeping an eye on the boy.

She accidentally ran into a young man carrying a rooster, both of which yelled loudly at her, and sent feathers flying. Valentina paused long enough to apologize, but when she glanced back at the kid she was trying to intercept, he looked right at her and darted left down a long alley, giving up his goal of the market building.

Valentina gave chase down the alley. The boy ran much faster without the crowds in his way and he soon pulled ahead of Valentina and jumped to grab the top of the wall at the end of the alley and scrabbled over it and away.

She reached the wall at the end of the alley, her side pulling in pain and her lungs on fire. The wall stood ten feet tall. There was no way she could jump to the top and pull herself up. She doubled over, trying to catch her breath and thinking ill thoughts of the boy who got away.

Valentina slumped against the wall in the shadowy alley until her side stopped hurting. After a few moments, she looked up and realized why it was so cool in the narrow space. While the alley ran between the two-story support buildings for the round main city forum, it was also close enough to the forum itself to stand in its shade. The forum towered over all those around it and reached at least five stories into the sky. Thus, no morning sun reached the alley.

The way the city was laid out made this particular spot as close to the exact center of the city as possible. The massive main forum sat between the palace complex and the central market buildings and courtyards, each taking roughly equivalent areas.

In the central area taken by the forum, a ring of smaller building encircled the larger structure. Those smaller buildings were used for vendors on market days, as well as specialty shops such as blacksmiths, wagon makers, and chariot experts. A large stable and field sat beyond the buildings to care for the horses on show days.

This is where Valentina found herself. Few people walked through the area. The main forum, nearly twice as large as its sister building on the school grounds, stood quiet.

All the crowds were at the market place.

A chill that had nothing to do with the cool air ran over Valentina as she realized how alone she was. The best thing to do would be to find Clelia so they could continue their day together. Now the fun of running after the boys seemed like foolishness she could have done without.

Pushing against the wall, Valentina stood upright and started walking back to the mouth of the alley. A crashing noise in the second story of the building above her startled her almost to falling.

The crashing continued in the building, and sounded like metal pots thrown down a large stairway. Valentina crept to the far side of the alley and past the building with all the racket, but she was too curious to just leave. She positioned herself on the far side of a large cabinet permanently affixed to the outside of a building across the alley from the one making all the noise. If someone came out of that building, she'd be out of sight, but she could also peer around the cabinet to see what was happening.

Valentina squatted low and waited.

Her planning paid off.

A few moments later, the crash happened again, except this time much closer and the double doors to the building flew open.

Hayden came flying out, his recognizable citrine orange tunic flying as he stumbled out into the alley. Coming after him, a man emerged that was at least a head taller than Hayden, and much more heavily muscled, wearing a soldier's outfit with markings she didn't recognize. The metal of his chest plates clinked and echoed in the tight quarters of the alley as he stalked toward Hayden.

Valentina held her breath. They were so close that she could hear the labored breathing of the tall man. There was something wrong with his face. It almost looked melted, especially his nose, which would explain the loud and strained breathing.

A moment later, a thin man in dark orange and white came out of the building. He watched impassively as the large man circled around Hayden. Hayden stumbled and swayed a bit, then steadied himself with visible effort. He spit neatly at the thin man, narrowly missing.

"I recommend you stop this recklessness," the thin man said oily. He didn't look impressed with Hayden.

"Call off your dog," Hayden said, an attempt at contempt in his voice, his unsteady stance somewhat ruining the effect.

The large man stepped up, a hand out to grab Hayden's neck. The thin man stopped him with a gesture.

"Not here," the thin man said. His eyes flicked around the alley. Valentina looked down, superstitious that he would find her face if his eyes passed over her spot. She held her breath and counted to ten before looking up again.

"How about not ever," Hayden said back. He wiped his mouth with one hand. It came away with blood.

"Reputation is everything. You cannot be seen to be weak. Ever," the thin man said.

"Then stop bringing your lackey around," Hayden said.

The tall man growled at Hayden's reference.

"Your man," Hayden said with a motion to the tall man. It seemed to satisfy the mountain sized man, for he backed off from Hayden.

"He is not my man," the thin one said. "He is your father's man, just as I am...just as he would be yours if you don't ruin this for us all."

"I'm not ruining anything. There is nothing wrong with competing fairly," Hayden said.

"There is not such a thing as competing. There is only winning. You have your instructions. Do not make us come here again. Your father has promised a personal visit if necessary."

Valentina thought she saw Hayden's shoulders jump at the reference to his father coming to visit. He did not look pleased about it.

"Tell him he need not bother. Everything is well." With that, Hayden turned and walked from the two other men toward the mouth of the alley. Valentina pulled back in her hiding spot, terrified Hayden would turn and see her there, now exposed to him from his new position by the alley entrance, but he didn't turn.

He walked with a halting limp and exited the alley, and then went toward the market square.

The two men went back into the building and pulled the door shut behind them.

Valentina sat back against the cabinet and listened to her breathing in the quiet alley.


Several hours later, Valentina sat in the second-floor courtyard of the main market building. Tables and benches filled the central space, while stone benches lined the walls under the archways that looked out into the first level of the market which ran well into the street below. Women with large arm rings and thick necklaces sat at tables, waited on by servants, while other tables had couples or groups of men. Just a few children ate there, quickly ushered out by their nannies as soon as they were done eating. Any disturbance of others was met with glares and hushes.

Valentina kept her head down and tried to avoid eye contact. The last thing she wanted was trouble on her day off. She'd found enough of that at the school.

She'd walked all the stalls of the market, marveling at the items for sale. Dates, nuts, plums, vegetables of all kinds, many she hadn't recognized, slaughtered hogs, duck, geese, leatherworkers, wool sellers, and other craftsmen. It had been overwhelming.

It hadn't taken long for the rich smells of the fine cooking to drive her to the courtyard to raid her bag for an early lunch. Cold bread and cheese were not nearly as appealing as the curries, stews, and pastries for sale by the market vendors, but she didn't have money for anything else.

She told herself she hadn't been searching for Hayden, but knew she was lying. He must have walked through the market and left. She didn't dare chase after him, especially not back to the school with Genedron hanging around and threatening to disappear her.

Besides, what would she say? *Hello, I saw that bully. What's going on?*

So she'd stayed close to the market, hoping Clelia would show up. It had been their plan, after all. Hopefully, Clelia hadn't gotten into trouble with the other kid.

Valentina thought she'd seen a few other students in the market, but wasn't sure so didn't talk to any of them, which was how she ended up eating the last of her cheese alone in the courtyard. She looked around. She'd have to find another fountain soon, for she hadn't thought to bring a cup for water.

A hand slapped the table behind Valentina, startling her.

"Ha! Gotcha!" Clelia said, smirking at Valentina's jump. Valentina turned, then narrowed her eyes at Clelia.

"Not funny," Valentina said.

"Says who?" Clelia answered. She held half a plum pastry and bit into it, relishing the taste, then sliding onto the bench next to Valentina.

"I thought you didn't have any money?" Valentina said, staring at the food in Clelia's hand.

"I didn't have money to waste on food, no, but I got some," Clelia smiled at Valentina. When Valentina didn't smile back, she slapped Valentina on the knee.

"Oh, be happy. It's market day! I'll buy you one too. Besides, I owe it to you. If you hadn't taken the other boy, they might have ganged up on me. As it was, I got the purse back, and those little kids' mom gave me a reward. The girl watching the kids was happy too. I thought the mom was going to whip her."

"Whip her?" Valentina asked, shocked.

"Well, they can be pretty rough with servants these days. Slavery is frowned on but..." Clelia popped the last of the pastry in her mouth, as if she'd not said anything unusual. "Come on. Let's get you some."

Clelia stood, grabbed Valentina by the wrist and pulled her along to the pastry vendors on the first floor.

They left the market just past the hottest part of the day. The sun hung midway to the horizon. The city had soaked up the heat, and now the white walls radiated it back at its residents. Everyone on the street walked slowly, and there were a great deal fewer people.

If it was a school day, this would have been the time for naps.

Valentina guessed it wasn't just a school custom. The heat made it unbearable to do much else.

Valentina sweated in the sun. She regretted the hat she wore and the heat it kept in. Clelia looked much more comfortable in her light linens that blew in the little breeze the city did have.

Valentina had forgotten all about her goal of finding Mercato and now she didn't have much energy for it. He hadn't been at the market, but that could be meaningless.

"Are there are a lot of markets in the city?" Valentina asked Clelia.

"Some, I think. None like that one, though. That was the emperor's special project for his wife."

"He's married?" Valentina asked, surprised, then wondering why she was surprised.

"Not yet," Clelia answered, then yawned. "He likes to plan ahead I guess." Clelia checked her bag and found a thin coin with a hole in the center. "I haven't offered tribute in a long time. Wanna come?"

"I have nothing," Valentina said, not sure what Clelia was talking about.

Clelia dug in her bag and pulled out another coin, this one a little smaller, but with no hole. She looked pained, but handed over the coin to Valentina. "Now you do. You helped, and so did the gods. We cannot forget them, or it will go badly for us."

Clelia steered Valentina to the other side of the boulevard, angling for the next large temple on their route home.

The tall pillared building stood on the hillside ahead, the grounds falling away and lush with greenery. Three braziers with open flames roared up between the four front pillars of the building. Valentina squinted, but could not see walls behind the pillars, only a shadowy darkness. Two guards stood at the entrance, careful to stand in the shadows of the square blocks that marked the boundary to the temple grounds.

"What temple is this?" Valentina asked.

Clelia shrugged. "It doesn't matter. A smart person gets to them all. The gods are a jealous bunch."

"Do you believe in them?" Valentina asked. A man passing by on the street looked at her sharply. She looked down and away.

"I always give them gifts," Clelia said, winking at Valentina.

They passed by the front guards, who waved them in once Clelia and Valentina held up their coins.

Once on the stone path set in the low green ground cover, the temperature dropped noticeably. The city noises fell away as they got closer to the building. Soon the roaring of the fires in their grates was the loudest sound.

Two priestesses stood behind the fires, in the cool shadows of the temple. They bowed at Clelia and Valentina and waved them into the inner room.

A large bronze dish, wider than Valentina was tall, lay in the middle of the room. Coins, jewelry and offerings of grapes, breads, and other household good lay on it, even a plant in an ornate ceramic dish. Fires burned in their braziers on either side of the dish, a layer of incense on top of the wood adding a heavy perfume to the air.

Four statues stood in the corners of the room. Valentina inhaled sharply when she spied the first one, partially hidden in the smoke and shadows. The winged headgear of the woman stood out. The other statues were variations of the same woman.

The goddess of war.

Clelia stepped forward, tossed her coin onto a pile of similar coins on the dish, then kneeled nearby. Valentina followed suit. She looked down, unsure what to do. She glanced nervously at Clelia, who had shut her eyes and now talked too quietly for Valentina to hear. Valentina quickly gave her own words of thanks, but then sat in silence, letting her thought drift.

Maybe it was the incense, or the hot, long day, but Valentina felt as if she were sleeping, floating on the cool air of a darkened forest. Light filtered in from the green crowns of the trees high above, so dim that little grew on the forest floor; instead it was covered with a thin layer of rotten leaves from prior years.

Valentina walked through the trees. She reached out to feel a branch. The rough bark tickled her fingers, the tree vibrating under her touch. Soon her whole body vibrated from the tree. The impossibility of that happening jolted Valentina out of her dream of the forest, and her eyes flew open.

The temple rattled as the ground moved and shook it. Coins on the offering place jingled, bouncing along the surface in strange patterns. Grapes fell from the edge of the plate and landed on the floor, rolling on the tiles. Screams filtered in from outside the temple.

Valentina lost her balance, unable to stay on her knees on the bouncing floor. She sprawled to one side, nearly landing on Clelia who stared back at her round-eyed.

"Earthquake! Get out," Clelia said. She crawled on her hands and knees, scrambling to the door. Valentina followed, nausea coming as the ground rolled and moved under them. Dust and bits of the building fell around them.

A larger chunk fell from the ceiling directly into one of the statues, sending the statue tilting over toward Valentina and Clelia crawling at the entranceway.

Valentina saw the massive piece of marble coming down and shoved Clelia forward with all her strength, sending the girl out to the portico of the temple, where the fires spilled over their braziers. The priestesses had already fled to the lawns.

Valentina scrambled after, but wasn't fast enough.

The head of the statue came down on Valentina's ankle with a crash and an explosion of marble bits.

# 19

Noise filled the air. The rumbling of the ground that sounded like a monstrous beast just below the surface. The fall of masonry onto stone tiles in the temple and all over the city. Screams. Even the hiss of hot coals sliding on the temple portico.

Dust rose from the city, dimming the brilliant white walls and the blue sky above.

Valentina had felt and heard the statue come down. A shooting pain rain up her leg, but not nearly the agony she expected when she saw the massive marble head coming down for her ankle. The last thing she saw before she squeezed her eyes shut was the wings of the statue's headgear hitting the marble floor by her ankle.

Those wings must have taken some of the weight off the falling marble piece and protected her ankle during impact. If it had landed directly on her leg, the bones would have been crushed to tiny bits.

As it was, it only hurt. A lot. But her leg looked intact when she pulled it through the rubble to inspect.

Blood, yes.

Flopping over in a mess of broken bones, thank the goddess no.

Valentina pulled herself down the shallow steps of the temple and into its lawn.

Already there, Clelia reached out and pulled Valentina closer. Valentina let her, biting her lip against the pain the jolting motion caused her ankle.

After what seemed an eternity, the shaking subsided to a low rumbling and then stopped.

Everyone sat quietly.

A bell clanked somewhere far off in the city. People moved again.

"There will be more shakings, most likely," Clelia said, her normally happy face grim.

"How much more?" Valentina asked. She'd never experienced such a thing before in her life.

"I don't know, but there is usually some," Clelia said.

They nodded at the priestesses who stumbled past them toward the temple. The priestesses looked dazed.

"Does this happen a lot?" Valentina asked after she watched the women go by.

Clelia got to her feet, a little unsteadily. "A lot? No. I can't remember it ever being this strong, but then again, I also try to forget. The worst is when it happens in the middle of the night." She grimaced at Valentina. "You may yet get that experience tonight."

Valentina sincerely hoped not. Her stomach felt like it was still moving. Putting off trying to stand up, she sat up and pulled in her ankle to inspect it. Cautiously feeling her leg, she could feel nothing terrible, just some puffiness and swelling. Then she felt two loose pieces of something hard.

At first, her brain tried to comprehend if she would not feel any pain if there were two broken pieces of bone floating around, then she realized the pieces were not in her leg, but in the ankle pocket of her pants.

Then a sinking feeling came over her. Her present from Mercato. It was in the ankle pocket Dante had custom made for her in the old pants. It must have broken when the statue fell on her. Dreading what she was going to see, Valentina untied the straps that held the pocket closed and pulled out the two pieces.

Amazingly, the medallion had split neatly, leaving the front and back facings whole. The deer carvings only had a few light scratches, but Valentina barely looked at them. Inside the medallion was a single gold coin set into the top half. It must have been a secret compartment. Somehow it had broken open in the chaos, but hadn't been destroyed.

The face showing on the coin took Valentina's breath away. It was the same face as on the statues inside the temple; A woman's profile, wearing the same winged headdress as the statue.

"What is that?" Clelia said, looking down over Valentina's shoulder. "That looks like gold. Winged mercies, that must be worth a fortune. You said you had nothing!"

"I thought I had nothing," Valentina said softly, not moving her eyes from the coin. She touched it gently. It had the same warmth as her knife always did.

"Where is it from?" Clelia squatted to get a better look, reaching for the medallion piece. She held the piece with the embedded coin up to the light and tilted it, squinting at the tiny letters embossed on the metal coin. "I don't recognize the language."

"You don't? It has the same goddess as inside the temple. Why would it be in a different tongue?" Valentina stared at the coin. The script was different. "Maybe we should ask the priestesses." Valentina stood, but before she could walk off, Clelia grabbed her wrist.

"No, don't do that. They'll probably find a reason you have to leave it as tribute. They can be very insistent," Clelia said. She narrowed her eyes at Valentina. "You don't want to do that, do you?"

Valentina had to laugh at that. "No, and not just because it was a gift from my friend. You don't think I like being poor, do you?"

"Hm, no," Clelia said, still looking skeptical. "You do like hanging out with the poor students."

"Would you like to go live with the Artis ones? You'd probably fight them all."

"Good point," Clelia ceded.

Another priestess came up the walk, looking at the two girls with a frown.

"Come on. We should go." Clelia held out a hand for Valentina, who pulled herself up after she carefully stashed the medallion pieces into her pants pocket. Much as she wanted to look at them, inside a city full of pickpockets was not the place. Anyone would be tempted to take that large piece of gold from them.

Valentina's leg hurt with each step, but not terribly, so they were able to go back down the hill and head back to the school. Valentina searched the crowds on the way back but didn't see a sign of Mercato or anyone who looked like the riders from Cerceion.

That night after dinner, Clelia came into Valentina's room and plopped herself onto the bed while Valentina worked at the desk by candlelight, trying to read the remedial history scroll she'd been assigned.

"They let you take that to your room?" Clelia asked when she saw the wood pins.

"Yes," Valentina said. She hadn't realized it was a special favor.

"Artis..." Clelia said it like a curse.

"I didn't ask—"

"Of course you didn't ask. That's the point. You don't have to ask. Everything is just handed to you," Clelia said. She laid back on

Valentina's bed with her hands behind her head. At least she hadn't stomped out. Of course, if Clelia got much madder, Valentina might want just that.

"Sorry," Valentina finally said.

Clelia relented. "Oh, it's not your fault. I should get you to get some of the army scrolls they only give me a candlemark with in the library, and only with one of those old men watching me the whole time like I might stick my finger in my nose and then touch the thing."

Valentina snickered, only because she could see Clelia doing such a thing just to be rebellious.

"Stop laughing," Clelia warned.

Valentina swallowed the last laugh with a snort and went back to reading. There was little time for her to catch up, and all the morning weapons training drained her enough to fall asleep nearly the moment the sun fell below the horizon.

Valentina read for several minutes, forgetting Clelia was there, until Clelia asked, "So, why did your friend give you that coin?"

"I didn't know he had," Valentina admitted truthfully.

"That coin is worth a lot. I can tell just by looking at it."

Valentina agreed with that, but not because it was gold, like Clelia was thinking. Valentina couldn't help but think it had something to do with who was on the coin. It was the same goddess as the temple, and to have it revealed on the sacred grounds of that temple had to mean something.

It was too much of a coincidence for Valentina to dismiss, much as she would like to, but the alternative was too much to accept; that someone or something intentionally caused an earthquake just to show her the truth about Mercato's gift. Impossible. Valentina pushed the thought away and tried to focus on the musty listings of the numbers of horses and supply wagons needed in the third battle of the Mercherness, a battle her teacher thought most important. There were so many battles in the beginning of the empire that memorizing them felt like counting the stones in the hills, an endless and meaningless activity.

"What language do you think it's in?" Clelia asked.

"I have no idea," Valentina said, pushing away the scroll to turn and face Clelia. "I'm considered remedial in the Valderhorn tongue, having only spoken my own language all my life. I don't know any other languages."

"Nor do I," Clelia admitted. She sat up on the bed. "You know, we do have two history majors. I think Luno had to learn languages for the oldest scrolls... Can't remember."

Luno was the most scholarly of all their little group. She'd been there the longest too, having come a year early as a special dispensation to her father, who was highly valued for his bookkeeping skills by one of the wealthiest traders in town. If anyone knew, it would be her. Plus, it felt safer to ask one of the students rather than risk a teacher, who, like the priestesses, might feel it their duty to take the coin in question. Or worse.

A few moments later, Luno sat at Valentina's desk, holding the medallion half with the coin embedded in it up to the light of the candle while Valentina and Clelia waited from their perch on the bed.

"Hmm," Luno said, then grabbed at the coin and tried to twist it out of the wooden medallion. It didn't budge.

"I don't want to ruin the carving," Valentina said, referring to the other side of the wood, the top of the medallion that had the delicate deer head carving.

"No, I wouldn't want to either. It would help to know what the other side looks like," Luno said.

"What about the writing?" Clelia asked, unable to contain herself any longer.

"It might be familiar. It would be nice to compare it with some scrolls," Luno said, giving Valentina a look. Valentina shook her head. She wasn't willing to give the medallion to anyone else, even for just an afternoon.

"Could we go see the scrolls together?" Valentina asked.

"We could, but they do supervise us with them," Luno said.

"I thought that was just Clelia," Valentina said.

Luno laughed. "No, she'd have you think that, but they watch all of us with them, at least until we have senior status."

"Or Artis status," Clelia said bitterly.

Dante knocked at the door, curious about the voices inside.

"Come in," Clelia called, then recoiled from Valentina's glare. "What?"

"It's my room," Valentina said in a growl to Clelia, but didn't tell Dante to stay out. He came in and saw the flash of gold in Luno's hand and went over to look immediately.

"Holding out on me? What prize is this?" he asked as he stared at the coin, then at their faces.

"I didn't know I had it," Valentina said. Dante nodded at this, seemingly unsurprised that she was the one bringing in yet again something new. He'd told her at least a dozen times they never heard of Hayden getting bested like that in a test. Even coming to the school, he'd been so well trained at his father's compound that it was now just accepted no one could beat him.

Until Valentina had.

To her bad fortune, it had not made her popular with anyone. The common students suspected her of cheating, and the Artis students hated her for disturbing their routine and pecking order. Having a special lecture from Master Silas had just cemented her status as an outsider and troublemaker.

"This is beautiful," Dante said as he accepted the medallion from Luno. He flipped it over and examined the deer carvings on the front face. "Is this part of a set?"

"It was just a single medallion, but somehow it came apart and this was inside of it." Valentina decided to skip the whole earthquake part of the story. She was sure Clelia would fill him in soon enough. Getting up from the bed, Valentina took the bottom half of the medallion from the desk and gave it to Dante. "I'm not sure if it was meant to come apart."

He took it from her and set the top neatly on the bottom. It fit perfectly.

"Oh, I'm sure it was meant to come apart," Dante said, looking at the fine carvings. "Whoever made this had a great deal of skill and control. You just didn't know how to work the mechanism. Where did you get this?" He turned to Valentina.

"It was a gift from some people I didn't know all that well," Valentina said.

He stared at her and raised his eyebrows.

Good point. Who gives gifts to mere strangers, especially ones filled with gold coins that apparently are worth a lot and are stamped in strange tongues? If she were them, she wouldn't believe that story either. It sounded far more likely she'd stolen it from somewhere.

"A guy living in the woods with an elderly woman who said she knew who you were gave this to you?" Dante asked as he and Valentina sat alone in her room. They each had half of the medallion and were rubbing oil into it. He worked at the desk, while Valentina worked on the floor, unwilling to risk spilling oil on the blankets. Clelia and Luno had left to get ready for bed. Tomorrow was a normal school day.

Dante hadn't been able to figure out how to put it back together, but said they could at least protect the wood. "We might be able to glue to back. It would ruin whatever way the creator had to open it again, but it would hide the coin."

Valentina shook her head at that. She'd keep the item with her, sleeping on it if she had to. It was important for a reason.

"You sure?" Dante asked. "This school is not always the safest, no matter what they say about Master Silas' protection."

Valentina concentrated on rubbing the oil in with her piece of rag.

"Fine, then, your risk. You've done well so far," he said.

He rubbed on the half of the medallion that he had. They worked in silence for a few moments.

"You sure you don't want to tell me more about—"

"Absolutely sure. I shouldn't have told you about them to begin with."

"Is it a secret?" Dante asked.

Valentina set down the oily rag and the medallion on the desk. "I don't know what's a secret. Can we just not talk about it?"

"Sure," he said. He examined the coin on his half of the medallion. "I have an idea, but we should have done it before we treated the wood. Wait here."

Dante ran out of the room and came back with a precious piece of vellum and a stick of charcoal. Setting the medallion wood side down, he set the corner of the vellum on the coin and rubbed gently with the charcoal. It made a neat image of the coin. Tearing the vellum in half, he made another image. Taking the two pieces of vellum, he folded them each in half to hide the images and protect the charcoal from smearing. "One for me and one for Luno. We'll figure out what language that is in."

"Thanks," Valentina said, suddenly nervous at his having that information.

"Don't worry," he said, "We won't tell anyone where it came from even if they do manage to see it."

Valentina nodded, unable to calm the jumping nervousness in her stomach.

Dante rose, collecting the vellum pieces, charcoal, and amphora of oil they'd been using. Just as he was about to open the door again,

Valentina asked him, "Dante, what do you know about Hayden's family?"

He paused. "They are the ruling family of Winsterson, the lands to the western interiors. Mountains mostly. They share as little as possible about themselves, while it's said their spies are everywhere. As sunny as he looks, they are said to be ruthless. Why do you ask?"

"Is that why no one has bested him before?" Valentina asked, hoping fear of his family was not the reason. If it was, she had stepped into something awful by doing just that.

He took a second. "Honestly, no. There is a reason the emperor line does not come by blood, and why the school is supposed to be a neutral territory. Anyone can be the next ruler. All they have to do is prove themselves, although most are slyer than to show their ambitions on the second day."

"I don't want to be ruler," Valentina said, shocked.

"That's probably not what most of the Artis kids think now."

Valentina looked away, a horrible new understanding coming over her.

# 20

The thunderous clouds rolled over the city sky, hanging heavy and threatening. The wind blew in the smell of rain, but none had come down over the school yet. The darkness made it hard to believe it was just midmorning. The air felt staticky and sharp, as if a thunderbolt hung above, about to be released any moment.

Valentina ate an apple on her way to weapons practice, enjoying the rare cool air, her practice sword tucked under her arm. A few of the gardeners nodded at her, the reward for her efforts to be friendly the first few weeks of being there. It seemed few of the students acknowledged the school workers at all.

Her blisters were finally healing into thickening callouses on her hands, and she found she looked forward to getting back to working with her practice sword after a day off. The exercise felt good, and she was getting better. The other students complained about doing the basic exercises alongside her, but Valentina liked them. She could see the usefulness of all the positions, and their weapons teacher, Master Chendris, took the time to explain transitions and where they would help. Those other students might have had trainers at home, but she had not, certainly not ones that thought to train a woman in weapons.

Much to her chagrin, Valentina exited the tunnel to the ground of the Forum Peti to find she'd arrived early. She'd tried to not do that ever since the first day of testing. The other students held no love for her, and being with them while there was no teacher around seemed like a terrible idea.

Genedron and a few of his cronies stood in the center spot of the forum. The only other student Valentina recognized was Alcorn. He stood slightly off to the side, but still was a part of that group.

None of the other female students were there, nor were most of the male students.

Valentina briefly considered going back into the tunnel, but Genedron had already spotted her. No doubt they'd run after her, and she would be worse off in the tunnels hidden away from anyone seeing. So instead, she walked calmly to the practice area as if nothing was amiss.

"Class canceled today?" Valentina asked, trying to say it casually and hoping they couldn't hear the tremor in her voice.

"Just a little delayed. There is a more important lesson to be had here," Genedron said, stepping forward. His cronies fell in behind him, even Alcorn who looked a bit sheepish at it.

"There is?" Valentina asked.

"Oh yes," Genedron said, pulling out his sword from the sheath at his waist, except this was a real sword, its metal glinting even in the dim, stormy day.

Whipping her apple core at his face, Valentina pulled out her own sword, its wood now woefully inadequate for what she needed.

Genedron ducked the apple core, giving Valentina just enough time to get into position. The others circled Valentina.

"Are you such a coward that you need both a metal sword and

your friends to do your fighting for you?" Valentina said to Genedron. She tried to put a smirk on it, but was afraid she just looked ridiculous.

It was better than looking like what she felt—terrified. There was no way she could fight all of them, much less if one of them had a metal sword. He'd cut through the wood of her blade, then he'd cut through her too.

But her taunt worked. Genedron huffed at her accusation, but flicked his head back, telling his guys to retreat. They did, all except for Alcorn, who walked close to Genedron and said in a low voice, but not low enough to keep Valentina from hearing. "We agreed no real blades. No killing here."

Valentina tightened her grip on her sword.

"Get," Genedron said to Alcorn, his mouth tight.

"What are we doing?" Valentina asked. "You've already threatened me once. Is this your pastime? Oh, I'm a little bored, I think I'll pick on the new student."

He growled.

Right. Maybe taunting the bully was not the right approach.

"Fun isn't it?" Genedron said, then came at her.

"No, not really," Valentina said as she danced out of the way of his charge. Whirling, she got back into position just as he skidded to a stop and turned to charge again.

This time he clipped her sword, her dodge not quite fast enough.

A chunk came flying out the middle of the wooden weapon, tossed high into the air and landing with a thunk behind her. The rest of her sword still held, but just barely, its strength greatly reduced by the damage he'd caused.

Great. So much for a pleasant morning. A pleasant morning to die, perhaps?

She turned to face him as he came around to charge again.

This time she didn't wait. She turned and bolted for the stands behind her, the remains of her sword swinging wildly as she ran.

A roar of rage came behind her. She didn't dare turn and look. If she stumbled now, it could be the last stumble of her life.

Her injury from the statue in the temple came to life, agony shooting through her calf and ankle at the unexpected hard use.

She ran on anyhow, ignoring the pain and promising her body a hot soak in the baths if it could just get her out of there.

Making it to the low stone wall that marked the beginning of the audience section, Valentina leapt up on top of it, fueled by adrenaline. She turned just in time to see Genedron's surprised face as she kicked out with her right leg, her foot connecting square between his eyes.

His head snapped back, even as his legs kept going, a combination that laid him flat. The air whooshed out of his lungs. His sword clattered on the stones.

Valentina looked up to see the rest of his gang staring at her with their mouths hanging open. All, that is, except for Alcorn, who stood and laughed, his hand over his mouth to cover the sound.

Below her, Genedron rolled his head to the side and moaned.

At least she hadn't killed him.


Hayden came out of the closest tunnel nearby. Had he been watching? Valentina wondered as he strolled into the forum, his own practice sword under his arm. He stopped, surprise clear on his face at the sight in front of him. He swung around slowly and took in the entire scene.

So no, he had not been watching.

Valentina jumped down from the wall and edged away from Hayden. On the far side of the forum, other students filtered in along with Master Chendris, all carrying very large shields that they started to set up on the far side of the forum. Master Chendris seemed unaware of Genedron on the ground.

Hayden came over to Genedron just as Genedron rolled to his side and then staggered to his feet. A large red mark blazed on Genedron's forehead and his eyes were swelling shut.

"Stop," Hayden called just as Valentina was about to jog over to the other side of the forum. She stopped, then looked down at her feet and then slowly turned to face Hayden.

"Yes?" she asked. "Class is about to start, and I don't want to be late."

"What happened here?" Hayden asked her. She stared back at Hayden. What answer did he want? Surely he knew these boys were trying to hurt her, if not kill her. Why was he asking her anyhow?

"Genedron is quite clumsy, it seems. He ran into the wall and I came right over to see if I could be of any assistance. He told me my help was not needed so I am going back to class."

"That is your story?" Hayden asked. Valentina could see Genedron's glare over Hayden's shoulder. Well, let him tell Hayden the truth then. She wasn't going to.

"It is my story, to everyone," Valentina said meaningfully.

She turned again and walked to the weapons master who was describing one of the shields to the gathered students. Her back itched every step of the way, but no dagger struck her in it.

Valentina looked out the second-story window of her student housing building. The deep gray clouds from that morning lay even thicker on the land, getting lower and lower in the sky. They looked almost low enough to touch the main forum in the city center.

Below, students ran through the school grounds. The gardeners had long fled for indoor tasks, and only the students coming back late from lunch still roamed the grounds. The air hung thick and still, waiting for the impending storm. It had not been this bad even ten minutes ago when Clelia and Valentina had come from the dining hall.

In the city center, a bolt of lightning flashed down and struck a tree in the palace courtyard, sending sparks shooting into the sky over the nearby buildings. Valentina jumped and backed up from the window just as the thunderclap reached their school house. A second later a sheet of rain came down, sending spray into Clelia's room and getting Valentina's face and tunic wet.

Clelia got up from her desk chair and slammed the heavier curtains shut against the rain, then ran to grab a piece of wood custom made to fit in the window opening and keep out the rain. She shoved it in, elbowing Valentina out of the way.

"Goddess' blessing we don't have to walk in that for lunch," Clelia said.

"Would you?" Valentina asked.

"I'm not missing lunch." Clelia patted her stomach. She was thin, but always wanted more to eat.

With the window blocked by the board, the room was even dimmer than it had been before. Clelia had two candles going to study with. "I can't sleep through storms," Clelia had said by way of explanation as she lit the candles to study after lunch instead of napping.

As exhausted as Valentina was, she couldn't sleep either, so instead hung out in Clelia's room to study with company. She left for only a brief minute to shut her own window after the downpour started before returning to her study spot on Clelia's bed.

"How well do you know Luno and Dante?" Valentina asked. Clelia looked up from the notes she had been staring at and peered at Valentina. "Well enough I guess. I mean, they aren't Artis students."

"Yes, but does that make them trustworthy?" Valentina asked.

Clelia shrugged. "Enough, I'd say. Why? Is it because of that coin? You're probably overthinking it. They probably gave it to you because they thought it was a nice piece of carving and had no idea there was anything valuable in it. You just got lucky."

Valentina bit her lip to stop herself from correcting Clelia. Apparently she had not told Clelia that Mercato had made it himself. Unless he found a discus of wood that just happened to have a gold coin in it, of course he knew what was inside, but it was probably best to not point that out to Clelia.

"I guess," Valentina said, trying to sound vague.

It was true enough that she had been lucky to find Mercato and Jessop in the woods. Without their help and guidance, she might still be in those dark woods looking for berries to eat, or worse yet, found by the riders.


Several days later, Luno came into lunch so excited she was nearly floating. The girl rarely smiled, but this day she wore a smile to rival the sun. Market day excitement had long worn off and the students going through the line had the rather dull look of too much to do and not enough time to do it, and any break being a long way off. Valentina held her tray in line and watched Luno at the door of the dining hall with amazement. Clelia glanced over, but didn't seem to notice the difference, being more interested in getting a large enough serving of the Mousitopitta. Valentina found the desert too sweet, but Clelia could eat three servings or more if allowed, which usually meant stealing it off her fellow students' trays.

Dante entered the line soon after and snuck up to Luno. He whispered something in her ear and the smile on Luno's face wavered, then disappeared. Luno's lips quivered in the effort to not smile and Valentina had to look away or she was going to start laughing herself.

Valentina and Clelia left the line and sat down at the table in the middle of the large hall that they'd taken as their regular table. Valentina sat facing the Artis students, with Clelia next to her. Clelia had also started bringing her knife with her to lunch and laying the large weapon meaningfully on the table. Valentina didn't think that would deter the Artis kids, but Clelia was not in the habit of listening to Valentina.

Soon after, Luno and Dante joined them. As always, they wore the plain robes of the common students while Valentina had on another of Dante's creations. It seemed supremely unjust he could not wear them himself, having to settle for the complex ribbons and knots he had in his hair instead.

"Valentina, my studies have been most interesting," Luno said in an affected way Valentina had never heard before.

"Oh?" Valentina asked, playing along.

"Yes, I found a wonderful old language with so much style that they used for all sorts of things, like coins and ancient temple designs and... stuff," Luno said, running out of steam for her eloquent phrasing.

"Oh, very interesting," Valentina said, drawing out the very. She couldn't help teasing a bit. Dante looked down to hide his smile.

Luno's mouth hung open, not sure if she should be offended or not. "I was just trying—"

Clelia kicked Luno under the table while eating her pudding.

"Ouch! Hey, I was just trying—" Luno said

"We know what you were trying, and how about later?" Clelia said as she looked up and put an enormous spoonful of food into her mouth.

"I was being careful," Luno said as she rubbed her knee.

"Carefully weird. That alone will get someone's attention," Clelia said just loud enough for their group to hear as she rearranged the items on her tray, as if very concerned with them.

Valentina kept from staring at Clelia with some effort. She'd had no idea Clelia was paying that much attention, nor could be that sly.

"Right," Dante said in a normal voice, as if simply continuing on the conversation and not changing the topic. "We are getting into the really juicy histories in our line of studies. Love, romance, betrayals..."

At that, Valentina scowled. "That's not the histories I've been getting... war, war, war."

"Well, the writer does get some control over what they focus on," Dante admitted.

Clelia looked back and forth between the two of them, then turned to Valentina. "So, exactly what historian are you studying? Do they give numbers for the troops and the supply lines?" The gleam in the girl's eyes was a tad terrifying. She probably dreamt about army strategies.

Valentina glanced up and her eyes met Hayden's over the crowd of students between them. He had been staring at her. He looked away quickly. Nereen saw and narrowed her lips, then scowled at Valentina.

Dante invited them into his room for an after lunch snack of sesame candy. Clelia did not have to be asked twice, despite having eaten nearly all of their lunch desserts. The candy had been a gift from a friend of his on market day.

Valentina loved being in his room. Like all the students, he had the narrow bed and tiny desk, but somehow he'd had the time and funds to decorate it, making the spare room almost luxurious with red tassel shawls decorating the walls, and hanging lamps made of intricate knotted threads holding a glass sheath and a place for tiny candles at the bottom.

And his beautiful fabrics hung everywhere. He studied history because there was no formal schooling for Dressiers. They learned from other masters if they were lucky. Dante had worked hard to get into the school, saving every penny he'd made helping style his mother's friends back in the small coastal school he'd come from so he could come into the school and have some time to learn the conventions of the big city. It was too easy to come from a small town and not get an apprenticeship, but taken in as an indentured servant, or worse yet, a slave.

Being at the school offered some protection from that, even if it also offered its own dangers.

The sesame snack was just an excuse for the four of them to get together and shut the door without others wondering what they were doing. Even so, Valentina greatly enjoyed the honey and seed treat. It was better than the overly sweet soggy puddings that Clelia loved.

Of course Clelia loved everything sweet.

Luno came into the room last, sitting cross-legged on the floor with the rest of them on the pillows Dante had scrounged from somewhere. "Okay, now we get to talk for real," Luno said.

"But quietly," Clelia added. "Unless it's about food or army stuff, then as loud as you want. They'd believe that."

"They?" Valentina asked.

Clelia motioned to the shut door with a thumb. Apparently snoops were everywhere. "It's a cutthroat school."

"So what is this language you found?" Valentina asked Luno.

"There's not much of it, but they found some scrolls in an abandoned ancient temple in northern Brehallan. At least that is what the records say. Just a few of them," Luno explained, her eyes bright. "They found them about a hundred years ago, but they think the scrolls are much older. They are extremely fragile, and only a few in the whole school can look at the originals."

"Oh," Valentina said, disappointed. "Then how did you get to see it was the same language?"

"Because they made copies the students can look at."

"Wait, isn't that only for senior students? If it's rare or old, it seems it's off-limits," Clelia asked suspiciously. She'd been trying to get the personally written Histories of the Generals for ages, and the librarians wouldn't even let her see a scrap of them, even if she just looked over their shoulders.

Dante smirked. "Valentina is not the only one that appreciates my creations."

Clelia's mouth hung open. "You dirty dog. You need to help me."

"Get me some coin for fabric and we'll talk," Dante said.

Clelia crossed her arms and set her mouth in an expression Valentina was starting to recognize as dangerous.

"Can you read the language?" Valentina asked to change the subject.

"Not much." Luno's face fell. "The only reason we read any of it is that there were some inscriptions on the temple walls in multiple languages. They think the inscriptions mean all the same thing, so supposedly those words at least could be known."

"Do you really think it really matters what is inscribed on the —" Valentina stopped herself from mentioning the coin.

"It did seem a bit more than Long Live the Emperor, or some standard stuff like that," Clelia said.

"Did they have emperors back then?" Valentina asked Dante and Luno, who seemed to know the most about that sort of thing.

"Not that we know. Lots of clans and tribes and gods," Dante explained.

"We have gods," Clelia said.

"Yes, well, they took theirs very seriously, and not just on tribute day for the alters. We found other old scrolls for other lands thought to be from the same period, and they all talk about their wars of the gods. If you had the right god on your side, nothing could stop you."

# 21

The late afternoon sun came in the windows of the building as streaming thick rays of light. Valentina longed to move her chair into one of the sunbeams, but that was strictly prohibited by the history master who sat at his elevated desk, reading a scrolling of his own while pursing his lips into a thin straight line.

Sunlight damaged the delicate scrolls, so the heavy wood tables all sat clustered in the middle of the large room, while racks of holders occupied the far walls. Why they didn't just put the scrolls in a windowless room as well, Valentina had no idea. At least they didn't have to burn as many candles with a bit of light coming in the window.

The afternoon students sat at tables around her, their heads down studying, or at least pretending to study. These were the newer students, mostly much younger than Valentina, and none of them Artis class. Whether that was by chance or design Valentina had never figured out. She'd managed to keep some distance to the other Artis students, so didn't know exactly how they worked. All the ones in weapons training were her age or older, or so it seemed.

She hadn't had to move in with them, thank the goddess.

Nominally, her staying in her assigned house with the other common students had been so she could keep working in the nearby stables as directed by the emperor, but Valentina sometimes wondered if Master Silas had other reasons. He could have easily moved her.

Thankfully, the order had never come, or not yet.

After several weeks of classes together, the afternoon students had gotten over their fear of her enough for a few to actually sit at the same table as she did. Valentina had become accustomed to having the vast work space all to herself to spread out while the others crammed at the remaining tables, so it was with some chagrin she had to start sharing.

One of the bravest, Lesel, sat next to Valentina. She had a ruddy look, unlike most of the other students. Maybe always being different had given her some of her bravery, for she'd been the first one to talk to Valentina, and the first to claim some of Valentina's table for her own use.

After nothing had happened to Lesel, a few others had followed.

Valentina shifted in her seat and pulled out a slip of paper. She stared at the inscription on it, laying it on top of the scroll of southern fishing customs. Luno had given her the translation of the coin just that morning after working on it all night.

*Those who honor the goddess,*
*Are known by their heaven mark*

Lesel leaned over and stared brazenly at Valentina's work. Valentina slapped a hand on top of the slip of paper, but it was too late.

"Private," Valentina said.

"That?" Lesel said, a confused look on her face. "How can a children's game be private?"

"Game?" Valentina asked, her turn to be confused. "What are you talking about?"

"That slip of paper. Didn't it say those who honor—"

"Shhh" Valentina said.

"It's not a secret," Lesel said. The kid across from them looked up and back and forth anxiously between Valentina and Lesel. Apparently this was where the famed Artis temper was supposed to come out of Valentina and crush the student next to her. Valentina gave him an annoyed look, and he went back to spying more surreptitiously, stealing glances up once in a while.

"What do you mean it's not a secret?"

"Where did you grow up?" Lesel asked. "Every kid in Brehallan knows that rhyme. It's how we eliminate people when picking teams. But you've only got the first half of it."

"What's the second half?" Valentina asked, holding her breath.

"I don't remember exactly," Lesel said. "Something about those who do wrong against the chosen ones getting smitten or something. As I said, that was how we eliminated people." She gave a smile that told Valentina just how much Lesel liked that part. It looked odd on the small girl. A chill ran down Valentina's spine.

"If I remember, I'll let you know," Lesel said.

"Great, thanks," Valentina said. She shoved the paper back in her pocket then rolled up the scroll and stood to put it back on the rack. She suddenly wasn't feeling so good.


"Did you know that was a children's game?" Valentina asked Luno as she lifted a pitchfork full of dirty hay into the wheelbarrow with a little too much force, sending bits of hay flying into the air, highlighted in the red of the setting sun. The horses nearby snorted and moved uneasily in their stalls. The closest horse rolled its eyes at the commotion and kicked at the stall door.

Valentina put the pitchfork down for a moment and leaned on

it, focusing on her breathing and calming herself. It did no good to get the horses upset. At least no palace attendants were still working in the barn to witness her upset. They'd finished their sections earlier and left for dinner, leaving Valentina to work out her frustration with the hay and the cleaning.

Clelia had sent Luno to the stables since Valentina had told Clelia it was urgent. Valentina still had to do her chores before dinner, but she'd wanted to talk to Luno as soon as Luno got back from class.

Luno stared at her. "What's wrong?"

"I don't know," Valentina said and looked up and gave Luno a weak smile. "Probably nothing."

"What are you talking about then?"

"The translation you gave me. Apparently it's an old kids' rhyme from Brehallan. I thought you said that was what the..." Valentina lowered her voice, "the coin said." She didn't think anyone could hear her here, but it didn't hurt to be careful. Besides, Hayden had been in this barn at least once, even if she'd never seen him there again.

"It could be both," Luno said cautiously. "Most kids' rhymes are based in something, sometimes something quite old. And Brehallan is pretty close to where that temple was found."

"How old a kingdom is Brehallan?" Valentina asked.

"I don't know. Pretty old. They claim to be the founding kingdom that proposed the empire."

"Who would know more?"

"More what?" Luno asked, confused.

"If that was really a nursery rhyme or not?"

"One of the Artis kids from there?" Luno suggested.

Of course. "There have to be others from that region besides the royals. They might not know the common rhymes anyhow," Valentina said, trying to convince herself more than Luno. Valentina really did not want to have to talk to the Artis kids about anything. She'd been surviving the weapons training so far, mostly because Genedron was more wary about getting another kick to the head, but that didn't mean they were friendly. If they found out she wanted some information, they would make sure to keep it from her, or give her the wrong information just for spite, and hopefully to really hurt her. They were not a nice bunch.

The best treatment she got from them was the cold shoulder Hayden gave her, although she'd caught him staring once in a while.

"That might be true, other students knowing better than the Artis ones," Luno said, graciously giving strength to Valentina's hope.

"That isn't the whole rhyme, by the way," Valentina said.

Luno's eyebrows went up and she waited expectantly.

"The rest is something about smiting the unbelievers."

Luno blinked.


Valentina sat through dinner watching the Artis kids. They sat at the back of the hall. The group of four that she and Mercato had met on the road sat in the center of their table, all of them facing out and looking into the room. Those four always wore the same colors, probably the colors of their house back in their home kingdoms. Genedron in ruby red, Nereen in shades of amethyst, Alcorn in sapphire blue, and Hayden in orange citrine.

The wall behind them had no window, and with their positions at the edge of the room it was probably the safest spot in the entire place, except for Master Silas' seat during the ceremonial dinners. The other Artis students sat around those four, many with their backs to the main part of the room.

Those must be the lower status students.

Valentina studied those other students to see if any looked like some she could talk to. Despite her gut telling her it was a terrible idea, she had to admit she might have no other choice if they could not find another common student from Brehallan to ask about the rhyme. Or have someone else ask about the rhyme, so it wouldn't be Valentina.

Alcorn was one student from that kingdom. They knew that because all the heirs apparent and their titles were announced at the formal events.

Alcorn had only laughed on the occasions when Valentina had seen him. Did that make him more trustable, or less? He didn't really seem to be on anyone's side.

Clelia noticed the direction of her gaze. "I'd love to have those seats."

Valentina looked at her, not entirely surprised. "For the great strategic placement?"

"Quick learner," Clelia said.

Valentina nodded at Clelia's smile and went back to studying the Artis students. She ignored Clelia's hand snaking out to steal her dates.

"But not quick enough," Clelia said, eyeing her prize before taking a big bite of the fat date.

"I let you have that," Valentina said.

Clelia opened her mouth to make a retort, then shut it again, sensing Valentina's serious mood.

"We could just assume that girl..."

"Lesel," Valentina said.

"Lesel was right. I mean, why would she lie?" Clelia said, then waved to Dante and Luno who were late as usual.

"That is a thought," Valentina admitted.


That night a full moon stood over the city. Valentina stood in her window and looked at the moonlight dancing on the buildings. The aqueduct, for that is what she'd found it was called, stood like a tall sentry over the sleeping buildings below, its arches adding a fine lace to the details of the capital.

The moon shone so brightly, it looked almost as light as day. A faint dizziness came over Valentina, as if her mind could not tell what time it was. Then, she spotted movement and stared, hanging on to her windowsill for support. Saddleless white horses ran through the streets, galloping with their manes flying. But no sound came with the horses racing down the stone paved streets. An impossibility.

She blinked her eyes and looked again. The vision was gone.

Nothing lay in the city below but the dim blue outlines of whitewashed buildings and the shadows of manicured trees.

Valentina drew her curtain against the moonlight and went to bed.


Two bales of hay stood, one on top of the other, the gold straws falling out of their bindings and making a mess on the stone floor of the Forum Peti. Two burly school attendants had brought them and set them to one side of the forum, then settled down to watch the practice from the stands, taking advantage of their unusual errand to the stadium. They looked like they spent most of their time working the school fields. A chance to enjoy the seats in the beautiful morning sun was too much to pass up.

On the other side of the forum, the other Artis students practiced their swordsmanship while wearing plate armor. All of them to a one had their own custom equipment. Valentina had nothing of the sort. Master Chendris' solution had been to send her off to practice on her weak javelin throwing until something could be done.

Artis students usually had money. Yet another way she stood out and made herself a target.

Just as she lifted the javelin to make another throw, her wrist already hurting from the previous throws, a trumpet blared from far away. It was followed by another and yet another. Valentina pulled up, holding the javelin instead of letting it fly. She'd not heard trumpets since the parade in the city. She looked around. The other students stood, their swords hanging limply, while they stared back in the direction of the city. Nothing could be seen through the high walls of the Forum Peti, but the urge to look at the sound was overwhelming. Even the two school attendants in the stands stood, then scurried down the aisle to disappear into an exit tunnel.

Master Chendris looked no less confused, blinking at the unexpected sounds.

Valentina set down her javelin and walked to the other students and Master Chendris.

"The emperor's trumpets," Master Chendris said under his breath,

"What does that mean?" Valentina asked.

One of the young girls tittered and hid behind Nereen so her laughter wouldn't be spotted by Master Chendris. Not that it was likely, judging by his slightly dazed expression.

"The emperor has special trumpets?" Valentina asked.

"For when he leaves and arrives," Chendris said.

"She knows nothing," one of the students said. Valentina whirled to see who said it, but no one made eye contact.

No one except Hayden. He stared at her in that uncomfortable way. It wasn't a dare, and it wasn't exactly... not a dare. Except this time he spoke. "The emperor is announced when he leaves the city, and when he arrives. Nominally we," he motioned to Alcorn and Genedron, "should at least attend the procession. That is the custom, unless something is amiss, or there is an urgent affair." He stalked off.

Valentina watched him go. That was helpful, except he delivered it with a deadpan expression. She liked the outraged look he'd had when she'd dumped hay on him better. At least that had been a feeling, and not speaking to her so coldly.

Why did she even care? Valentina looked away, rather disgusted by the sudden question.

With Hayden's departure, Master Chendris snapped out of his confusion. "Yes, yes, the heirs should go. Actually, we all should."

Go where?

But before anyone could get to the tunnels, Master Silas emerged. Hayden came after him. Master Silas must have caught him in the exit.

"No need to go anywhere," Master Silas said. "The emperor ordered the trumpets afterwards as a courtesy. He left at dawn. There has been an urgent matter he must attend to."

"Alone?" Genedron said, his face reddening.

Master Silas stared at Genedron as if seeing him for the first time. Genedron took a step back.

"I was not informed how many liege he took. I would never presume to ask," Master Silas said.

Genedron nodded and looked away, his face going even redder.

Master Silas looked over the group, assessing each member slowly, but instead of speaking further, he turned on his heel and left.

The students broke out in whispers.

Valentina looked from face to face. They all seemed surprised. An ugly feeling roiled in her stomach.


A scroll lay open on Valentina's desk, but she had not seen a letter on it in many moments. Instead, Mercato's medallion lay in her palm. The oil had finally soaked into the wood, but she still did not dare set it down on the scroll in case she was wrong and any errant greasiness ruin the borrowed scroll. Artis or not, the Master in the library had promised to skin her alive from her feet upwards if she so much as got a speck of dirt on the thing.

Maybe she shouldn't have taken it.

Setting the medallion down on the floor carefully, Valentina wiped her hands on her pants, and then rolled up the scroll and set it leaning against the wall.

"Oh, we missed it," Clelia said, as she entered Valentina's room and threw her books onto Valentina's bed.

"Hello?" Valentina said, swooping down to grab the medallion off the floor before Clelia accidentally stepped on it. "What did we miss?"

"The emperor's procession. One time when Emperor Severus came back, they'd made an entire new arch for him." Clelia flopped down on Valentina's bed, then laid on her side to look at Valentina.

"Arch?"

"That fancy thing by the palace we all walked under," Clelia said, lazily waving her hand in the direction of the palace.

"How long was he gone for?"

"A few years I guess,"

"A few years?" Valentina asked, surprised. The emperor was her champion. He had stood up for her when those riders had wanted to come and take her away and test her, which sounded suspiciously like killing her. Even Master Silas had not been near so vocal. If the emperor could be gone for years, how safe was she really in the school?

It had been the emperor's word that threw the attackers out. He had been the one outraged at their proposed test for her.

"It can take a while to put down rebellions," Clelia said.

Feeling suddenly cold in the warm afternoon, Valentina stared at the medallion in her hands. "Will he be gone for years this time?" she asked.

"I wish I knew. If I was a general, I'd be in the war rooms right now," Clelia said, laying back to stare up at the ceiling and kick one leg over the other. "That is my destiny, I can feel it. Protecting the lands."

"You just hate being inside or anything called studying," Valentina said.

"Yes to the first one, but you're wrong about studying. I'll happily memorize any scrolls that tell me how to win a war, or form or supply my troops. I'll study whatever I must to be the emperor's right hand."

Valentina did not doubt it.

# 22

Valentina limped to class. The morning sun blazed down on the city, even in the early morning hours now. Insects screeched in the decorative high dry grasses, while the birds hid from the heat. Valentina now only heard birdsong through her windows in the predawn chill, and at dusk, but no longer during the day.

She wished she could hide with them.

A gardener carrying a rough sack of trimmings from one of the gardens nodded at her. His rough clothing and dirt encrusted hands spoke of many hours already working. Valentina longed for work in the quiet cool hours before the sun rose. Instead, she had to go to classes with students who would just as soon see her dead. She couldn't tell them she had no designs on the empire, because isn't that exactly what she'd say even if she had? They wouldn't believe a word she said.

So instead, she endured elbows and knees. Accidental slips in the dining hall that ended with her wearing that night's stew, the lumps of stringy meat and mushy vegetables falling off the precious clothing Dante had made for her.

It had grown worse in the weeks the emperor had been gone. The cat was away and the mice were murderous.

Clelia had warned her to stay away from the sides of tall buildings. Valentina scoffed at such strange advice at first. "Have you seen any piles of roof tiles smashed on the ground lately?" Clelia had asked.

"Yes, but isn't that normal? They do need repair once in a while." Valentina said, exasperated.

"Do you really think they need that much repair? And always when you're around?" Clelia smacked her hands together, imitating the thick red clay tiles sliding off the roof and exploding on impact on the stones below.

Valentina frowned at her.

Then, that very afternoon, she'd narrowly avoided tiles that came down and broke three of the body sized urns of flowers that lined the path to the history building. Too slowly she looked up, only to see the back of someone's tunic disappearing from the edge of the roof.

She'd followed Clelia's advice to the letter after that.

Afternoon classes had been even worse.

Lesel claimed there were few other students from Brehallan when Valentina asked. Then Lesel had stopped showing up in class entirely. The other students glared at Valentina, as if she had something to do with the feisty girl's disappearance.

"Where is Lesel?" she'd finally asked the timid boy who still sat across from her.

"Gone," he said, thrusting his chin out at her.

"Where?" Valentina asked.

He didn't answer. Another girl, one table over, said to Valentina, "We don't know." The other students all stared at Valentina like it was somehow her fault.

Maybe it was.

Valentina had not gotten much done that afternoon.

. . .

Even with the heat, weapons practice still happened in the Forum Peti. The solid gray stone seats and walls did not reflect as much heat as the whitewashed walls of the other buildings of the campus and city, but they reflected enough for heat to shimmer in the air, making it difficult to focus on anything too far away.

"No, no, no," Master Chendris said to Valentina, showing her how to stand in first position so that her plate armor protected her. Instinctively, she stood at an angle, something that worked best when one didn't have any protection and had to rely on minimizing the size of the target their body made. Fighting in armor was much more difficult, and stranger than she'd guessed it would be.

The Artis students stood in a group around her, watching Chendris instruct her. This was the very basics, which they all knew well, but Chendris beamed with their attention and solicitous questions. Valentina looked down and scowled. Whether their staring was to intimidate her, or make her too uneasy to learn, it didn't matter, the result was the same—she struggled to ignore them. She finally settled on focusing on a bench in the stand ahead of her and pretending the other students were furniture.

"Back into one," Chendris said, directing Valentina and her sparring partner, one of the lower status boys who stood close to her own height. Chendris motioned for them to begin. The boy struck Valentina's parry, moving his weapon in an unusual angle, subtle enough that Chendris might not notice, but effective enough to slide near Valentina's hand if she wasn't careful. He smirked at Valentina, then glanced at Genedron for approval.

Genedron's expression was inscrutable, as if watching an orator in the marketplace.

The boy looked away, not sly enough to hide his disappointment. Valentina caught Hayden's frown at the interaction, but didn't have time to ponder it before Chendris gave the reset command.

Valentina got back into position. Her arms ached from the bruises she'd received this week. This practice promised to give her a few more.

"Master, Master!" a guard called, interrupting the group. He ran from one of the dark tunnels that led into the forum floor from the passages under the seats. It was one of the formal guards from the front of the school, the blue-dyed horse hair in his helmet bouncing as he ran and his cape flying behind him. A sheen of sweat covered his arms and neck, and his face glowed red with exertion. He must have run from the front entrance.

Chendris turned to face the guard, his brows furrowed. "Yes?"

"There is an urgent message for one of the students to come to the palace," the guard said. He stopped in front of Chendris, breathing hard.

"The palace? But the emperor is gone," Chendris said.

"It is the message we received," the guard said.

"Do you have it with you? What does Master Silas say?" Chendris asked.

"Master Silas is gone for the day, visiting the member farms in the north. He left no instructions of this," the guard said. He pulled a slip of vellum from a slit pocket in the wool tunic beneath his armor. A broken seal of purple wax had held the folded vellum together, but had been opened.

"You opened this?" Chendris asked, his eyebrows raised as he took the vellum from the young man.

"Protocol for urgent messages in Master Silas' absences."

"Ah yes, that's right," Master Chendris said in a low grumble, "not that I've ever agreed with that particular one."

The guard said nothing to that, instead looking down and waiting for Chendris to read the message.

The other students had pulled closer into a tight circle around

Chendris. The closest tried to peer at the paper. Chendris did not notice.

"This says to bring them now, with no explanation, signed by the captain of the palace guard," Chendris said, finally. "I do not like this. It is most unusual. The emperor makes a point to not interfere with the school."

"As you said, he is not there," the guard pointed out.

Chendris examined the letter again, staring intently at the seal.

"It is the seal of the captain of his guard," Chendris finally said. He sighed, lowering the letter. "Ah, there is no help for it." He turned back to Valentina. "Valentina, it appears you are going on a field trip."

If the other students had been glaring at Valentina before, they absolutely seethed now. Genedron looked ready to strangle Valentina, his face flushing.

Despite the vast space of the empty Forum Peti around them, Valentina felt suddenly claustrophobic. She wanted to be anywhere but at the center of the tight circle of students around her. Terrifying as the palace was, it had to be better than this.

Hayden stepped forward to the guard and Master Chendris. "I will go with to assist the guard," he said.

"Hayden!" Nereen said, then quieted at the dark look Hayden sent her. She glared at Valentina with naked fury.

Valentina stared at Hayden. What could he mean by this?

"You will do no such thing," Master Chendris said. "Students leaving the school grounds at non-approved times is not a light thing. Having an heir apparent leave is especially forbidden. Do you understand?"

"No," Hayden said. A hush came over the students. Master Chendris turned to him.

"Then you will have to suffer without understanding here on the school grounds. Is that clear?" Master Chendris said, an unusual firmness to his voice that Valentina had not heard before.

Hayden pressed his lips together until they were nothing but a thin white line, then nodded once. He stepped back, his entire body rigid.

"This could work out well," Genedron muttered, earning a shocked look from the guard. Nervous titters of laughter came from his cronies. Master Chendris said, "Enough", with a low growl without even looking at Genedron.

"Go with the guard," Master Chendris said to Valentina. "Now. Don't delay."

Master Chendris turned to the guard. "Bring others with you. Three should do it. And report back once she is returned to the school."

"Yes, Master Chendris," the guard said. He waited for Valentina to come with him.

She nodded and stepped forward. The Artis students slowly parted for her to leave.

The guard and Valentina waited just within the campus grounds at the foot of the large building marking the entrance to the school grounds. Shade stretched out on this side of the building, giving her and the guard a chance to cool off as the other guards were called from the barracks to accompany them and to fill in at the front gate.

Other students walked by, staring curiously at Valentina in her armor and carrying her sword—a real one this time, as real swords were used for armored practice—and at the armed guard next to her. It was an unusual sight. Weapons were normally restricted to the Forum Peti or the training fields at the back of the campus. Their interest was probably normal, but Valentina was in no mood for it. She glared back at the offending students until they finally looked away, then she turned her back to the campus and focused on the stone steps ahead.

It didn't take long for the other guards to join them. They set off into the city streets, the four guards in a square around Valentina, giving the impression of imprisoning her.

"I'm not going to run away," Valentina said under her breath.

The lead guard who had come and retrieved her had excellent hearing. "That is not our fear," he said.

Valentina reddened. She really must work on not saying exactly what she thought.

The city streets were only moderately populated with pedestrians, the heat keeping many inside even though it was hours before the afternoon period of rest.

Sweat trickled down Valentina's back as they walked. The heat coming off the white walls pressed against her face like a hot iron. The peppered smell of someone's lunch cooking came from one of the few nearby compounds in the area. Valentina's stomach growled despite her anxiety. One of the guards smirked, but quickly wiped the expression away when Valentina glared at him.

The pedestrian traffic remained sparse even as they got closer to the central plaza. Even on non-market days, some vendors had permanent stalls to sell essentials, drawing business from local compound slaves and house attendants. Food stalls provided lunches for other businesses in the central area of the city.

But the heat of this day had discouraged most residents from leaving the cool shade of their homes, leaving the city feeling strangely empty.

Distracted by the food smells, Valentina almost missed the subtle scent of musk that she walked through. The scent was so familiar she didn't think much of it until an image of her old court and the day they dragged her to the tower popped into her head. She had not thought of that day in ages. Why now?

Puzzled, she looked around, then smelled that scent again. The only ones close to her were the guards, and the few city residents in familiar white robes, scurrying on their way and leaving a wide berth for the armed guards around Valentina.

Then she stared down the street ahead. At a point where the street narrowed between two temporary wooden vendor buildings stood a sedan chair, uncharacteristically still with its curtains closed, blocking the street. The breeze had come from that direction.

Valentina narrowed her eyes, trying to see the chair better.

The men carrying it still held it high, which they would not if the passenger had disembarked, but they were not moving either. They also wore heavy thick leathers in the heat, not the usual thin short robes the bearers wore to let their sweat cool them.

The familiar smell had come from them.

"There is something wrong," Valentina said quietly to the guards. The one who had fetched her turned back to look. She flicked her head forward to the sedan chair.

On a hunch, she glanced back the way they had come. Another sedan chair stood in the middle of the road, also held up by six men in leathers. Quick looks found a third and a fourth chair in the side streets facing in toward Valentina and the guards.

"Let me guess," Valentina said, "you always take the same route to the palace."

The lead guard cursed and barked an order to the other men. They turned their backs to Valentina, circling her for real this time. While the protection was nice, they blocked her from using her own weapon.

A sick dread came over Valentina. Even four highly trained men could not do much against six times their number. Valentina's heart raced as hot adrenaline shot through her. She crouched into first position without thinking, Chendris' voice in her head.

Seeing the change in the stance of the guards around Valentina, the men carrying the sedan chairs abandoned all pretense of being household attendants. They dropped the chairs and thrust back the curtains to pull out long metal swords that flashed in the sunlight.

Only one of the chairs had a person inside of it. It was the dirty blond Valentina recognized as the leader of the riders in black who had tried to kidnap her from the parade.

King Elgar's man from Cerceion.

Osian.

He'd come back for her and brought reinforcements.

# 23

Valentina licked her lips nervously and looked around, her sword ready in her hand. The four guards around her crouched, their own swords at the ready. Their dark midnight blue capes faced her, giving her the strange feeling of being in a deep sea.

Only a few pedestrians walked the streets between the tall buildings. It was a hot day, and not an official market day, so only those with urgent business braved the sweltering heat. A larger man in a toga ahead, and a house attendant pulling two young boys with her behind. No one appeared to be on the side streets.

The large man in the toga stared at Valentina and her crew, then slowly turned around to see what they were facing. He gave a surprisingly high-pitched squeak when he saw the seven men in leathers advancing toward them. He squeaked again when he saw the three other groups of men with swords and then wasted no time scurrying into a nearby building.

A yelp from behind, and a woman's urgent scolding told Valentina that the attendant was equally making herself and her charges scarce.

At least they wouldn't have to worry about innocents getting injured.

It also meant there would be no help coming, not immediately.

The lead guard in front of Valentina held his sword wavering in his right hand and fumbled with a chain at his neck with his left and pulled out a thin metal whistle attached to the chain. He blew on it, the shrill tone screaming in Valentina's ear.

The men in leathers charged. The lead guard dropped the whistle to concentrate on sword work with the men coming ahead. Valentina bit back a scream.

Their only advantage against the oncoming men was that their tight formation made it difficult for the others to fight them effectively. The twenty-five attackers could not fight the four standing so close without slashing each other.

All Valentina could hear for a few minutes was the sound of sword against sword, the ringing making a sickening sound and echoing off the close by buildings. More whistles, barely audible in the racket, went off in the distance.

The smell of sweat and fear flooded Valentina's senses. She whirled, repeatedly, but there was no room for her to strike; The four around her moved flawlessly to protect her against the onslaught. First one attacker went down, then another.

A pool of blood formed at their feet. The tiles became slick.

At a motion from the blond, Osian, the attackers pulled back. Two of them dragged along their wounded, leaving smears of blood.

Nausea pulled at Valentina.

"Surrender the girl," Osian called. His sharp accent triggered memories of home to Valentina—a home she desperately did not want to return to.

"No!" the lead guard called out. "You dare disobey the emperor in his holy city?"

Osian smiled wickedly. "The emperor is not here to object."

The guards around Valentina muttered angrily at his answer.

Osian motioned up sharply with his hand.

Four of his men ran back to the Sedan chairs and pulled out bows and sheaves of arrows from the curtained center. Holstering their swords, the men quickly notched an arrow in their bows. All four of the men aimed directly at Valentina.

Valentina didn't know which way to look.

"You cannot block all the arrows. Do you want her killed now, or let us take her and have the possibility of saving her later?" Osian called out. His wicked smile said the chances of saving Valentina later were miniscule.

But a chance was infinitely more hope than becoming a dead body now.

The lead guard hesitated, looking at the men with the bows and then at Valentina.

An arrow let loose from behind them with a whistling noise.

It landed with a thunk in the calf of one of the guards protecting Valentina. The guard faltered with a howl but did not go down, his eyes bright with pain.

Before Valentina had even turned around to look at the shooter, he had another arrow notched in his bow.

"That was your one warning," Osian said. "Surrender the girl."

"The Captain of the Guard of the palace expects us," the lead guard yelled. "You'll never make it out of the city alive."

Osian only laughed.

"I'll come!" Valentina yelled. The guards around her protested.

One grabbed her arm. "There is no sense in your getting killed for no reason," Valentina said in a hiss as she twisted her arm free.

She pushed against the guards' backs, forcing her way between them.

Osian smirked at his victory.

Just as Valentina set one foot down outside the protective circle of guards, a scream came up from behind them.

Valentina turned to look at the horrible sound, as did everyone else. One of the attackers behind them was pulling off his tunic, potatoes and meat falling off his shoulders. A second later, an iron pot flew down and hit him in the head.

From another window, a stream of boiling water arced down and hit another man.

More hot food, or sharp or heavy objects, came from other windows, all aimed at the attackers.

The city residents were not agreeable with Osian's plan, and were letting the visitors know in no uncertain terms.

"Run," the lead guard said in Valentina's ear. He pointed to a break between the two sets of attackers.

Valentina nodded an assent. All the guards ran with him, trying to keep their formation while also avoiding the assault raining down on the attackers.

They made it halfway to the side street before Osian yelled a command.

A few attackers managed to cut them off, bring up their swords. The battle was fierce, but quick. Valentina had her sword up to help, but she wasn't needed.

Still, she moved around as much as possible, just in case anyone still managed to have an arrow aimed at her back.

The attackers moved away from the windows and ran after Valentina and her guards.

Three attackers stood ahead of them. The rest were running up from behind. The lead guard took out one attacker.

Another guard got a second attacker, leaving Valentina in front facing the third attacker. The other two guards ran up behind Valentina to help her, but they would be too late.

Valentina got into the position she learned just earlier that morning and held her sword ready. It shook in her hands.

The attacker raised his own weapon, his massive muscles bunching under his leather tunic.

Even if she held form perfectly, she didn't have the strength to parry someone of that size.

Making a split-second decision, Valentina dropped and rolled to the side.

The attacker swung his weapon in empty air. He lost his balance with the unexpected result, having brought all his weight down to bear down on her.

Only now she was gone.

One of the guards coming up from behind had to hop over Valentina to keep from trampling her.

He turned to face the third attacker, while the trailing fourth guard faced the mob of men coming up from behind them, the arrow still in his calf.

Valentina didn't know what to do. She should go back and help the man.

"Run!" the lead guard yelled at her.

She hesitated.

"RUN!" the guard yelled again. His opponent tried to circle him to get to Valentina, then slashed at the guard, sending the guard's helmet flying.

Valentina ran down the side streets, her feet pounding painfully on the stones, her armor bouncing and jangling and her sword sweating in her hand.

She ran and ran.


The sounds of swords crossing and men yelling faded into the distance behind her. Her feet thundered on the paving stones, echoing back at her from the stone walls.

Valentina thought she should be at the market complex by now but only saw more white walls of residential compounds, their high walls pushed up close to the narrow boulevard. Behind those walls were gardens and then further back, houses, but the street itself seemed to be deserted. There was no one to help her.

And she was completely lost.

Slowing, she turned to look behind her. No one came after her.

She stopped to listen, trying to still her raspy breathing, and heard no one.

A child called to someone as if it was a normal afternoon.

Valentina wanted to cry. It had all happened so suddenly. She wiped her face with the back of her hand. No time for that now. She had to get to safety, and to do that, she had to figure out where she was.

Resuming her run down the boulevard, she looked for landmarks, but the walls were too high to see far. Ahead, a small shed abutted the wall of a huge compound. It was lower than the wall, and bricks lay in a pile below it. Valentina ran to it and used the bricks as stepping stones to climb to the top of the shed and then to the top of the wall above that.

Inside the wall lay a massive garden of cultivated flowers and exotic plants. Thick shrubs formed a maze deeper in the yard, and beyond that, a fountain tinkled, only the edge of the pool visible through the greenery. The house loomed in the background. It was an immense amount of wealth for a single household.

Pulling her eyes from the place, she looked upwards for the familiar tall wall of the large forum, or the sprawl of the quad buildings of the palace. Finally, she saw them off to one side. She thought she'd been running toward them, but she'd only been running deeper into the city.

To make things even worse, the Forum Peti marking the school grounds lay even further away. She hadn't even had the sense to run back to the school.

Suddenly conscious of her visibility against the sky for anyone who happened to be looking her way, Valentina dropped down, but it was too late.

"What do you there?" an angry voice yelled from inside the compound walls. A house servant came running through the backyard of the house, a water pitcher in hand.

"Nothing," Valentina called as she ran along the wall to get away from the man. She reached the end of the wall where it turned the corner and jumped to the boulevard beyond just as the water pitcher flew through the air, smashing into the paving stones a short distance beyond her and smashing into shards. It landed close enough for water to spray her face.

She ran on, not bothering to look behind at the angry servant.

When the stitch in her side pulled too sharply to go on, Valentina slowed to a walk. She'd worked her way closer to the main marketplace that marked the edge of the central square and the location of the main palace. The streets were wider here. Citizens walked them wearing cool white robes against the warm sun. Servants ran back and forth, most carrying goods of some sort.

Valentina stood out with her armor and her sword, both rare things to begin with, but even rarer on a woman. People stared. She could not afford to ignore them, instead checking their glances and constantly looking around for either her guard or the attackers trying to find her.

It had been too quiet. Running away too easy.

The attackers had to be somewhere close. It seemed unlikely her four-man guard would hold them for long. Valentina's shoulders twitched with the thought of an arrow coming out of nowhere and striking her.

What she wanted more than anything was a safe place, and if not that, a disguise.

But she had no money, and no clothing shops seemed open anyhow, even if she'd the nerve to stop and look for something to buy to disguise herself.

Valentina had chosen to come this way since the message from the captain of the guard was probably a forgery. If the captain had been in on the scheme to capture Valentina, the attackers would have just waited until she'd been delivered.

Besides, she'd seen the emperor and his captain. Unless something dramatic had happened, the emperor was still protecting her, and by extension, so too was his captain.

Still, she had to get there if she wanted any chance of safety.

Valentina kept close to the walls by the street so she would have something at her back if she had to fight someone. The walls were few here, replaced with storefronts and the temporary tents of the few vendors doing business on a non-market day.

Ahead, the tall form of the main forum loomed. Just past that was the palace. She just had to get past the marketplace, the forum, and then she was at the front of the palace compound.

Birdcalls sounded loudly, the first she'd heard in a while.

She wiped sweat from her brow as she walked. A rock kicked out from under her foot as she walked. Suddenly, Valentina realized how quiet it was. Even the day insects were quiet.

The bird called again.

A bird, in the heat of the day. Real birds did not call in the middle of the day.

Valentina turned quickly. A man ducked into a shop behind her.

She took off running to the forum. The man came out of the shop behind her and gave chase, his feet pounding on the stones. Startled citizens got out of Valentina's way.

She ran past the market building and past the small structures surrounding the large city forum.

Another chaser joined the first. He came at her from the left side while the one behind pulled back.

They were trying to herd her to the rest.

Fighting the gut instinct to run directly away from them,

Valentina cut left and then ducked down a side street. She lucked out in that it had an exit and wasn't a blind alley.

Her luck ran out when an attacker in leathers waited at the end for her.

She turned and ran back the way she'd come, barely getting ahead of the original two chasing her.

They ran after her through the forum complex and then blocked her from the palace by another six of them standing in a line with their swords held high.

An elderly man in long yellow robes tried to scold the waiting attackers into leaving, and for the crime of having weapons out in the city, but one of the attackers reached out a straight arm and shoved him over. Rage fill Valentina at the sight, but she could do nothing but keep running. If they caught her, she doubted they would restrain themselves from hurting her, especially if they got a reward either way.

She had no choice but to run back to the main forum. They'd managed to corral her after all.

The forum itself stood empty, no event planned for the day.

Valentina ran into the forum, up a ramp that led to the main complex.

The men chased after her.

The layout of the forum was different from the Forum Peti. She couldn't find the tunnels she knew must exist underneath it, but instead only the main walkway for the spectators. She ran on the walkways, then through the stands, trying to buy time to find an exit.

Meanwhile, more and more attackers came in behind her, and from other entrances she had not seen.

She was running out of options.

She climbed higher and higher in the stands as the attackers converged on her. Some jumped over the seats in a direct line toward her, others ran through the aisles.

Valentina dropped her sword in her exhaustion. She stopped and looked back at it, but there was no time. One of the attackers would reach her if she went back for it.

She ran on.

Tears ran down her face. She climbed higher as they fanned out in a semicircle behind her.

Reaching the top of the forum stands with the back wall six feet above her head, she turned to face the dozen men chasing her.

She reached into her tunic and pulled out her small knife, slashing it at them to keep them back.

They stopped in a semicircle around her, swords and knives held high.

# 24

The sun did not reach the section of the stands where Valentina stood with her back to the wall. The same wall shielded her and a small section around her from the hot yellow light.

The rest of the forum baked in the blazing sun. The stone of the spectator stands had been in full light for a few hours already and radiated a heat of its own. Not a cloud graced the blue sky above. Even the air felt still.

Valentina panted, breathless from her run. The men smelled of a foul mixture of sweat, body odor, and that sickly musk she recognized from her time back in Cerceion. They grinned at her. They were also out of breath, but there were twelve of them and one of her.

And they were all much, much bigger than she.

Not to mention the half dozen swords they had. Even the knives were larger.

A manic laugh threatened to bubble out of Valentina. She swallowed it back.

"You risk the emperor's wrath by coming here," Valentina said, looking from face to face. Which one to talk to?

One man grunted, but none of them replied.

A birdcall sounded. The only clean-shaven man of the group put two fingers in his mouth and gave out an answering call.

A moment later, Osian appeared in the stands below. He looked around until he found them.

The group waited, no one moving until he reached them.

He looked over the shoulders of his men and smiled at Valentina. "We've caught you at last. Our king will be most pleased."

"Your king wants war with the empire?" Valentina asked.

Osian laughed. The men around him hesitated, then laughed too, a bit more uncertainly.

"No one goes to war over a girl," Osian said, then spit into the stand next to him, his laugh gone completely.

"You're here, aren't you," Valentina said.

Fury crossed Osian's face. He waved forward one hand, signaling the attack.

The men moved forward slowly as a group, none racing forward to attack.

"Cowards," Valentina called. "Are you afraid to go one-on-one with a girl?"

She looked at the man directly in front of her. "You're afraid, aren't you?"

He grimaced back at her, but didn't rush forward ahead of his mates.

Valentina looked to her left, picked the man at the end of the line. "What about you? Are you as much of a coward as this one over here?" She flicked her head at the first man she'd taunted.

"Steady!" Osian yelled, but it was too late. The second man Valentina taunted flushed, then raced forward, his knife out. Valentina lunged to meet him and grasped the wrist of his knife hand and pulled it down.

He stumbled forward. Valentina used her momentum to step

on top of him while putting her knife handle in her mouth and leaping up to grasp the top of the wall of the forum behind her.

She kicked the man back into the other attackers, then, pulling up with all her might, she swung one leg up to the top of the wall, and then the other.

She lay on the wall for a second, panting, while her muscles spasmed.

The men below bellowed and cursed as they untangled themselves. Some tried to jump up and grab her.

One man grabbed another to climb on his shoulders. He would reach her for sure.

Valentina forced herself up. She made the mistake of looking over the far side of the wall. The wall stood five stories high. Her head buzzed and her feet felt light.

It was taller than the tower she'd been imprisoned in for three years. She could easily fall to her death, a fear she'd had all her life. Now she was even higher and in more danger. Paralysis gripped her.

No no no.

"Kill her," Osian called. As if in a dream, Valentina slowly looked to him, forcing her eyes away from the ground to stare at the naked hatred in his. Everyone moved so slowly.

He really wanted her dead.

He screamed his hatred. Wads of spittle flew from his mouth and arced like tiny jewels in the brilliant sun.

The other men shared similar expressions. The ugliness of their emotions was horrifying.

It was all an ugly, terrifying, slow-motion dream.

No.

She was not going to let that happen.

Tearing her eyes away, Valentina forced herself to focus on the wall itself.

She exhaled, and the world went back to normal speed.

"Get her," Osian yelled. The men inside the forum scrambled over the spectator seating in an effort to get her.

Valentina ran as fast as she dared along the narrow wall top.

She made it about halfway around the circular forum when she stopped. If she kept going, she'd come up to the men again. The only way down from the wall was off the five-story drop off the forum, or dropping back into the spectator seating with the attackers.

Death either way.

Her feet froze with indecision as she stared at the men inside the forum. Could she get past all of them somehow?

An arrow whizzed by her head. Valentina jumped, then looked back to the other side of the wall and the city beyond.

A man in leathers stood on the grounds outside the forum, another arrow already notched and aimed at her.

Valentina ran along the wall.

Another arrow whizzed by.

Ahead, the cluster of support buildings for the forum stood in a group just outside the forum. Banners ran between the buildings for an upcoming festival. Another building had a large awning over the seating area in front.

Inside the forum, the men inside raced to intercept her path.

She saw one way to possibly escape, but she'd have to outrun the men inside the forum, as well as the shooter outside.

She ran faster. There was no other way.

The men inside raced to meet her.

Finally, the next arrow flew past. She leapt off the building.

The hot air rushed up at Valentina as she sailed through the air in a long arc racing toward the buildings below.

Pulling the knife handle from her mouth, she twisted in the air, trying to face and grab one of the banners slung between the buildings.

She missed the first one. Then, with a glancing blow, she hit the second. Stabbing her knife into the fabric, she tried to hold on to the banner, but she was not strong enough.

Instead, she slid down the material, her knife slicing it on the way down. It slowed her fall only slightly as she smashed into the awning below, and then through to the chairs and tables beneath.

She landed on her back with a clatter of broken wood and falling awning supports. The debris rained down around her.

Women screamed. Men yelled. Valentina had a vague sense of trampling feet but could not see anything from beneath the awning fabric.

Off in the distance, more whistles blew.

Valentina tried to breathe but couldn't. Her body refused. Panicking, she rubbed her stomach until her diaphragm released with a painful spasm. She coughed as she pushed away the torn awning and bits of broken furniture.

Shocked citizens stared at her.

Valentina scrambled to her feet. Thankfully nothing was broken. The man with the bow would have seen her jump and was probably running to her now. She had to get out of there.

Pushing the people aside, she ran down the narrow alley between the support buildings and around the corner.

She had to get to the palace.


As if they could sense the chaos in the streets, the citizens of the city had come out of the buildings and houses around the central business area. The whistles of the school guard's alarm echoed through the city. The school guard had no authority in the city proper, but the city guards also knew to not interfere with a chase.

The school had the patronage of the emperor, and that was not to be taken lightly.

At least one school guard had run into the central area, searching for Valentina. She'd seen the helmet decorated with blue-dyed horse hair while running atop the forum. It seemed an insignificant detail in the heat of the chase, but now it stood out as greatly important to find at least one person on her side.

Even her sword was gone, dropped in the stands of the forum.

Valentina peered around a building. It was the last in the cluster of support buildings for the city forum. Ahead, a wider boulevard that ran down to the palace. It was the main route for parades and city festivities. There were few hiding places on that run.

Luckily, the increased pedestrian traffic helped.

Running footsteps echoed in the streets behind Valentina. She decided to not wait to see if they were friendly, but instead ran ahead, weaving in between people.

The adrenaline from the chase was wearing off. Her exhaustion made her clumsy and she ran into more than one person, earning glares. One man looked as if he would strike her, but the heat and her muttered apology were enough to dissuade him.

Ahead, the four buildings of the palace grounds stood so close. The smell of the fragrant blossoms from the fruit trees planted in the palace gardens filled the area.

She made it one block, reaching the back corner of the palace.

Pedestrians stared at her. Sweat soaked her clothes, along with yellow dust and dirt from the awnings and banners all over her hair and skin. Wood bits from the destroyed furniture stuck in her hair.

There was only one more stretch of street and she could turn the corner to the main guard house. She might even be able to yell for help.

Turning to look behind as she ran, Valentina saw the bobbing head and top of the bow of the archer back in the crowd. Too many people stood between them for him to take a shot at her, for now. She turned back and pushed herself to run harder.

Skittering around the corner to the front of the palace, Valentina ran. Ahead, a crowd gathered, blocking her path to the front gate. She cursed her luck and looked for a way around the group. A slight gap opened between the palace fence and the people. She ran for it.

"Valentina," a voice called her name. "Val—" the voice called a second time, this time stopping in a racking cough and then a scream.

Valentina focused on the crowd for the first time.

It wasn't a gathering of citizens in the varied robes of the city like on the side streets, as she had assumed.

There were robes, yes, but they covered men with leathers underneath and rough beards and hateful eyes glaring at her.

In the center of the gathering, one man held Mercato by the hair, a knife to his throat. Next to him, another man had Clelia. The girl had a black eye and blood ran down the front of her tunic from her nose.

*Clelia?* How had she gotten here?

Valentina skidded to a stop, unable to take her eyes away from the two prisoners.

Footsteps came racing up behind her. Valentina turned and backed up, keeping a distance. Osian and one of his archers came up then stopped to stare.

Osian shifted his gaze to smirk at Valentina.

She stared back and forth between the prisoners and Osian.

"Ah, you've found our bargaining chips, have you not, Valentina?" Osian said.

Her name sounded foul in his mouth.

A shiver of revulsion passed over Valentina.

"Let them go. They have nothing to do with this," Valentina said.

Osian smiled at her. He crossed his arms. "Are you sure?"

Valentina looked back at Mercato and Clelia. Mercato had given her that strange coin in a hidden way. What did that mean? And what had Jessop meant when she said she knew who Valentina was? Could that little old lady in the woods possibly have anything ill against the king? Not any more than Valentina herself, and look what that had earned her.

She faced Osian again. "Yes, I'm sure," she said. "Let them go. You could just shoot me, could you not? You don't need them." Valentina pointed to the archer next to Osian, now with his bow notched.

"Yes, I could, I guess," Osian said, making his way carefully toward Valentina. She held her knife up between them. "But you see, now *I'm* pissed. My king might not care if you arrive dead or alive, but I very much want you alive for the return journey, no matter how you end up arriving there."

He smirked at her, letting her think of all the horrible reasons he might want her alive for at least part of the journey. None of them were good.

"Run, Valentina," Clelia called, earning a punch in the gut from the nearby attacker. Clelia doubled over as blood flew from her mouth. She coughed on the blood, nearly going down on her hands and knees.

Rage filled Valentina. "Stop that!" she yelled.

"Drop your knife and surrender," Osian called.

"Let them go first," Valentina said.

Osian sneered. "You're hardly in a position to make demands, are you not?" Over his shoulder, the archer aimed an arrow at Valentina's heart.

"Kill me then, and miss all your fun," Valentina said. She'd never been so angry in her life. She could have stuck her knife clean through Osian if he had been just a little closer.

Osian's eyes widened for just a second at whatever expression was on her face before he got control of himself again.

"The palace is right there. The guards are right there," Valentina said, pointing just beyond the group, although it made a liar of her. No guards stood at the guardhouse of the palace.

No city guard stood anywhere close.

Goosebumps rose on her arms and scalp.

There were no guards.

The palace was the exact wrong place for her to have fled to. She turned back to face Mercato and Clelia; the leverage these men had brought here because they knew she'd flee to this safety.

Although it was not safe at all.

She'd been imprisoned in the tower for three years because the powerful people in her kingdom of Cerceion couldn't bring themselves to kill her.

Or failed trying.

Now, not only had they come to do just that, but two innocents were going to be killed too along the way.

Perhaps more.

Dante and Luno and Lesel had all helped her. Lesel had already disappeared. Did these men do something to her too?

Or had Genedron done that? Another enemy who wanted her dead.

Or all the enemies of her family back in Cerceion. It all came back in a rush. All the things she couldn't remember before.

NO!

If she was going to die, she was not going to let others die for her.

Not today.

Turning back to Osian, she yelled, "*I FORBID IT!*" then for the first time in her life she called on that feeling she'd known fully only in her dreams, and held her breath.

The world stopped.

# 25

Valentina's cry echoed out from the square into the city. Far away from the commotion in front of the palace, people turned at the sound of her yell. Men in tunics, women in stolas. Vendors set down their vases and turned from their customers. Even servants in the palace felt the cry, and the floor vibrated underneath their feet. They ran to the windows to see what was happening, but not one made it before the world stopped, and they hung frozen in midstride.

In the tableau that lay out in front of the palace, all stood still except for Valentina's moving eyes.

The blood dripping from Clelia's lips hung in midair.

The arrow launched by the archer glinted in the sun, its tip pointed and still in the hot air.

Dust motes hung still, bright shimmers in the sunlight.

The only sound was the rush of blood in Valentina's ears as her heart beat. *Thump. Thump. Thump.*

Valentina bolted for Mercato and Clelia.

Grabbing the knife from the man holding Mercato, she shoved the man away, then kicked at the man holding Clelia. The two men hung suspended in the air, like a mouse caught high in a cat's paw.

She grabbed both Clelia and Mercato. They were too heavy to carry, so she dragged them as far as she could before her vision started to blacken. She couldn't hold on for much longer. Tears streaming down her face, she pulled further, then fell to her knees. Her body forced her to breathe.

The exhale came out like an explosion, and then she sucked the air back in.

The world started again.

The men that had been holding their prisoners suddenly fell to the ground in a crash,

The arrow completed its arc to skitter on the stones in the place Valentina used to be.

Osian turned in a fury, unable to find the girl that had just been in front of him.

Clelia and Mercato blinked, confused and off-balance in their new positions outside the circle of the leather clad invaders. Valentina had each of them by the sleeve and pulled. "Run!" Valentina yelled, getting to her feet. "Run!"

They ran.


The people in the square all faced toward the direction of Valentina's yell, blinking as it was gone as soon as it started. Merchants in their rich robes, house servants come on errands. All dazed in the brilliant sun of midday.

Confused, the citizens of Valderhorn now faced the group of attackers in their leathers, having long since thrown off the camouflaging robes, standing defiantly in front of the palace.

Valentina, Mercato, and Clelia ran past the city folk, dodging to avoid collisions. Valentina dragged Clelia along. The girl was even more exhausted than Valentina.

It didn't take long for the scramble of men running after them to sound. The slap of leather sandals on paving stones echoing throughout the square.

Then the sounds of trumpets rang out over everything.

The emperor's trumpets.

Where was he when they needed him? Valentina gritted her teeth and pulled harder on Clelia. They would be caught if they didn't hurry. The girl could barely see out of her swollen eyes and ran blindly, hanging on to Valentina.

Ahead, Mercato skidded to a stop.

"Don't stop! Run!" Valentina yelled before she came around Mercato and saw what stopped him.

The emperor and a small group of twenty guards in parade dress. It could be no one else but the emperor, with his black hair slicked back, the gold and silver plate of his uniform, and his black eyes burning directly at Valentina.

Further down the street, more guards ran to catch up, their formal helmets with the red-dyed horsehair crests of the guard bouncing over the pedestrians in the way.

Valentina turned. The men from Cerceion kept coming. They had not seen the emperor.

"Get behind me," the emperor said.

Valentina didn't hesitate. She pulled Clelia with her as she and Mercato ran to the center of the twenty guards behind the emperor. A trumpet called out a lone, long note. Immediately afterwards, archers appeared at the top of the palace buildings. Those closest aimed directly at the men in the square.

A woman screamed somewhere and the citizens ran, the normal celebration of the trumpets of the emperor leading to something darker and more dangerous this time.

The men following Valentina pulled up, but not in time, coming face-to-face with the emperor and his men.

"Where are my guards?" the emperor called out, his face red with rage.

The front of the palace still stood empty of them.

A moment later, men in the same parade uniforms of the guards came through the door of the main palace, pushing ahead several men in more informal uniforms. At the same time, guards in the parade reds came up the smaller side streets leading to the main boulevard, corralling in more attackers in leather.

Soon, Osian and his men were surrounded by a massive company of guards in the plaza in front of the palace. Another several dozen guards in informal brown uniforms were pushed into the circle with the attackers.

"Is this all, Terif?" Emperor Severus asked.

A guard with a phalera of gold on his breastplate stepped forward. "It is, Imperator, with the exception of the men from the north gate."

"Ah, the north gate," the emperor said. "That was the only one that was corrupt?"

Captain Terif nodded.

"Hold these men," the emperor motioned to the group in the center of the guards. He turned to face Valentina, who still held up Clelia.

"My apologies, Valentina of Venancio. We had laid a trap here, but even my most esteemed advisors," he looked back at Captain Terif, who stared stalwartly forward, although with a burning red face, "misjudged the extent of the corruption in our own forces. We now have the information we need to correct that for good. My only regret is how close to danger you got."

Valentina stared at him. She almost died for a trap? Gratitude at being saved warred with wanting to kick the man who put her through it. She forced herself to bow. "Thank you for your rescue," she finally said.

The emperor laughed. "Is that all you want to say?"

Valentina nodded, refusing to look up, knowing her eyes would reveal it was most certainly not all she wanted to say, but for once she was going to not blurt it out.

The emperor surveyed the captured men, then turned back to Valentina. "Do you have any preference for how these men are treated?"

Valentina shook her head. If they were going to suffer, she wasn't going to weigh in on it. Let the emperor and the laws of the land deal with them.

Something did bother her, though. "Was the message from the captain of the guards real?" Valentina asked, then blushed at her forwardness.

The emperor looked serious at that. "No, it was not. I have information it had the official seal on it."

Valentina nodded. "That is what my master of weapons said."

"Yes, well, I am sure we will find out how that happened soon." The emperor looked at the captain of the guards. "Meanwhile, ask my treasurer for a new seal. We will make the master keys to go out."

Terif nodded at the command. "Now, Imperator?"

"No, after this is settled," the emperor said, waving to the captured men.

"I knew it wasn't real," Clelia said. Her voice sounded weird, as if through water. She still bled from her nose and dabbed at it with a sleeve.

"Who is this?" the emperor asked?

"Clelia, your next general," Clelia said and gave a bow. "I figured it out before anyone in the school did."

The emperor laughed again. Valentina thought he had no idea who he had just met.

.   .   .

Once again Valentina sat on a couch in the plant filled room behind the palace throne courtyard, now accompanied with Clelia and Mercato as Physician Flaraite tended them. Once again Physician Flaraite's formal outer robe lay crumpled on the ground, earning even a smile from Clelia, who otherwise complained loudly at every ministration.

"Ouch, ouch, ouch. Why does it have to hurt so much?" Clelia said, leaning back as Physician Flaraite dabbed at her face with a solution-soaked ball of linen gauze.

"Because you managed to injure yourself quite well," Flaraite said.

"I didn't do it, they did. Tell me you are torturing them just as much," Clelia said.

"I can honestly say they are not so lucky as to get my help," Flaraite said.

"Hrmp," Clelia said and crossed her arms.

"Clelia," Valentina cautioned. She really didn't want to talk about the attackers. Besides being exhausted, Valentina felt fine. Clelia was the only one really hurt.

The elderly attendant Isagani entered, passing by the two guards at the arching entrance of the room. He came to stand in front of Valentina and gave a small bow, his gray hair falling forward. "The emperor would like to see you now," he said.

Valentina nodded and got up from the couch, while Mercato did as well. Clelia tried to push the physician away, but he simply pushed her back on the couch and kept applying the tonic to the lacerations on her face.

"Just you, Valentina," Isagani said.

Valentina exchanged a look with Mercato. They had not had a chance to speak in private yet. She had no idea why he had been taken, again, by the attackers, or what he had meant by the coin he'd given her what seemed like ages ago.

· · ·

ALEX LINWOOD

Isagani led Valentina past the open courtyard with the fountains and the gardens. It was night now, so stars twinkled above instead of blue sky. The plants around them were dark shadowy shapes with the sounds of water falling from somewhere within their foliage. A chill had settled over the courtyard, and Valentina immediately missed the roaring fire of the room she'd just been in with Mercato and Clelia. She missed them for other reasons as well as she followed the attendant to face the emperor.

The emperor had not allowed any of them to return to the school, instead insisting on hosting them at the palace, but somehow it felt less like hosting than being held, even without Clelia's loud complaints. All day there had been the sounds of running footsteps and whispers outside their room, but the guards had gently motioned for them to return to their seats whenever they went to the doorway to look to see what was going on. One guard had not so gently picked up and carried Clelia back to her couch when she didn't take the hint.

Isagani took her back through a wing of the palace that must extend into the back garden, for they walked for longer than she thought possible, even in the vast building. Finally, they turned into a small room dominated by a large round table, inscribed with an enormous map on it. Emperor Severus sat at the table alone, along with a large goblet of wine.

He motioned for Valentina to sit next to him.

Valentina nodded and awkwardly pulled out one of the enormous chairs. Isagani rushed to help her, surprisingly strong for his thin frame. "Thank you, Imper..." Valentina struggled with the address.

"Imperator, but we don't have to be that formal right now," the emperor said. He gave a wave and Isagani brought another glass for Valentina, then excused himself. The two guards at the door followed the attendant out and closed the door behind themselves. There was no window in the room. It was safe as long as the guards

244

remained outside the door alert for danger, but now there was privacy between the two of them.

Valentina looked at the glass but decided she was too nervous to pick it up in front of the emperor and forced herself to ignore it.

"So so so, shall we talk about what we've learned this day?" he asked

A cold sweat came over Valentina. "I'm not sure I understand what you mean, except for that my king still does very much want me dead."

The emperor stared at Valentina. "Do not be coy with me."

Valentina sat up in her chair, suddenly wanting to flee anywhere but there.

"I'm not being coy," she said.

"Aren't you?"

The emperor took his goblet in one hand and took a sip, staring at Valentina over the rim the entire time.

"What happened?" he finally asked. "My witness says he saw you, then he didn't. You moved instantaneously."

Valentina's face turned a deep red, then white as the blood drained from it. What witness?

"That trap wasn't just for those from your old kingdom. Had that not yet occurred to you?" the emperor asked as he leaned forward and tapped Valentina on the knee.

# 26

Valentina stared at the emperor, her mouth hanging open. She knew she looked like a bewildered imbecile, but still could not bring herself to do anything about it.

Maddeningly, when her brain should be working on something to get her out of this situation, all it could do was focus on the surroundings. The heavy wood table they sat at. The layers and layers of maps on the wall, hanging from thick wood dowels and twisted ropes of colored threads from gigantic iron hooks high in the walls above.

The whole room looked like a war room. Heavy wood cabinets lined the back walls, making the room feel even smaller and more claustrophobic that it already was. The lanterns were all shaded as if to protect the highly flammable contents of the room from a lick of open flame.

They probably were shaded for just that reason. It gave the room a dark menacing look, even with half a dozen lanterns strewn about the place.

Emperor Severus stared at her, patiently waiting for an answer she didn't know how to give, the dark shadows under his black eyes making him look almost like a skull staring back at her.

Valentina wanted to throw up.

He wanted to know something she had refused to even admit to herself. That something strange did happen sometimes. Something she didn't understand. Only today, for the first time in her life, had she intentionally called upon it, and only out of utter desperation.

No, that was a lie. She had called upon it one other time. To save herself. And then she'd spent two days in shock and coldness, unable to understand what had happened, ready to die anyhow because she could not move in the new world it had shown her.

And now the emperor wanted her to explain it all to him, as if she could explain what was inexplicable.

Impossible.

A sharp pain shot through her skull at the ridiculousness of it all, and how trapped she was.

"I cannot explain it," she said, finally.

He stared at her, then nodded, as if agreeing with her, and not condemning her to death or torture for the answer, which she had half expected. Who dare refuse anything their emperor demanded of them?

Instead, he said, "Perhaps not," agreeably. "Let us try another approach. Let us talk around the edges and see what we can explain, shall we not?"

Valentina nodded. If anything, she had Mercato and Clelia to think of. There was no reason to make them suffer if he was willing to do the unthinkable to get the answers he wanted.

She had no reason to think the emperor so ruthless, except her own experience with those in power in her past kingdom. And his admission to what happened today had been a trap—one that almost killed her and those she cared about.

"Where do you go when you disappear?" the emperor asked.

Valentina stared at him, confused. "Disappear?"

"The witness said you were there one minute, and then gone the next. It happened so fast they thought they had blinked and missed you, but no one can run that fast."

"I don't go anywhere," Valentina said.

"Do not lie to the emperor," he said.

Valentina flinched.

"I don't go anywhere special," she stammered, trying to figure out how to say it. "I just go to the next place I want to be like I would normally."

"Normally?"

"Walking, or running..." she said weakly.

"That fast?" He looked at her disbelievingly.

"It's not that I'm fast, it's that everyone else is so slow."

He stared at her.

She sank back in her chair.

"Do it now," he said.

Panic gripped Valentina's heart. "I don't think I can. It just happens sometimes." She had sudden visions of a test called 'The knife' or whatever Osian had meant by that, involving some sort of torture to make her do something she barely understood herself. Was she a coward to not want to face that?

Clelia would probably say so, but Clelia seemed to be fearless.

"Is it always like that?" the emperor asked.

Valentina had to look down. "No," she finally admitted. "I was able to call on it today. Usually it just comes."

"When you are stressed or in danger?" he asked.

She nodded.

"I see. So you really don't want me to test this because it might be painful or frightening for you?" he asked.

She looked up and nodded. Perhaps admitting that was a mistake and only sealed her doom, but now that she started talking about it, it felt impossible to stop. She'd never talked to anyone in her life about it. Part of her knew without being told that is why those in her kingdom wanted her dead years ago. There was something terribly wrong and evil about it.

About her.

"I'm not going to lie and say it isn't tempting," the emperor said.

Valentina gripped the wide wooden armrests of her chair, suddenly feeling trapped in the tiny room much as she imagined a coffin felt like.

"But one doesn't get to be emperor by not having any self-control," he said, then giving her a wink.

Valentina could not find the humor to laugh, even smile at his joke. If it had been a joke.

"Ah, yes, I guess not funny from your perspective," he said.

They sat in silence for a moment. He drank his wine. Valentina wanted a sip of whatever was in her cup, but her hands shook so much now she didn't dare try to lift it. She shoved them under her legs instead.

"What is it?" he finally asked, open curiosity on his face.

Valentina tried to answer the best she could.

"It's like the whole world is holding its breath. Even the air. Nothing moves. I can move, but anything I touch will just stop the moment I stop touching it."

"So you could kill me in this moment and nothing would stop you. I can see why your king wanted you dead."

Valentina shook her head, but then realized he was right. If she could control her powers, she could kill the man in front of her. Getting out of the room alive was another thing entirely, for the power was so short-lived, she could not escape before he was discovered.

"But there are limits, are there not?" he said, astute in his observations. "For otherwise you would do it all the time and get whatever you want."

"I don't know how to control it, not really," Valentina said.

"For now," he said.

"For now," she admitted.

They talked for several more hours, and sometimes Valentina did not understand the questions he asked, but her answers seemed to illuminate things for him, for he grew more comfortable the longer they talked. Isagani reappeared after a bit, leading in several other attendants who set the table with a cloth and then several courses of a meal that Valentina barely tasted, even though she ate all of what was given to her.

Her head bobbed with sleep by the time the emperor was satisfied with his questioning.

"Go, rest," he said. "We have much to discuss in the morning."

Valentina followed Isagani out of the room, too tired to even ask about Mercato and Clelia, only following him to a well-appointed bedroom of the palace, where she laid down on the covers and fell asleep fully dressed.

Two quiet female attendants showed up in the morning and knocked on Valentina's bedroom door. They were dressed in rich robes of pure white linen, the purest of whites that spoke of plenty of expensive laundering, and trimmed with pinks and light purples. Both of the women barely spoke as they laid out fresh clothes for Valentina and then waved in two burly palace male attendants carrying a large copper tub.

Mercifully, they allowed Valentina to bathe on her own while they waited outside. She had a lot to think about. When she'd asked about Clelia and Mercato, the attendants only shook their heads and refused to say a thing. Valentina thought of that and sank down in the tub, fully immersing herself in the warm soapy water.

The quietness of being below the surface of the water calmed her. She was there as long as her breath lasted her, feeling the water in her ears and over her face.

When she came up, she knew what she needed to do.

Isagani led Valentina to an outdoor table in the central palace garden, the one that lay in the spaces between the four main buildings of the complex. Fruit trees filled the air with their spring blossoms, and gardeners walked the grounds, cleaning the debris from the winter months. The landscaping held much larger plants, and stranger ones too, looking both more wild and exciting than the repressed grounds of the school.

It fit the impression she had of the emperor. He did not beat the garden into a sad imitation of wildness, instead cultivating it for his own.

Guards stood within the arches of the four buildings facing the garden, as well as at regular intervals on the stone path she walked with Isagani. It seemed there were more guards than she had seen all the previous day.

Was this because of her talk last night with the emperor?

She found him at a breakfast table with another place set. Isagani motioned her to it. She bowed formally this time before sitting, having remembered her manners after the chaos of the previous day faded away.

"Good morning, Valentina," the emperor said.

"Good morning, Imperator," Valentina said.

He drank a steaming cup of coffee and waited for Valentina to be served her own before starting.

"Did you sleep well?" he asked.

"I did."

"Do you know why I've kept you here?" he asked.

Valentina laced her fingers together and kept them on her lap. She was not going to let him throw her today.

251

"No, but I have a feeling. First, though, can I ask a question?" she asked.

He nodded permission.

"Where are Mercato and Clelia? No one would tell me anything."

He wiped his mouth with a napkin and set it on the table. "Ah, your friends."

"My friends," she said.

"They are safe, back at the school, for the moment."

"Mercato too?" Valentina asked.

"Yes, him too. Why do you ask?"

"Master Silas would not allow him on the grounds last time," Valentina said. Or had it been the emperor? She could not remember.

"He is there now," the emperor said, and waited for Valentina to say more. She did not.

"Well, now that your curiosity is satisfied, I have a royal request of you. Do you know what that means?"

Valentina nodded. It meant it was not a request at all, not unless she wanted her head on a pike. Still, that ending was a choice, and she had that. She gripped her hands into fists, then forced them open and relaxed when he glanced down at them, then looked up with one raised eyebrow.

She blushed, then spoke, "Yes, Your Imperator."

When she looked up, his face was not as she expected it. Instead of fury, there was a twinkle in his eyes, and his lips were pressed together, repressing... *laughter*?

Confusion overcame Valentina. What was he laughing about? She could see no humor in anything at the moment.

"You do not seem to know what you can do means," he said once he had control of himself.

"No, Imperator," Valentina said.

"It means you are the marked one of a god. A goddess, to be exact."

Valentina stared at him, not sure she was hearing correctly.

"Do you not know this?"

She shook her head.

He pulled a pouch from a nearby table and undid the drawstring, then put his hand inside and pulled out a coin. Opening his palm with the coin on it face up, he extended it to her.

"Do you recognize this?" he asked.

It was the same coin face as the coin Mercato had given her. Was it her coin? She fought the urge to check her pocket for it. Might they have taken it while she slept?

She nodded numbly, afraid now for real.

"It is the goddess of war. What you can do matches the lore of what her chosen one can do. Do you know this?"

Valentina shook her head.

"I thought not. Even if you knew, you could not do the feats you do without the assistance of the goddess. You are well and truly marked."

Valentina gripped her chair as she looked up from the face of the coin to the smiling face of the emperor.

"I want you to be my lead heir apparent," he said.

The world roared in Valentina's ears.

# 27

The late summer sun shone into the barn, highlighting the familiar golden flecks of hay as they flew up into the air. Valentina finished shoveling the fresh hay into the stall and admired her handiwork.

The stall itself was one of the larger ones near the end. Not the largest at the end, but large enough for a good sized animal to be comfortable. Everything gleamed from a good scrubbing, and the only dirt was the fine layer of dust from the dried hay.

The horses in their stalls along the long aisle of the enormous building only snorted occasionally, or shifted their feet. They were long used to Valentina's hours in the barn, and the smell of her was as familiar as the hours in the fields they enjoyed every day.

"I don't know why you still do this," Clelia called as she entered the barn. "You, of all people." She walked down the aisle to join Valentina admiring the stall. "For your horse?"

"For my horse," Valentina confirmed. "And why shouldn't I do this? I, of all people, should know how everything works."

"Everything?" Clelia asked. She grinned, thinking no doubt of some unpleasant task she could set Valentina to in the name of 'education'.

"Stop that," Valentina said. "You know what I mean."

Clelia crossed her arms. "You are getting to be no fun."

Valentina picked up her shovel and walked down the barn to the tool rack to put it away. Clelia trailed after.

"When was I ever fun?" Valentina asked.

"Oh, you're right. Never, I guess."

"Ouch, you're mean." Valentina exited the barn, then held the door, waiting for Clelia to follow.

"That's the thanks I get for trying to save your life," Clelia said with a pout.

Valentina shut the door, then faced Clelia, her smile gone. "Thank you, Clelia."

Clelia blushed and turned away. "Oh, don't go and get all serious on me now."

They walked in silence to their school house. Just as they reached the door, Clelia turned to Valentina. "I'm going to miss you," Clelia said.

Valentina pushed back the emotion she'd been avoiding all day, then finally gave in. "I'm going to miss you too." She grabbed Clelia in a hug.

They stood there for a minute until Clelia pulled away and cleared her throat. "Well, if you need saving at the Artis house, just call me."

"I might do that," Valentina said with a laugh.

Clelia opened the door to the house for common students and gave a flourish for Valentina to enter.

Valentina raised an eyebrow, then entered the building.

They climbed the stairs to the long row of rooms.

"Can you help me with one thing before you go?" Clelia asked as she held the door to her room.

Valentina nodded and went to Clelia's door.

Instead of entering, Clelia turned the door handle and shoved the door open. Inside, Luno, Dante, and Mercato shouted "Surprise!" as they threw flowers at Valentina.

Valentina put a hand over her racing heart, then laughed as she entered the room.

Valentina sat at the place of honor on Clelia's bed, along with Clelia, while Dante sat at the desk and Mercato and Luno took spots on the floor in the tiny room. Luno had brought a cake she had bribed one of the cooks to make in exchange for translating a family scroll. It had late summer berries covered in cream. A rare treat for the poorer students of the Stanasbrisson.

"So, will you be ready in time to be my general?" Valentina asked Clelia. "Or have you been spending all your time planning how to harass me?"

"They say I'm a very quick learner at the palace, even if they don't let me take those scrolls home either," Clelia said with a pout.

"They are state secrets," Dante pointed out as he cut himself another piece of cake.

"So? One of these days I'm going to have the privileges to take scrolls home!" Clelia said.

"You are never satisfied. At least you get to study with the real military now," Valentina said.

"And you should be happy I'm never satisfied, if I am going to protect you on your campaigns," Clelia said as she shoved an enormous piece of cake in her mouth.

The group muttered their agreement with that.

"Don't forget, I'm getting your room," Mercato reminded Valentina. "Don't let some other student grab it."

"Why would I do that?" Valentina asked.

"Just making sure," Mercato said with a laugh. He'd been admitted to the school as a condition Valentina had made so he would be protected and thus protect her from blackmail in the future. There were things to be learned at the school, even for a merchant, and Mercato had agreed to the plan for Valentina's sake as well as his own. Master Silas had not even complained when Emperor Severus explained it to him. The last-minute addition to the school roll had left Mercato in an even smaller room than normal, more the size of a closet the gardeners might use.

"One last gift while you are still here, though I am sure I'll get to make more as an official Dressier, right?" Dante asked Valentina meaningfully.

"Yes, of course. Why would you even have to ask?" Valentina said with a laugh.

"Because I'm careful and methodical, and you know that," Dante said as he rose and left the room. He reentered a moment later with a red wool dye undertunic for armor, heavily embroidered with the wings of birds, and a helmet with feathered wings fashioned on it. It looked like a spitting image of the woman on the coin. He gave it to Valentina. "So no one forgets who you are and tries to kill you again."

"This is far too presumptuous," Valentina said as she took the beautiful garment. "That is a goddess. I could never."

"According to the temple priestess and the emperor, you can, and you will."

Valentina swallowed the rest of her protests and looked down at the garment. The embroidery grew fuzzy as her eyes watered.


Valentina packed the few things she owned into two canvas bags Dante had loaned her for the occasion. Most of it was clothing he had given her, and the armor Master Chendris had made. Pulling out the drawer of her desk, she felt in the back for her hiding spot, just in case. Something tickled at her fingers. It was not empty as she had thought.

Getting on her knees so she could reach further, Valentina struggled and then finally grasped what was back there. She pulled out the small light bag of herbs, or whatever it was, that Jessop had given her ages ago but refused to tell her what it was. It still had a slight fragrance to it.

Sitting on the bed, Valentina stared at the bag in her hands. Considering how important the medallion Mercato had given her had been, it was foolishness to think this tiny bag was not somehow important too. She could not just get rid of it.

Still, she had no time to learn more. It was moving day. She would just have to hide it well in her new home until she could figure out what it was.


Dante, Luno, Mercato, and Clelia walked Valentina across the campus, helping to carry her bags, and armor and scrolls. It felt like a small army, but still not nearly enough for Valentina.

The gardeners stood by the walk, not working on the beautiful late summer beds. Many flowers still bloomed, and other heartier plants that could take the summer heat—mostly grasses and thin leaved plants—stood neatly trimmed, not needing any more work. It took Valentina a moment to realize that the gardeners were standing outside to see her as she walked across campus with her group to the Artis house, each giving her a respectful nod. She nodded back at each one, gratitude filling her heart.

The emperor had allowed her to delay this transition until the end of the summer, but said it could go on no longer. If she was to be a part of the empire, she had to forge bonds with those also destined for leadership; those close to or destined to become the heads of the member kingdoms of the empire. Valentina had not spoken a word of the attempts on her life from that group, but the emperor had seemed to know, and despite that, had been implacable in his insistence on this change. He said such conflicts made it even more called for.

Valentina's dread grew greater with each step they took across the campus.

The Artis house stood deep within the campus grounds, at one of the safest spots if it was to be attacked from outside the gates.

That did not help Valentina much if the attack was coming from within. But she had her duty, and her agreement with the emperor.

And she would still see her friends at classes and exercises. It was not yet the true isolation that leadership could bring. It felt like small consolation.

The Artis house rose high above the neighboring buildings, almost as high as the grand hall at the entrance of the school grounds. Six columns graced the front and eleven the sides. School guards stood at attention, the only school building with specific guards besides the gates. The late afternoon sun framed the building in an orange glow, as if blessed by the gods themselves. The students living there would have the others so believe, Valentina thought bitterly.

Now she was one of those students.

Outside, waiting for her, stood all the Artis students of the school. Near three dozen. In front, the other heirs apparent stood; Hayden, Alcorn, and Genedron. Nereen stood close to Hayden, as if to protect him.

Genedron stepped forward to meet the group, a scowl on his face. He stood directly in front of Valentina and forced her group to stop.

"Have a care. This will not be so easy for you," he said in a growl to Valentina, rage and hostility bristling off him like a red-hot brasier.

Valentina nodded at him. She had nothing to say. She was sure it would be anything but easy.

Stepping around him, she led her group to the room designated her new home deep within the lair of the lions called the Artis students.

# AUTHOR'S NOTE

While this work calls up many elements of Ancient Rome, any and all events, people, and lands are fictional. This book is fully a work of my imagination and is not a historical document.

That said, I had a great deal of fun pouring over images and accounts of what life was like those thousands of years ago. I hope you have as much fun reading this book.

ALSO BY ALEX LINWOOD

THE GODDESS OF DESTINY

The Queen of War

THE JACK OF MAGIC

Red Jack

Moss Gate

Black Raid

Iron War

Gold Crown